BAZAAR OF THE IDIOTS

by

GUSTAVO ALVAREZ GARDEAZABAL

BAZAAR OF THE IDIOTS

by

GUSTAVO ALVAREZ GARDEAZABAL

Translated by

SUSAN F. HILL AND JONATHAN TITTLER

Introduction by

RAYMOND LESLIE WILLIAMS

LATIN AMERICAN LITERARY REVIEW PRESS
SERIES: DISCOVERIES
PITTSBURGH, PENNSYLVANIA

YVETTE E. MILLER, EDITOR

1991

The Latin American Literary Review Press publishes Latin American creative writing under the series title *Discoveries*, and critical works under the series title *Explorations*.

Library of Congress Cataloging-in-Publication Data

Alvarez Gardeazábal, Gustavo.
    [Bazar de los idiotas. English]
    Bazaar of the idiots / by Gustavo Alvarez Gardeazábal: translated by Susan F. Hill and Jonathan Tittler: introduction by Raymond Leslie Williams.
        p.   cm. -- (Discoveries)
    Translation of : El bazar de los idiotas.
    ISBN 0-935480-48-X (paperback : acid-free)
    I. Title   II. Series.
PQ8180.1.L9B313   1991
863--dc20   90-49121
                                              CIP

This project is supported in part by grants from the National Endowment for the Arts in Washington, D.C., a federal agency, and the Commonwealth of Pennsylvania Council on the Arts.

Financial support was also granted by the Department of Romance Studies at Cornell University.

Translated from Spanish title *El bazar de los idiotas*.

Permission to translate from the Spanish text given by original publishers, Plaza & Janes Editores, Bogotá, Colombia.

Cover by Francisco Bedmar

Bazaar of the Idiots may be ordered directly from the publisher:

    Latin American Literary Review Press
    2300 Palmer Street, Pittsburgh, PA 15218
    Tel (412) 351-1477 Fax (412) 351-6831

INTRODUCTION

When North Americans know anything about Colombia, it usually relates to either Gabriel García Márquez or drug trafficking. Nobel Laureate García Márquez entered the consciousness of U.S. readers in 1970 with the publication in English translation of *One Hundred Years of Solitude*. In 1982 he was awarded the Nobel Prize for Literature. The 1980s also witnessed the worldwide attention paid to Colombian drug trafficking by the international media, to the extent that the Medellín Cartel's ringleader Pablo Escobar is probably a more familiar name to many North Americans than even García Márquez or the President of Colombia.

Literary and economic activity in Colombia, of course, has a much broader base than the work of García Márquez and Pablo Escobar. Colombians wrote two of the most renowned novels of the Hispanic world—*María* (1867) by Jorge Isaacs and *The Vortex* (1924) by José Eustasio Rivera. Colombia's venerable (and largely untranslated) literary tradition remains as unknown to most North Americans as its impressive economic record, which includes establishing the first national airline system in the West (in the 1920s), becoming the world's second largest coffee producer, and currently having one of the smallest foreign debts of Latin American nations.

Another of Colombia's best-kept secrets outside the Hispanic world is the novelist Gustavo Alvarez Gardeazábal. The author of nine novels, numerous short stories, and essays, Alvarez Gardeazábal burst onto the Colombian literary scene in the early 1970s. A precocious and controversial figure in his mid-twenties, he published three novels and began to compete with García Márquez for readers in Colombia. In 1974, in fact, *Bazaar of the Idiots* was the best-selling Colombian novel in the country.

Alvarez Gardeazábal is one of the most controversial intellectuals in Colombia. We met in 1975 when he was living in Cali, in the western part of the country. He was enjoying high visibility, primarily because of the recent success of *Bazaar of the Idiots* and two previous novels. His life was typical of many young Latin American intellectuals: he taught some classes at the local university and wrote a regular newspaper column. I spent two days in Cali and was impressed with Alvarez Gardeazábal's mental quickness and incisiveness. He was usually direct and down-to-earth in one-on-one conversations, and more presumptuous and supercilious when in large groups. I noticed his interest in matters such as ecology and human rights issues that were more North American than Colombian at the time. He had recently created a controversy over the local Cali zoo, claiming in his newspaper column that the animals were being abused. As I eventually realized, he has lived for the controversies that he has created.

Gustavo Alvarez Gardeazábal was born in 1945 in Tuluá, a town of approximately 80,000 inhabitants near Cali. When only a young child he witnessed one of the most horrifyingly violent periods of Latin American history, the civil war usually identified as La Violencia in Colombia. Historic conflicts between Liberals and Conservatives broke into bloody conflict on the streets of Bogotá on April 9, 1948, with the assassination of the popular Liberal candidate Jorge Eliécer Gaitán. Violence continued for a decade throughout the country, but was particularly acute in a few towns of the Valle del Cauca region such as Tuluá. Alvarez Gardeazábal has spoken publicly on numerous occasions of looking out the balcony window as a child and seeing corpses below in the morning. Bandits usually attacked at night and often left mutilated bodies on the streets.

The experience of La Violencia left an indelible mark on Alvarez Gardeazábal and was successfully fictionalized in his novel *Cóndores no entierran todos los días* (Condors do not bury every day, 1972). The remainder of his childhood experience was less exceptional and more typical of middle-class life in the provinces of Colombia during the 1950s. His family had roots in the region of Antioquia, his mother descending from the Basques that came to that area of Colombia in the nineteenth century. His father was a hard-working *campesino* who, in the tradition of the independent Antioqueño pioneers who settled western Colombia, found economic success in clearing and farming land. The young Gustavo attended a private Catholic school in Tuluá, as did the children of most of Tuluá's respected families.

According to family accounts, Gustavo was the model Colombian and Antioqueño child throughout his adolescence: an outstanding student, disciplined, and Catholic. His mother, a profoundly conservative Catholic, was the dominant parental presence. He was reared with the ideal of becoming an engineer and father of a large Catholic family. Upon completing secondary school, he was sent to study engineering at the university in Medellín. As the eldest son, he seemed destined to fulfill the family's expectations.

Everything changed radically for Alvarez Gardeazábal, however, during his freshman year. He came to the realization that he could not accept the role that his family and traditional Colombian society had assigned to him, for he was neither a *macho* desiring to marry a woman and have several female lovers (still the common model in Colombia), nor intellectually attracted to engineering, nor spiritually inclined toward Catholicism. The twenty-year-old rebelled against everything that had constituted his life until then: he accepted his sexuality and assumed a gay lifestyle; he quit his engineering studies and began writing; he totally rejected the Catholic church. The most immediate result of these radical changes was the publication of a short novel (or "pamphlet", as the author calls it) that resulted in his expulsion from the university after one year.

The satirical little booklet that Alvarez Gardeazábal published as a freshman, *Piedra pintada* (Painted stone), is virtually unknown and does not appear in the published bibliographies of his work. Since Alvarez Gardeazábal found such rapid success in the 1970s, few people realize that he had been writing constantly (but not publishing) during the 1960s. As an unknown author, he was also submitting stories to contests during the 1960s. At the same time, he was studying literature at the Universidad del Valle in Cali. He completed his degree there by writing a thesis on the Colombian novel of La Violencia.

In the early 1970s Alvarez Gardeazábal's literary career blossomed in Colombia and the Hispanic world. During this period, from 1970 to 1974, he published what some critics have identified as his "cycle of Tuluá," five books set in Tuluá with similar themes and many of the same characters in each of the stories. Two of these books deal primarily with La Violencia: the short fiction of *La boba y el Buda* (The fool and the Buddha, 1972) and the novel *Cóndores no entierran todos los dias*. Much of the prior Colombian literature of La Violencia had emphasized the physical brutality and the ideological conflicts of the phenomenon. In his short stories and *Cóndores no entierran todos los días*, however, Alvarez Gardeazábal portrayed La Violencia more as a result of long-standing family traditions and feuds than exclusively class or ideological struggle. *Cóndores no entierran todos los días* has appeared in successive editions in Colombia since 1972, has been adopted as a standard classroom text in Colombian schools, and is widely considered a modern classic of Colombian literature.

Despite the enthusiastic local reaction to Alvarez Gardeazábal's polemical analysis of La Violencia, the novels that have drawn a broad spectrum of readers, particularly beyond Colombia's borders, have been *Dabeiba* (1973) and *Bazaar of the Idiots* (1974). *Dabeiba*, the inventive story of a town's response to an imminent disaster, was a finalist for the Nadal Novel Prize in Spain, one of the most prestigious literary prizes in the Hispanic world. The imaginative and humorous *Bazaar of the*

Idiots, an immediate best-seller and later a TV soap opera in Colombia, constitutes Alvarez Gardeazábal's most forceful satire of Colombian social and literary institutions.

In the late 1970s Alvarez Gardeazábal's life and writing once again underwent a radical change. During the early 1970s he had been teaching at the Universidad del Valle, the state university in Cali, and was writing a regular column in newspapers owned by the local oligarchy. By the late seventies his critical stances toward the ruling oligarchy led to his dismissal from both positions. He became involved in local politics and served as an alderman in Cali's municipal government. In 1977 he also published his most daring experiment in narrative technique, *El titiritero* (The puppeteer), a novel which moved beyond the setting, themes, and techniques common in his cycle of Tuluá.

The 1980s were turbulent years for Colombia and Alvarez Gardeazábal, yet they also represented a period of great vitality. Colombia witnessed the curious juxtaposition of the rise of the cocaine cartels with its first Nobel Prize; increased political and drug violence was accompanied by a publishing boom and the emergence of new novelists, such as R. H. Moreno-Durán, Alberto Duque López, and José Luis Garcés González. In 1985, Alvarez Gardeazábal was awarded a Guggenheim Fellowship, which he used to reside in Ithaca, New York, in order to complete *El Divino* (The Divine One, 1986). Before that he had published two novels that launched an unrelenting attack on Cali's oligarchy, *Los míos* (My people, 1981), and *Pepe Botellas* (1984). More recently, he published *El último gamonal* (The last boss, 1987), a modest contribution to the sub-genre of the Latin American dictator novel.

Perhaps it was inevitable that an intellectual career so intimately involved with Colombian politics would eventually lead to a political campaign of his own. In 1988, Colombia held the first mayoral elections in its history. (Mayors had previously always been appointed by the governor.) The new system resulted in the assassination of scores of mayoral candidates. Incredibly enough for an individual who had created numerous enemies on both the left and the right, Alvarez Gardeazábal survived the campaign and was elected the Liberal Party's mayor of Tuluá in 1988. One of the most dangerous political positions to occupy in Colombia from 1988 to 1990 was that of mayor, and at least one of the new generation of democratically-elected mayors was assassinated weekly. Alvarez Gardeazábal not only survived his term but also gained the respect and admiration of many citizens of Tuluá as well as Liberal Party regulars. They were impressed by his bold and honest style during a time when relatively few Colombian politicians demonstrated these qualities.

The publication of *Bazaar of the Idiots* in English marks yet another turning point in this unorthodox Colombian's career. The North American reader unfamiliar with Colombia and Alvarez Gardeazábal should not encounter any significant barriers to understanding this novel in English translation. Nevertheless, some minor points beyond the general introduction already offered may be useful. Above all, one should be aware that Alvarez Gardeazábal's intensely Catholic family and upbringing are typical of Colombia, one of the Latin American nations in which the church as an institution has been historically the strongest. Consequently, Alvarez Gardeazábal's satire of this institution is probably more irreverent when read in Colombia than in the United States. It might be of interest for North American readers to know that beauty contests (see the rear cover) are a vigorously promoted national institution, far more so than in the United States and other Latin American countries. *Machismo* is as alive in Colombia as anywhere else in Latin America, and the idiots' patently unmasculine and anti-heroic behavior is one of the most perversely humorous spoofs of *machismo* to be found in contemporary Latin American literature.

The day after I met Alvarez Gardeazábal in 1975, we took a train from Cali to Tuluá to talk about *Bazaar of the Idiots*, Tuluá, and Alvarez Gardeazábal's writing in general. I remember a pleasant ride through the lush sugar-cane plantations between Cali and Tuluá, and actually meeting many of the special people who appear in *Bazaar of the Idiots*. Most of them, of course, had been transformed in this work of fiction, although many had the same names as in the novel. Although Tuluá and Alvarez Gardeazábal proved fascinating in many ways, the trip did not significantly alter my understanding or appreciation of the novel itself. Rather, I returned to Bogotá thinking that Alvarez Gardeazábal's fiction, particularly *Bazaar of the Idiots*, should hold for North American readers much of the same appeal found in the critical and humorous work of writers such as Kurt Vonnegut and García Márquez. Fifteen years later, with the first English translation of Alvarez Gardeazábal now available, I still find that idea reasonable.

Raymond Leslie Williams
University of Colorado at Boulder

I

Perhaps Marcianita Barona managed to sense the whole conclusion to her story. Impassive, she has contemplated the outcome of the vengeance she nurtured in her solitude as the sole hope in a life destined for submission and scorn. Endowed with the ability to see even the impossible, she will, starting tomorrow, confront the same town that assailed her as a child of sacrilege, until it finally forgot her past in exchange for a backlog of resentment and crass business deals. It will not be the same confrontation of her infancy, much less the one her mother had to endure to assure Marcianita's birth. If she were still alive, and if Tuluá remembered all she stood for, surely nobody today would believe the explanations that have been concocted to justify the wonder that emerged from her body. For the past hour, reporters, television cameramen, hysterical daredevils, and speculators who see their chances of enrichment thwarted have been bemoaning the end of their prosperity. No one remembers Marcianita as the wife of the construction engineer of the Pacific Railroad. Everyone claims to see in her only the survivor of what has been blown to smithereens.

Nevertheless, things now are very different, and they will have to remain that way because destiny has ruled over Marcianita Barona since one October thirty-first, many years ago, when she decided to appear between her mother's legs. That was when the town of Tuluá, the angelic choirs of heaven and earth, the cherubim of the main altar of San Bartolomé's, and the cold mouths of every last one of the houses that then existed, bellowed, begging heaven that the punishment of eternal fire not descend upon Tuluá with the same ease with which Father Tascón had convoked it.

No one uttered a doxology, much less a simple prayer. "The world is ending," Miss Paulina Sarmiento must have screamed from the depths of her hoarseness when she spread the news. Although she was what the ladies of the Association, who never spoke to her, called a liberated woman, she was so upset by this story that she lost count of the bottles of milk she had been distributing since dawn. This job of hers had served, some months before, to alert Tuluá to the fact that in Manuela Barona's house not only was there a passion ripening. It was a sacrilege, and probably a damnation that would rule the streets forever, occasioning a loss of the blessing that Pope Leo XIII had bestowed on the centennial of Buga's basilica, and of the many graces which for one reason or another the pious people of Tuluá had been accumulating through years of prayer and sacrifice.

No one understood it during those first days because Miss Paulina was not known for her good sense. But since neither could anyone understand the appearance of the gray mare on the main square, which Miss Paulina devoted herself to documenting and explaining in her leather-bound diary, her explanation did eventually take hold, becoming an obsession that many tried to destroy, annihilating its originator once and for all.

Doña Manuela must have gotten wind of what was going on because while her pregnancy was visible she managed to stay off the streets and administer her affairs from the farthest point of the jasmine patio which now, with all this miracle working, has been reduced to graceless sterility. Only Miss Paulina Sarmiento, personally distributing some containers of milk, succeeded once, after attempting a thousand ruses, in catching a glimpse of her. She then tore through the streets besmirched with ashes, shouting like an idiot that not only were her previous warnings accurate—about what the mare symbolized and what she had imagined—but also that the shamelessness that swelled within the woman's body would sooner or later amount to the seed of Tuluá's destruction.

The cycle which seems to have ended today began on the day that Father Severo Tascón, recently ordained in the Popayán Cathedral, arrived in Tuluá and took lodging in the house of Doña Manuela Barona—and not in the rectory, as had been the custom of all the previous parish priests. When he was seen dropping off his suitcases at the house of the jasmines, he hardly needed to explain that the comforts of a good boarding house were never equaled by the cold, faded rectory, replete with stormy legends. No one knew who had told him that his residence should be this particular one and not Miss Benilda's hotel, which would have been more in keeping with his position. But he so imposed his judgment that within a few months Manuela Barona was called Sister Manuela. Instead of paying for her services, Father Tascón had the children from the catechism classes invade the house to weed the jasmines, put white stones in the flower beds, and even cook, while invoking the name of the good father. As time passed, the news reached the bishop, perhaps carried on the ever-estimable tongues of the ladies of the Association. Father Severo Tascón was then obliged to hire a maid, have the rectory cleaned, and buy his own pots and pans in order not to further inflame the animosity that had grown against him and Doña Manuela. People quieted down, the rumors were eventually forgotten, and Father Tascón, a model of purity and virtue, capable of resisting the strongest temptation, succeeded in converting himself into a candidate for canonization. Or at least that was how things looked until the day Miss Paulina, by a sheer stroke of luck, saw him leave Doña Manuela's house at dawn, heading for the church to celebrate the five o'clock mass.

At that time Miss Paulina had just been widowed and people greeted her explanations with ridicule. But the mare had already begun to appear, and she was convinced that she could confirm her story and prevent the catastrophe that would befall Tuluá if the necessary measures were not taken to put an end to the gestating submission to Satan.

Ready to break down the walls or roof if necessary, the first thing she did was to rent the house next door. But since Doña Manuela's house always seemed like an infinite tabernacle of jasmines, Miss Paulina was stymied for several months. She then decided to buy a dozen firecrackers from Don Ignacio Kafure. She set them off that very night—waking up half the town, distressed at the thought of the volcano erupting. She was sure that Doña Manuela would come to the door, or at least to the patio, to wail like everyone else. But Doña Manuela did not come out; she only coughed as if to let her noisy neighbor know she had not been disturbed and would go on sleeping.

The next day, a bewildered Tuluá commented on the cloud of dust Miss Paulina had raised, but no one believed her chatter about Doña Manuela and Father Tascón was completely true, the fruit of meticulous observation, and not the result of her own lack of a husband. She was certain of it and resorted to the kinds of tricks, which, though they had made her a wealthy woman, so corrupted her life that about a year ago, still climbing in and out of the English jeep she had bought from Tito Uribe, she decided to die. In fact, she did not have to resort to much subterfuge. On her second bold attempt, having climbed up the bamboo ladder of the chicken coop with a telescope aimed at the bathroom of the neighboring house, she succeeded in convincing herself that Doña Manuela Barona was indeed carrying Father Tascón's child.

That was the day she went out into the streets whooping, shattering the silence with tremendous shrieks, and preparing the way for the eternal moments that the concubine of Tuluá's parish priest, determined not only to survive but to save her child as well, would live from that day on.

There was no meeting of important people, nor did the lines at the confessional at San Bartolomé's shorten. On the contrary, they seemed to grow with the town's awakened curiosity. Only the ladies of the Sacred Heart Association, Miss Paulina Sarmiento, and the invalid

Doña Magdalena de Pérez met to voice their complaints and to plan havoc. The moral obligation, the respectability they were convinced they incarnated, was often dramatic, and the conclusion they reached was that without a second thought they must eliminate the unborn child. According to the explanations the invalid Doña Magdalena emitted from the upper half of her body, if the child breathed the air of Tuluá, the whole atmosphere would remain contaminated for seven successive generations. The solution could be none other than to subject Doña Manuela to an abortion for the honor and salvation of Tuluá. Some of the ladies should go to her house, convince her of the imperious necessity, and take her where the operation could be performed with a minimum of fuss. That was where the plan bogged down. From the first moment, all eyes turned to Miss María Mora, a relative of Doña Manuela, but she was no problem. The difficulty stemmed from the fact that no one wanted to take responsibility for finding a midwife or quack to perform the abortion. They all thought of the ingenious possibility of offering the chance to the town gossips, to see if one of the curers from the red-light district would appear, one of those adept at inducing someone pregnant to vomit on the spot. But the superlatively chaste club, never bereft of gossips, proved to consist of mere idlers, and the affair was thus prolonged. Doña Paulina Sarmiento began to lose hope because the days flew by too swiftly, and even though they met two or three times a week, no one would take the initiative to arrange the pertinent details; assuming leadership of the group, she described the heap of calamities that would descend upon Tuluá if that woman gave birth before the nine months had elapsed and they were not yet prepared. Taking María Mora by the hand, she headed for Doña Manuela's house.

It smelled of jasmine; the breeze blew in and out through the damp brick galleries with reckless ease, and Doña Manuela, her belly big enough for her to give birth in less than a month, received them with the solemnity that infected the whole house. Miss María wanted to control the situation, but Doña Manuela ably took over the conversation, establishing Manuela's due date and not allowing anyone to get a word in edgewise. Doña Paulina grew weary of seeing herself converted into the useless thing she refused to become and hastily provoked a farewell. Nevertheless, she did not miss a detail of the house while listening to its owner speak. She reviewed the possible entrances, established elementary details of security, and engraved in her memory the number of steps between the door and the gallery. When the time came to sell her milk, she mounted her gray mule that was replaced years later by the English jeep and, straddling it like a man, headed for the market in quest of the Huitote Indian who would supply her with some poisonous herbs. With them wrapped in small leather bags, she went home, built a bonfire in the middle of the patio, boiled rosemary water to cover any telltale odors, and in a vessel full of smoky ashes she prepared the potion that would not only make Doña Manuela expel the child but would surely carry her to her grave in less than the six hours required to make her stomach function again. With everything ready, she ran from one closet to another, blinded as she was, looking for a hiding place for the nocturnal labor she herself would undertake. She leaped about the yard unaware that Doña Manuela, alerted by the smell of rosemary that emanated from her neighbor's house, was peering out, observing the whole operation.

When the night was just right, Miss Paulina, carrying in her hands the bottle with the potion, mounted the bamboo ladder she had propped against the roof of her sacrilegious neighbor's house. The objective of the hysterical milk-maid was neither Miss Manuela's room nor the roots of the jasmines on the patio. She had carefully observed the large clay water jug that was hidden between a vine and the dining-room wash stand. If she simply threw her little bottle into the carafe, everything would be set. If she managed to empty it, so much the better. If they heard her, she would probably be confused with the grieving souls that hovered about the water jugs at midnight to slake their purgatorial thirst. No man lived with Doña Manuela. The maids were always in their rooms, and there were no dogs or locks. Tuluá seldom had thieves, and when it did, they came from the outside and robbed during the day. Miss Paulina was thus certain of being able to accomplish her villainy, even though the next day she would have to run like crazy to fetch the doctor—who would be busy—to assuage her neighbor's infinite suffering and to wait for the moment of final destruction. She was so sure of herself, so confident that everything would turn out precisely as she had planned and as none of the ladies of the Association had been able to accomplish, that she forgot about the possibility of making a mistake. Upon hearing a voice that she identified with a certainty more absolute than her certainty of not being wrong, she was so startled and upset that she broke out in a cold sweat and dropped the flask before reaching the jug to complete her task.

"Paulina Sarmiento, why are you trying to take the place of destiny?" was the only thing she could make out. The voice was not that of Manuela Barona, but rather seemed to belong to Father Severo, she said much later. Neither one nor the other, however, made mention the next day of what had happened: Father Tascón, because from then on his sermons were only simple explanations of the sin of calumny—in order to help the faithful see the way—and Doña Manuela, because she did not leave her house or receive any guests other than the breeze that rustled the jasmines.

It was then that Miss Paulina and the other ladies of the Association decided to be more devious and to sprinkle poison elsewhere. They made it more dilute than the bottled potion (which had left a hole in the brick where it had fallen the morning of the fright) and resolved to sprinkle it about the vegetable garden of the lady of the house of jasmines, who, already fearful of the insidious reaction of a dead village, bought nothing at the market.

This attempt ended differently. Instead of poison, what they concocted was pure lye. The goal was to make the plants poisonous, but that did not work out because the overdose of the caustic they applied at night ravaged the garden, and Doña Manuela, unwilling to die of hunger, went out to the market absolutely unembarrassed about her bursting belly. Miss Paulina Sarmiento almost lost her mind. She had been incapable of executing the annihilation; she had precipitated Doña Manuela's exit into the streets to spread damnation and destruction on every corner. The ladies were so taken aback that not even Doña Magdalena de Pérez, who, owing to her partial infirmity, did not miss a detail, was able to protest or to initiate the measure they had planned in the event of the sinner's departure for the out of doors.

She did it with such elegance, with such extreme dignity, wrapped in a fringed shawl and carrying an immense basket on her arm, that when she arrived at the first market stalls, near which Miss Paulina had spent days before spreading her story and from which it had surely begun to spread throughout all of Tuluá, no one was capable of filing a protest or raising the kind of fuss that so often vendors have made over any little thing that might attract attention.

With Doña Manuela it was as if nothing had happened. The respectful silence the bishop instilled in them on confirmation day invaded the market place. Aphasia accompanied her slow parade in search of vegetables and fruits. She did not hear a murmur; she did not rub elbows with anyone. She was about to say hello to the only person she bumped into near the plantain stand, Doña Carmentulia Bueno, with her bulky cloth shoulder pads which were said to cover a living cancer on each shoulder. But she hardly touched her from afar with her fringed shawl because the woman, seeing her approach, blanched and fled for home. She arrived there as livid as they say she was on the day the progressive cancer was diagnosed. She consumed three gallons of alcohol, a bottle of cologne, and ended up by gnawing on the wood from the Holy Land that someone had brought her from the pilgrimage-that-almost-did-not-return.

Upon leaving, Doña Manuela heard the only voice, that of a little boy who could stand no more and looked fearfully at her to warn her not to take the groceries home. He rolled his eyes just as he did when he was vaccinated or forced to take a dose of goosefoot, and screamed and screamed so insistently that Doña Manuela almost lost the calm by which she was accompanied that day and on subsequent days, as she washed with hot water, inspected, and many times discarded the foods that she obtained through her faithful servant.

She had wanted to keep on going out to impose respect and to force all of Tuluá to accept her as she was, and not as what the rabble was maliciously proclaiming on the street corners. But another slander of the old ladies of the Association—who could barely overcome their fright with prayer—converted her into the prisoner she had feared becoming since that distant day when her father died, the victim of tuberculosis run amok. In those days in Tuluá, tuberculosis was something worse than syphilis. Since her father had evaded their diagnosing it and told only his daughter, however, she was able to save herself from that prison, but not the prison that misfortune had imposed on her for simply expecting a child.

She endured longings, nausea, hopelessness. She could not sleep, anticipating Tuluá's vengeance in every shadow. Miss Paulina's story—that all the market vendors she had bought fruits and vegetables from had at least one illness per family the following week—crushed her, isolating her completely from the events in Tuluá, which considered her a sinner and a scourge. Day after day, filled with ire as she made clothes for the unborn child and cooked to entertain herself, she imagined the forms of vengeance she would take against each and every one of the inhabitants of this town that had been convinced by a crazy old lady, an impudent thief like Miss Paulina Sarmiento. Every moment of her child's final gestation was also a moment in begetting her vengeful plot. Parallel with the growth of her belly, her mind, clouded as it was by the frustration she felt as a woman and as a Catholic, was making way for every possible plan of retaliation; this she declared as she pruned the jasmines on the patio, sure of being overheard by her neighbor.

She would not accept the treatment she was accorded. She had no intention of explaining her feelings to anyone, much less of trying to disavow the rumor. Inasmuch as the townspeople were entertained every night by trying to catch the mare that pranced through the park, she would rest, seated in front of the jasmines, gazing as if hypnotized. Only after ten o'clock, when either the people would get tired or the mare would disappear across the Abad's dark pasture, would Doña Manuela manage to snap out of her trance, go to bed, and begin her recurring nightmare of awaiting, wrapped in a shadow, the arrival of the vengeance that Tuluá plotted minute by minute against her, against the child in her belly.

No one, not even she, could explain the elusive night-mare that appeared in the Boyacá Park every evening at seven, when the street-lights were barely lit. The gray mare could never be clearly identified. Some maintained it was charcoal, others saw it as black, but no one was capable of finding some mark or sign that would prove it came from Chucho Zafra's or Don Jesús Sarmiento's herd. Making herself almost invisible at the moment the lasso was over her and running when everyone saw her standing still except for the one who had thrown the rope, the mare was classified by Miss Paulina as the clearest demonstration of the sin that was gestating. She had wanted more than this denomination. The meddling neighbor would have preferred to organize a protest and then a public burning of the sinner, à la Joan of Arc, but no means she used to try to promote such an outcome proved effective. She could not even destroy the mare because no one was capable of catching her between seven and ten at night, the time of her parsimonious promenades through the park. Desperate, Miss Paulina went to her brother for help, and two nights later, exactly five nights before Father Tascón was to pack his trunk with the ornaments, Don Jesús Sarmiento's cowboys arrived in town.

There were more than fifty of them, and they all carried lassos. Their assignment was not limited to capturing the mare, dismembering her, immolating her, and dispersing her ashes under the hoofs of their horses. It included also harassing Doña Manuela Barona, who was expecting the anti-Christ in her belly. Don Jesús had been charged with convincing them all. Spurred on by promises of free liquor and veal before and after, the cowboys descended upon Tuluá, raced about, spat in the streets, broke down even the resistance of the druggist who had refused to sell them muriatic acid, and began the hunt for the gray mare.

It was not yet six o'clock, but they were all ready, seated with their whips on the stone steps of San Bartolomé's vestibule, or riding about the park on their steeds. According to information from uncertain sources, the mare appeared immediately when the lights were lit. At the time of our story there was nothing in Tuluá but four light bulbs in the park, one at the railway station, three along Sarmiento Street, five at the river bank, and one apiece at the houses of Don Alfredo Garrido, Don Nicolás Lozano, and Dr. González. In the rest of the houses either the townspeople could not afford the electrical service or, like Dr. Uribe, they chose to remain in the dark rather than pay Agobardo Potes, the owner of the power company. Doña Manuela was one of those who still used candles, and maybe that was why her complaints were heard by no one, surrounded as they were by darkness.

At about seven, a few minutes after the lights went on, at first with a twinkling glimmer, then with the intermittent surges of the local plant, and finally with the permanent brilliance with which they had been proudly represented by their owner, the mare appeared near one of the corners toward the Abad's pasture. No one saw her pass until she reached the park, where they glimpsed her running round the electric lantern like a moth flitting about a candle. At that same moment, Doña Manuela sat down in her wicker chair and, rocking gently, began to enter the gloomy state in which no one saw her but which she never forgot and engraved in the mind of her unborn daughter. With the passage of years, and with many of the circumstances forgotten, the daughter and only the daughter could indulge herself the way she perhaps does now.

That night Doña Manuela suffered more than on the day of the birth. The gray mare did too. Don Jesús Sarmiento's cowboys, with an hour-and-a-half's worth of *aguardiente* under their belts, their hands cramped from so much waiting with their ropes at the ready, their palates longing for the veal they would taste upon returning, and the pride each one had in being the best, were befuddled by the little mare who traced odd circles around the first light. Those who initiated the first assault were already so drunk they could hardly throw their lances. Those on horseback attacked the mare without throwing a single rope. Doña Manuela, bathed in sweat, writhed in her wicker chair as if the dénouement had arrived. An infinite heat enveloped her, capable of scorching her clothes, her self, her child. Unable to escape the concentric rings around the post, the gray mare circled, each time faster than before, lost to the inflamed eyes of her would-be captors. Doña Manuela was tiring little by little, and a long, mysterious, profound moan escaped her lips, symptomatic of childbirth for anyone who might be listening, and potentially the maximum expression for Doña Paulina, if she had been keeping vigil at the neighboring house instead of watching the mare revolve at full throttle around the lamppost.

The cowboys were stunned; not even one of Don Jesús Sarmiento's many unbroken colts would have been capable of such a feat. During an instant of inattention, the mare broke free and instead of encircling the first post galloped about the whole park. At the fifth turn they seemed to shake off their astonishment, and the mare seemed to show what they ingenuously believed was a symptom of fatigue. Doña Manuela Barona, moored to her chair as if it were her only contact with reality, stopped moaning but was drowning in such incredible agitation that if Miss Paulina had heard her, she would have believed the mare was inside her neighbor's house and not in the park, where at that moment the mare had stopped, completely exhausted and kicking. Don Nicolás Lozano, the prominent patriarch, had sprinkled on her what everybody believed at first to be holy water because the mare writhed, wanting to remove something very annoying from within. Later, when a drop fell on the arm of the nearest onlooker, they discovered this substance to be some muriatic acid that the cowboys had bought from the pharmacist. In pain, the mare defended herself, kicking at the ropes that miraculously fell short of her, no matter how many Don Jesús's expert cowboys tossed at her. Doña Manuela lost control of her hands anchored to the wicker chair. The cowboys charged, sure of being able to strangle the mare, tired and spent as she was, but at that instant the bell tower of San Bartolomé's chimed the night Angelus, and she miraculously was able to break loose from her circle of captors and lose herself in the Abad's pasture. Doña Manuela collapsed on the floor of her house, and only the next day, when the maid who watered the jasmines awakened her and carefully picked her up, was she able to figure out all that had happened. Perhaps because of the immense suffering or maybe because in reality Don Jesús's cowboys had made the floor of her house tremble so (and continuous tremors unsettle any stability), at that time Doña Manuela mentally initiated the birth process. She preferred that pain a thousand times to the pain of seeing herself again in the bitter peril of the night before. The mare would inevitably return, and even through Don Jesús's cowboys would not, the possibility of her capture still existed. No one had been able to catch the mare; everyone had seen her, Don Nicolás had bathed her in muriatic acid, and she had writhed in pain. It was no devil, as Miss Paulina had tried to say while witnessing the inability of her brother's cowboys, but rather an animal ridden with vices and aided by celestial powers.

They will return, thought Doña Manuela. But no one, transfixed by the hunt and engrossed in the expanding racket of hoofs and shouts, had noticed the chime of the Angelus. In the end they were all convinced that the mare was a devil, and with such supernatural beings it was better not to interfere. The mare must not have felt or thought the same, for in the midst of the pregnant woman's anguish and the terror of the inhabitants of Tuluá who glared at her with hostility, around seven o'clock the mare returned. Instead of running rings round the post she had encircled the night before, this time she ran straight for Don Nicolás Lozano's house and deposited on his doors and walls a clear sign of her displeasure.

At ten that night, when the mare had again disappeared in the Abad's pasture, the Barona woman came down with a fever, and in Don Nicolás's house there was not a single piece of china left intact. The mare's kicks against the walls cracked all the decorations, and it almost shattered the lives of Don Nicolás and his wife to see pieces of the ceiling fall. In order to drive the mare down the road to the Abad's pasture, they recited all the prayers they knew, entrusted themselves to all the saints they found in the Bristol Book, and took recourse to water from Lourdes that Don Alfredo Garrido had brought back from his pilgrimage to the Holy Land.

Doña Manuela's stupor turned to delirium; Tuluá...the terror of sleeping...and Don Nicolás and his wife at home. The next day when the mare returned, Don Nicolás was at his mother-in-law's house, and the mistress of jasmines collapsed again. The birth seemed imminent but did not take place. The mare still had some unfinished business to tend to: to go to the rectory to kick insistently on the wall as a plain confirmation of what had transpired; to further intensify Doña Manuela's pains until she believed either she would see heaven or die in childbirth; and especially to provide Miss Paulina with the joy or terror of hearing the groans of the mother of what she continued to consider the devil renascent. Not one of the other inhabitants lifted a finger. Since the mare was definitively the devil incarnate, no one dared go out doors either that night or any of the following nights. The pilgrims to the Holy Land, whom the town had given up for lost three times in the four-and-a-half years they spent going and coming, recited this adage with the air their adventure had lent them: whosoever sees the devil will be condemned to eternal fire. And no one so much as peeked out a window while the mare was up to her old tricks, continuing to kick the rectory and finally stopping the next night at the house of jasmines, where she left at the door the most extraordinary quantity of manure that any animal could have shit in its life. Then, after taking twenty laps about the park at an infinite gallop, she vanished, not to be seen again for years either in the Abad's pasture or on the streets of Tuluá.

Everyone remembers the insistent pounding on the doors of the rectory and of Doña Manuela's house that last night. Everyone recognized the stench of excrement that persisted for days and weeks at the door of the house by the park. No one forgot the inexhaustible gallop, the noise of hoofs against cobblestones, the last ride of the gray mare. Prayers of thanksgiving rose from every house, incense was burned in honor of the Divine Majesty, numerous penitents came forth, but Father Tascón did not have the bells rung. The next day, just one day before Marcianita Barona was born, Tuluá saw him collect his belongings, climb the tower of San Bartolomé's, ring the bells himself, carry his suitcases to the station in a hand cart, and wait for hours and hours for the train that finally came for him.

Father Tascón said farewell to nobody. He gave no one any explanation for his departure. With a suitcase full of valuable ornaments and a few other items that neither Doña Manuela nor Miss Paulina could ascertain, the father stopped for one minute at the house that had generously received him, looking at his quarters for the last time. He perhaps said good-bye not only to the woman who had facilitated his departure, but also to that child in her belly that a momentary lapse in his celibacy had begotten. It was the punishment of a family and a whole town that, although they considered him the father of the child about to be born, never lacked respect for him nor disbelieved his words and deeds. Bent not by the years, which weighed little on him, but by an infinite shame that coursed through his arteries and which Tuluá later attributed to the monstrous kicks that the mare had administered him the night before leaving, Father Tascón crossed the park and reached the door of his church. As his final act, in full view of everyone and without so much as wrapping them up, he sent Doña Manuela the dishes from the rectory and an immense trunk.

It was October 30, 1916. Unfortunately, Tuluá has forgotten it with the years and perhaps because of that failure of memory can find no distinct explanation today for recent events. If someone really remembered the story behind the pair of idiots, no one would be doing what they are doing today. They would be thinking of Father Tascón and his multi-colored ornaments made of gold leaf, his dishes, his trunk, and his long wait at the railway station in order finally to get on the train for Buenaventura and to leave Tuluá forever.

The train was scheduled to arrive at midday. Father Tascón started waiting for it at ten in the morning. Seated at first on the wooden bench on the station platform and then pacing the length of the brick pavement from the warehouses to the water tank, Father Severo waited alone for noon to come. Not a single one of his flock had gone to accompany him to say at least one word of gratitude or to repay him for the many sessions spent awaiting some news of those on the excursion to the Holy Land, which had left in December and did not return until July four years later. He never wanted to celebrate mass in posthumous homage to those whom Tuluá had given up for dead; he insisted instead on a series of Gregorian masses to provoke their reappearance. On that same platform, several years before, he had felt sorrow and frustration when faced with the silence of his faithful pilgrims. And the day they arrived, they did it so secretively that neither the father nor Tuluá, which grieved for its dead without having forgotten them and wanted to offer them the heartfelt tribute it nurtured, noticed their return.

Also silently on that thirtieth of October, the father withdrew from his parish and left the mother of his child suffering the first pangs of childbirth. The sun beat forcefully down on the solitary soutane and on the jasmines of the Barona patio. Miss Paulina, already certain that the event could not be deferred and that Tuluá had neither prepared for nor avoided it, returned to her task with the lye. And at high noon, almost before the eyes of Doña Manuela, who withdrew into herself in order to bear her labor pain, she climbed the adobe wall separating her house from that of the sinner and sprinkled the jasmine patio with caustic soda. If no one had been able to make Doña Manuela abort, at least Miss Paulina could make her suffer at the culminating moment of every unwed mother. The jasmines, feeling in their entrails the fire the soda produced, hardly withered. The quasi-parturient either did not see it or did not let on that she did; clutching her abdomen in the breeze that could no longer carry the odor of jasmines that afternoon, she made her own way to bed and awaited the moment.

Alone because no midwife was willing to help her, she watched the hours pass on that day which Tuluá neither understood nor was capable of even noticing. Undressed, with her legs spread, taking refuge in the darkness of her room, perhaps reliving her indigenous ancestry, she was ready for the birth of her child of sacrilege. On her night table, two bottles of alcohol, three clean rags, a pair of scissors, and a glass of water. On the station platform, the long, black figure. It was past midday and the train had not yet arrived. The other passengers, sure of having seen him awaiting the train that would finally carry him away from Tuluá, canceled their journeys or kept a prudent distance, so as not to say a word to him, not to shout a blasphemy, not to offend his sensibilities in any way.

When the train arrived, three hours late, and he boarded his suitcase and climbed nimbly into the last car, he tried to look through the window at Tuluá, but the suffocating smoke from the locomotive and the irrepressible swell within him made him lower his head and breathe deeply. He opened his breviary and waited.

He had been anticipating that moment from the first instant he climbed into Manuela Barona's bed, when wind and history stood still in Tuluá, opening a gap that only today, many years later, seems to be closing definitively. It was three-thirty in the afternoon on October thirtieth when the midday train pulled away.

II

A month after the press had reported as a miscellaneous and innocuous news item the case of the Swiss man, Brother Andrés arrived in Tuluá. The Marist Brothers billed him as the main attraction for a grand bazaar to benefit the construction of their school. They, as well as Tuluá, remembered him from the days of the reign of Inesita González, when he produced a great spectacle with his trained spiders and double-tailed lizards. That day he arrived with a new array of spiders. Many years had passed; he now wore darker glasses and he was starting to go bald. From the moment he entered into the community of the Marist Brothers, in his remote, comfortable childhood of precocious vocation and smelling like the coffee of his native Armenia, Brother Andrés was characterized by his large eyes and his special ability to manage to stand out from the crowd. First, during the days of his novitiate in the Torobajo seminary, he was always a great athlete. In a place like that, where the altitude causes great shortness of breath, with the strength of a Quechua Indian he won all the track events. He was nothing less than a wizard at chess, a champion at ping pong, the basketball team center, the soccer team goalie, and the one who could put the most communions, sacrifices, ejaculations, and meditations on the little card that all the seminary students had to fill out and add to the spiritual bouquet before the Virgin's altar every Saturday. Surely, as he ran, as he thought about a chess move, and as he smashed the ping pong ball, Brother Andrés would recite the ejaculations that earned him indulgences or would meditate on Mary and her original sin or her immaculate conception. Anyway, he was without equal in those areas of endeavor. His academic work was not especially impressive, but since seminary education emphasized a healthy mind in a healthy body, the professors took it upon themselves always to give him the best grades, even though they might reflect what he had earned on only the first answer of five on an exam.

After his third year, when athletic triumphs had become as easy for him as they were undistinguished, he discovered the strange world of hypnotism. Starting with the instant he could hypnotize a hen, he tirelessly sought to learn all there was to know. He read one book after another, talked with Killer, Fu Manchu, and whatever first-, second-, or third-rate magus he could find. From his grandfather's library he rescued a book they assured him had belonged to the Wizard of Oz, and from writing to newspapers so often in order to obtain the address of Mandrake, he finally contacted an Indian guru who gave him the instructions that brought him fame in the novitiate. He never received his letters through the concierge because they were all opened and read before being distributed to the seminarians. In a thousand ingenious ways he made use of the people of Torobajo so that amongst his laundry, in the pocket of a recently ironed shirt, or as he did his morning calisthenics and training around the seminary, he could deliver or receive the correspondence that gave him all the broad knowledge he utilized.

His companions noticed him on the day of a geometry exam when neither he nor they knew anything of the subject matter. He approached Brother Tobias, and with a piercing gaze he created the great scandal. It was as if Brother Tobias were trapped in time. The future Brother Andrés tiptoed toward him, took the exam, read it carefully, copied it as best he could, put it back in Brother Tobias's hands, and, with a snap of his fingers ten minutes later, when everyone together had solved the five problems, brought the brother-professor back from his trance. Brother Tobias was unaware of what had happened, and even those without a chance of passing excelled. The brother-professor was dumbstruck. He had made up the test only five minutes before entering the class, and no one had seen it. He finally explained it as a consequence of the miraculous intervention of the Holy Ghost.

So Brother Andrés decided to become a magician. Hypnotizing chickens made him famous, and hypnotizing young men made him infamous. When an order from the Universal Vicar of Religious Congregations arrived for him to cancel all his activities as a hypnotist, the whole country already knew of his feats and imagined what he was likely to do as a Marist Brother, a friend of youth. He had learned to control himself, to feel self-confident in public and this, together with the fever he still felt from his days as an athlete seeking adulation, led him to climb all the snow-covered peaks in Colombia. From Mt. Ruiz, where he began what he himself was to call a major feat, to the insignificant Puracé, all bowed to his prowess. He appeared in one newspaper after another, he filled entire columns with his mellifluous declarations, and he was even decorated by the Japanese government for having found on one of his ascents the remains of the princely heir, who had disappeared some twenty years before in the midst of the uproar of the Second World War.

After conquering all the Andean peaks, he took up his ancillary profession as trainer of insects and reptiles. When he first arrived in Tuluá, he was the famous scaler of snow-covered mountains of the tropics and a novice trainer of hairy spiders, double-tailed lizards, and suicidal scorpions. The day of his appearance to raise money for Inesita

González's trip to Cartagena, he carried some covered flasks containing his little animals. He put them on top of a table covered with a green tapestry, and one by one he would remove them by hand, without being bitten. He would put them in the sleeves of the soutane he wore at that time, or they would leap about the stage to the terror of the spectators, who remembered how one of those chicken-spiders, when the flooding river rose as far as the park, hid in the toilet in Don Jesús Sarmiento's house, killed his eldest son, and left the second one sterile. Brother Andrés handled his animals gingerly; he had not yet acquired the mastery derived from so many years of mountain climbing. But when he finally chose this career and spiced it with trips to conventions on American fauna and Amazonian flora, he carried his act off with the greatest aplomb.

The day the Marist Brothers brought him as their benefit show's chief attraction, Brother Andrés was already a national celebrity. To his deeds as an alpinist he had added his talents as a hypnotist and his ingenious ability to train insects and reptiles. The bazaar was jammed, perhaps an omen of what Tuluá's fate would be a few days later. Brother Andrés appeared as the evening's grand finale. They placed him again on the same table covered with the green tapestry, but on it he put not the covered flasks he used to take his animals from, but rather some crystal and metal cubes with spring doors and some special pincers. His hair was white and now covered only half his head. He no longer wore a soutane, although he continued to be a Marist Brother and a professor of literature at Christ Academy in Manizales. Before going into his act, he gave a long lecture on his accomplishments as an alpinist, details of his decoration as a member of the Order of the Rising Sun, incidents with his spiders, his world record as a conqueror of the unknown summit of Tolima. Finally, he emphasized his friendships, making note of what positions *his* friends occupied and who had been *his* friends at various times in his life. At last, when people were about to burst with impatience before the only arachnologist in the world, he turned to the table where he kept his animals. He presented each one of the cubes, descending from the stage to the first rows. The women screamed to see the spiders pressed against the glass of their containers; some men trembled, but others were able to hear the explanations of each animal's poisonous characteristics, the place where it had been caught, the number of months it had been in captivity, how often it ate each week, the foods it consumed, and a thousand and one details that only the supple mind of Brother Andrés was capable of retaining or inventing without anyone's being the wiser.

He took off his jacket, and all those attending the bazaar saw him in the short-sleeved black shirt that highlighted his hairless arms, burned by a sun that was not exactly the sun of the beach.

The first animal to come out of its box was a lizard with two tails, one black and one white, and a tongue that resembled that of St. George's dragon. The spotlight focused on his hand, and the lizard went up and down the Marist Brother's arm, flicking its forked tongue, red and threatening. It was said to be one of a nearly extinct species of poisonous lizards unable to grow longer than eleven centimeters, but capable of killing a horse by simply pinching it between the two tails. The size of the tiny animal and its inoffensive appearance upset no one. When he opened the second box and a lizard almost fifty centimeters long came out, and with the ease of a trapeze artist he avoided touching its tail, the eyes of many spectators began to pop. He had it jump to the stage, climb back up his pants leg, coil up on his stomach, climb to his head, and from there, as he announced in a cracked baritone voice, take the great mortal leap of Pepi, the lizard of the Orinoco. The crowd applauded, the whispers grew, and more than one lady sat with buttocks tensed on the edge of her chair.

He opened the third box and with no warning, with no kind of explanation, a yellow spider with paws that resembled bulldozer treads ventured half way onto the green tapestry, looking defiantly at the audience. Brother Andrés touched it with his hand and stroked it with a wand that sometimes looked like metal and other times like rubber. He had it jump over coins he had stacked up and finally subjected it to a bath in the aquarium he had brought. He dunked it in the water over and over until it stayed in the depths of the aquarium for more than three minutes, only to emerge as energetically as it had left the glass and aluminum cube at first. It shook off the water like a dog, walked with the speed of a turtle, and when Brother Andrés tapped the table it once again entered the box it had left so blithely. The auditorium broke into applause and murmurs. A few minutes later, that applause would turn to screams. A fuzzy black-and-white spider performed like a dance master, walked like a horse, crawled under a jar lid, carried five kilograms for three meters, dove into the aquarium after fearfully dipping in one paw like a bather afraid of cold water, and when it grew tired, it dried itself on a towel, rolling about like a bathing beauty. The shouting, the applause, the laughter, the hysteria, and the astonishment of the crowd produced great delight on the face of Brother Andrés. They say it was because of that weakness that he had already cast aside one financial offer from a Japanese television network which, knowing that the Order of the Rising Sun already dangled on his chest, wanted to exploit that decoration and his ability to train insects and reptiles. The truth is that the Brotherhood, fearful of losing him if they allowed him to go to a heretical, Masonic country, summarily prohibited him from having any contact with the public other than through benefit performances. He did not quit the Community, as so many of his compatriots have recently done, because his traditional spirit forbade him to. He obeyed the letter of the law of his superiors and cast aside the temptation of flesh and lucre.

If he had fallen into temptation, surely what happened to him that day of the benefit performance would not have transpired. After three or four years of exploiting television programs or private shows, he would have been able to save enough money to buy a little house at the foot of those mountains that still beckoned to him. He could have retired and lived off the profits of his talents, those abilities that have always sustained the brothers of the Community. But he did not fall. He remained faithful to what he had promised on a remote morning in the Torobajo seminary before a wide-open Bible; and in Tuluá, before an audience that had seen him only one other time in its life, Brother Andrés began to live his death.

The next act, brought from the Amazon, was the spider *Metropolus*, with a hook on its forehead that made it look like a multi-colored beetle or a rhinoceros, and which meant for him the beginning of the end. It was absolutely domesticated. It was not so aggressive or refined as the one that had bathed for three breathless minutes, but it never took a false step nor was it necessary to subject it to the discipline of the wand. It walked up the brother's hand, tickled him with its gaff, jumped to the floor, approached the spectators, and produced screams; women left their seats and the first rows emptied, until it returned to climb up the hand of its trainer. It had never played a mean trick on Brother Andrés, who trusted it implicitly. He thought he knew it because almost no one before had ever found a specimen of such a temperament, and one who had done so, a French scholar of the turn of the century in Leticia, had died, assassinated by all the spiders that had left their open jars and rolled down from their shelf one afternoon. The records on this spider indicated that at a certain age it behaved unpredictably, but the brother had either noticed nothing unusual or believed that his spider was still very young. He did not remember the accounts of the Frenchman until the little spider, upon its second leap from the table to the floor, instead of jumping perfectly happened to fall clumsily. Brother Andrés squatted down to retrieve it as the people applauded, and then came the hecatomb. The spider, blinded, instead of clambering up the hand that it had climbed in every performance, leaped and grabbed the nape of his neck.

The spectators saw Brother Andrés collapse, trying without success to get his hand to his neck; the spider let go of the nape of his neck but grabbed onto his left hand, and there—in the midst of a dreadful scream from the brother, like the scream he might have let loose when he ascended to the peak of Tolima and found the airship of the heir of the Japanese Empire—it buried its barb once and again. The spectators screamed. The doctors in attendance rushed up to help him. The spider, losing a lot of blood through its unicorn, was flaccid on the stage's parquet floor. Meanwhile Brother Andrés tore his black shirt into shreds and made a tourniquet high on his forearm. He was prodigiously calm. He walked among the silent crowd that was dumbstruck with awe. They saw him pass by, climb into a car, and head for the hospital to await his death.

There, the doctors tried to give him the treatment for snakebites, but they discovered that the gaff had destroyed the whole palm of Brother Andrés's hand, and there was nowhere from which to suck anything. They trusted that since it was hemorrhaging, the blood would expel the poison. Then, subject to his consent, they loosened the tourniquet that he had made with his shirt. That was a mistake. Blood gushed down from the wound, but the poison flowed up from the tourniquet. A half hour later, unable to prevent the spread of the inflammation, the doctors administered snakebite serum to him. The arm was as big as an elephant's. His temperature rose and the spasms characteristic of all bites overtook brother Andrés's robust body. They injected him with the antidote to the bite of the X snake, the one with the most deadly poison known to mankind, but it scarcely stirred Brother Andrés from his stupor. The spasms abated for an hour; when they returned, they surged with such force that, desperate for the first time since the climactic moment on stage, he screamed for a mirror.

They left him alone in the emergency room of the hospital, looking at himself in the mirror. He remembered that at moments like this, what could make the blood flow stop was hypnotism, and while waiting for someone who knew about such bites to arrive, or while his ham-radio friends broadcast calls to Brazil in order to preserve the national glory by finding someone who might know how to save the victim of the *Metropolus* bite, he tried to use it. Otherwise he would be dead in six hours. He knew it better than anyone.

The first attempt failed. He was left hypnotized with the mirror in his hand, and when the force of the blood flow diminished, the mirror fell to the floor and broke into a thousand pieces. The crash returned him to his normal state, the doctors rushed into the room, and he, in one last attempt, implored them to have faith in his powers. It turned out to be more difficult to convince them because they believed that any extra movement would spread the poison through his whole body, a half hour after which there would be no salvation. Nevertheless, by insisting he got them to bring a new mirror, and with it in front of him on the stretcher, he slowed his blood flow and staved off death. The doctors could then put him to bed, and there, immobile, he remained for twenty-four hours. The news that arrived from Brazil was extremely discouraging. No antidote for the bite of the *Metropolus* existed, but a call had been made to all the international news agencies in order to obtain from an experimental center some universal antidote that might save him. When the Emperor of Japan heard, he sent a chartered airplane from Tokyo with an all-purpose serum tested on soldiers from New Zealand during the war. The flask arrived on the third day of Brother Andrés's agony. The doctors injected it into one leg. His arms were already so swollen that they began to split like carrion about to explode. The pinprick awakened him from his cataleptic state, produced a certain improvement in the electrocardiogram the doctors were monitoring, but increased the blood flow he had been able to maintain at an extremely slow rate, thereby eluding death.

All hope was lost at this point. The Marist Brothers prayed. The newspapers spoke of the death throes of the passionate alpinist decorated with the Order of the Rising Sun. The radio stations broadcast the final minutes of the Marist Brother who suffered in Tuluá, bitten by a *Metropolus* spider. The people were speechless, and they timidly viewed the remains of the blood-drained spider on the stage of the benefit bazaar. On the fifth day, Brother Andrés's head was already swollen and only one leg was left not yet part of the devastation. The doctors said that when the left leg swelled, it would be all over. The results from the lab arrived on that fifth day and were a complete disaster. Instead of decreasing the spasms and the swelling, the serum gave death a larger foothold in the alpinist brother, trainer of insects and reptiles, decorated with the Order of the Rising Sun, first arachnologist of the world.

It was at that moment when someone decided to take him to the idiots.

III

When Nemesio Rodríguez arrived on the midday train, Marcianita Barona was on the station platform, wearing the same complacent expression she must have worn when she emerged screaming from between Doña Manuela's legs. In the solitude of her room, perhaps she had tried to tell Miss Paulina and the ladies of the Association that in spite of them and their attempts to annihilate her within her mother's belly, she was indeed alive. It was the thirty-first of October of 1916, and Tuluá should have felt something akin to what was felt every time the Barragán volcano's tremors shook them to their bowels. It was nine-thirty in the morning. Miss Paulina, sure that the event was imminent, kept her ear glued to the wall of the room that, with millimetric precision, she identified as the borning room. At her side was Magdalena de Pérez, president and treasurer of the Association. Everything was foreseen. Peeking over the wall, they had established that jasmines no longer thrived along Doña Manuela Barona's limitless patio. Accompanying the ladies were three bottles of holy water, a dozen palm branches from the previous Holy Week, and a bag of blessed pebbles with which to attack the devil, should he appear with his sulfurous odor, his chains, and his mission to corrupt them, Tuluá, and the atmosphere that for centuries had breathed of purity.

The moment they heard the yowl, all the ladies reviewed the procedure they had agreed upon in the previous days. No one uttered a word. Hardly exchanging glances, they took up their holy water and prepared the blessed pebbles. Five minutes later, since neither did the devil appear nor did the infant cease its bawling, they exited like robots through Miss Paulina's door and, sprinkled about the town like army ants, broadcast the news that was reflected twenty minutes later in the curious gazes of thousands of *tulueños* coursing continuously past Manuela Barona's door. The child continued to cry, and the most righteous ladies of the parish interpreted that bawling as Satan's blubbering, which always sought to draw sympathy from the unwary. They stopped at the doorway, and when Miss Blanquita Lozano, the only friend that Marcianita Barona was to have in Tuluá for many years, tried to enter, the ladies blocked her way. They were the vanguard of Tuluá's salvation, and they were not about to stand idly by, permitting the demonic reincarnation merciful succor.

Doña Manuela learned of it while still in childbed. Assisted by her maid but unable to give her child even a drop of milk, she tried to make herself comfortable despite her weakened condition for having given birth practically alone. With her breasts bursting but unable to nurse her child, because at some time the doctor had told her that a newborn should not be fed for twelve hours, she did not know what to do about her daughter's intermittent wails. At one-thirty in the afternoon she could no longer stand the already almost agonizing cries of her little girl, and in spite of the prohibitions she observed with such distrust, and before the astonished gaze of her maid, who had not finished washing her hands in alcohol after having been smeared to the havelocks with blood, she gave breast to her child.

The ladies at the door almost howled when silence was imposed on their zeal to embody the vanguard. They looked at each other, proposed to go to Miss Paulina's, abandoned the portal they were so avidly guarding, felt they were soon to receive Satan's whip, and, blessing themselves, desisted from impeding the already diminished flow of people past the door. Father Severo Tascón's daughter then seemed to breathe more easily. Doña Manuela's maid could go out to buy the alcohol they needed, food to replace what the lye had ruined, and, most important for a house wherein flowers had great meaning, a bough of white jasmines.

Blanquita Lozano almost caught her as she left. She had had a basket ready ever since Miss Paulina had run through the streets spreading the news, and she gave it to the maid as she returned. At the bottom was a note: "Don't worry, Doña Manuela. If your daughter were a little Martian, the town would fear her no more." And from that day on, having no one to baptize or register the child, Doña Manuela called her daughter Marcianita, little Martian. She wanted to give her the surname Tascón, but she thought it better to avoid future problems. As long as she continued to be named Barona, her daughter would be safe from tongues like that of Miss Paulina Sarmiento, who, ready to run the ultimate risk of repeated failure, took to the street, stood at the door, and, abetted by the chorus of the ladies of the Association and Doña Magdalena de Pérez, raised a ruckus with shouts of "Lucifer must be destroyed."

An hour later they had almost a hundred people gathered together, and at five-thirty in the afternoon, when folks from all over the countryside were reaching the park, the tumult turned into a demonstration with Miss Paulina at the head, a torch in her hand and a howl on her lips. Lucifer had to be burned. Before the gray mare again appeared, before eternal punishment for Tuluá erupted from the beyond, she—and everyone supported her with shouts as if hypnotized—was going to burn alive the demon engendered by Manuela Barona. She forgot, or

wished to forget, that in Tuluá there was a mayor and that Blanquita
Lozano was his betrothed. It was almost seven and all eyes were on the
Abad's pasture, from which, on the night of the thirty-first of October,
the gray mare would appear—the night-mare that would nourish the
demon that Manuela Barona had just given birth to—and Miss Paulina
Sarmiento already brandished on high the torch that would purify Tuluá
of all contamination. Just then, from the depths of the demonstration
and with a rifle inherited from the War of a Thousand Days, the mayor
scarcely ordered Jesús Sarmiento's sister to drop the torch, and the
crowd began to disperse, breaking the spell. In the confusion, the ladies
of the Association could not protest. They had spent the whole afternoon supporting the fiendish Paulina Sarmiento, but when the time
came to act with the greatest alacrity, their gullets scarcely emitted the
sound of a plague-infested goose. When the mayor threatened to lock
them in their houses and to serve them a summons the following day,
they went obediently home and were no longer seen about town until
many months later. By then all was forgotten, and only Don Jesús
Sarmiento's sister tried to launch a new offensive that would liberate
Tuluá from harboring, at one hundred scanty meters from the altar of
San Bartolomé's, the demonic offspring.

In order to be able to nurture this idea in her mind and in those of
the ladies of the Association, Miss Paulina managed to get them to
describe strange sounds, like moans from beyond the tomb and death
rattles, the smell of sulfur, and secret movements of immovable
objects—all in letters that many residents of Tuluá received in her
handwriting, apprising them of the existence of the demon in the house
of jasmines. No one paid much attention, but little by little, or far in the
depths, the idea was sinking in. As Marcianita took human form and
moved her arms and legs like any neighborhood child, and her mother
decided to run the risk that she had never run when the child's body was
united with her own, one fortuitous error encouraged Miss Paulina to
make her malevolent move.

The day after Three Kings' Day, Doña Manuela decided that her
daughter needed the morning sun and that she should take a stroll,
having completed (at least in her memory, since she had risen from her
bed on the fifth day) the forty days of bedrest that any doctor would
have prescribed at that time. She opened the door of the house and the
warm breeze of all Tuluá mornings entered, wafted through the
galleries, and once again lightly stirred the first sprouts of the new
jasmines she had planted to replace those burned by the harpies. She
took the carriage she had bought months before the birth and, with a

dignity that even the Duchess of Windsor might envy, went outdoors, took a turn around the park, greeted Don Nicolás Lozano (more dead than alive), made a bow to Mother Delfina and another to Mother Leocadia, who were leaving the convent, and returned to her house. She did not tarry so as not to arouse the gossips. Only Miss Paulina saw her just before she re-entered the door, because Don Nicolás had rushed to inform her. She cursed not being prepared to incite Tuluá into pursuing the demon but got ready to do so the next day when Doña Manuela, with the same dignity of the previous morning, again took her daughter for a stroll in the baby carriage. Miss Paulina followed her and, helped by peons she had engaged for the occasion, scattered ashes and lavender disinfectant. Doña Manuela did not notice anything until she turned the first corner at the park and found the eyes of so many people on the sidewalk looking behind her. She wanted to react, to stop in the center of the park and confront Miss Paulina, but the docility she had displayed for years, which had so exasperated Father Severo Tascón, allowed her only to continue her stroll around the park and to return to her house.

The next day she could not take her daughter out for a walk. That night she had heard all of Tuluá coughing. She was sure she recognized the penetrating odor of sulfur at midnight, but since Miss Paulina said at dawn that Tuluá coughed because the demon's daughter had passed along the streets and not because of the loads of sulfur that had been burned on Picacho Hill, Tuluá believed Miss Paulina's version, applied grippe remedies (sugar-water, lemon, and steam), and cursed the demon's presence on their streets.

Surely the milk vendor had burned sulfur immoderately and what Tuluá felt was an overdose. At six in the evening, when the weather cooled down, the coughing intensified, the anginas multiplied, and Tuluá felt the demon's claws in the depths of its bronchia. Only Baby Marcianita did not cough. The coarse linen and gauze curtains her mother had always used acted as a filter for the sulfur, which did not touch her delicate, diminutive lungs. That night in Tuluá, four babes-in-arms died, and Jaime Pérez and Don Alonso Victoria were afflicted with embolisms. At dawn, the mayor, who in the end did not marry Blanquita Lozano, was at Manuela Barona's door. He did not break it down because by such means was dignity measured in those days, but he knocked so forcefully that he frightened Baby Marcianita, and her wails shocked the mayor's whole entourage. In the name of municipal hygiene Manuela Barona and her daughter should be examined by Dr. Simeón Jiménez Bonilla, medical lawyer, surgeon, and Freemason, as they later discovered. Perhaps because of this last detail, Dr. Simeón found nothing wrong with the child and stressed to the mayor that the cough that invaded Tuluá was probably due to the subterranean emanations of the Barragán volcano, dormant since the times of Lemus de Aguirre.

The mayor looked at him, indifferent and incredulous, but since Dr. Simeón was Dr. Simeón and not Miss Paulina, Manuela Barona could remain in her house, and Miss Paulina, suffering from an attack of limitless ire that drove her to sell her house, retreated to her farm at La Colorada and never again had anything to do with Father Tascón's daughter.

Five more children died, three Franciscan nuns suffered strokes, and the streets of the Boyacá Park had to be disinfected with balsam from Tolú. In her retreat Miss Paulina forgot about it, but for many years Tuluá refused to forget, and to speak then of plague or shock, of the evil eye or sorcery, was to speak of Marcianita Barona.

When Manuela again dared go outside, the child was taking her first steps and trying to say her first words. Thin but upright, or stiff, rather, Marcianita planted her tiny feet with the same satisfaction with which her mother had cleared her throat ever since the sulfur-scented night. It was the only memory Doña Manuela had of those early times, but every day from then until her death, she cleared her throat whenever she could, and felt vindicated, not forgetting what Tuluá and Paulina Sarmiento had done to her so spitefully. Not even the very emptiness she experienced each time she went out in public view could prevent her from imparting this above all to her daughter. At all costs and regardless of what might come, Tuluá had taunted her when she was a defenseless child, and she should never forget it.

She used all manner of trickery. She brought Marcianita up so evasive of people, so stubborn in a dialogue, so distant from the caresses that all children her age seek, that when she walked with ease but stiffness, marked stiffness, she would flee from whatever person she saw, or at least would wrinkle her nose as if smelling something foul. The days when she went out in public were either Sunday afternoons, when Tuluá took shelter (until the miracles began), or Monday mornings, in the midst of the marketplace swarm. The solitude of the Sunday afternoons and the long white dress she wore made her look like an untouchable lady who strolled with her daughter of sin. In addition to there being practically no one who would pass through the park on that afternoon, her mother taught Marcianita to smell people. Scarcely would they see her before she launched into meteoric flight to her mother's white gown, and from there, like a native plunked into civilization, she peered out at the world she had been taught to hate. Mondays turned out to be just the opposite, but Marcianita learned at that early age to distinguish between a Sunday afternoon and a Monday morning, and then acted with the wistful antipathy which year after year she has impassively shown. On those mornings, she would not run because there were so many people, but since everyone recognized the devil's daughter, a passageway would open as she went by, holding her mother's hand. For many years Doña Manuela Barona strolled that route without mishap. Only once, when Marcianita already spoke fluently, a lunatic, influenced perhaps by the thousands of tales spun about Señora Barona and her daughter in Tuluá and the surrounding regions, tried to harm them.

Marcianita saw him approach. He was dressed in a monk's habit with half his face covered. They were not frightened because those brothers had been about for some time. Nevertheless, seeing him scream like a savage, brandishing his guava wood staff, Marcianita clung to Doña Manuela, who started to shout, "Brother, Brother, Brother," uselessly trying to remind the in-habitant that she had been a benefactress of the sect since the first member arrived in Tuluá, back in the days when she had not even thought of becoming Father Tascón's mistress. The frocked one paid no attention, and Marcianita, in spite of her tender age, understood what he was up to. Forty-four years later her sons would strangely repeat the action, but without the same result. That day she was no more than two-and-a-half years old. She tore herself from her mother's skirts, opened her arms as if begging for clemency, and looked at the brother in his habit. Absurdly impelled by an extraordinary force, he stopped short, falling on his knees before her. Doña Manuela looked at her as frightened as if she herself were the brother, took her by the hand, and shut herself up in the house for several weeks.

During all those days, she examined her daughter carefully from head to toe, bathed her in holy water and in sulfur water, rattled chains near her ears, and touched her all over with the crucifix, but she observed neither convulsions nor any other evidence that would convince her that her daughter was really the devil that all of Tuluá believed her to be since the day of her sacrilegious birth. She found no explanation for the subduing of the in-habited brother, nor did she allow herself to overlook the possibility that her daughter might be a demon. She took charge then of not only giving her the education of resentment that she had planned to pass on to her in order sometime to take vengeance on Tuluá, but also of training her so that at specific moments in her life she could make use of her terrifying power. She ordered books on witchcraft from Germany and pornographic drawings from Denmark, contracted whatever Indian happened to arrive in Tuluá to bring her stories of necromancy, and was sure to receive all the instructions pertaining to these matters in Marcianita's presence.

But the days and years passed, and Marcianita neither seemed to learn these teachings nor to exercise her power anew. She limited herself to being one more of the many little girls who went to Luisita Tascón's school. She could not go to the Franciscan Academy, as Doña Manuela had at one time intended. Mother Delfina not only did not welcome her but went so far as to detain her at the door of the convent, with cries of "In the name of God, Satan, I tell you once and again, you shall not pass," directly below the portrait of the Immaculata, who impassively presided over that shameful deed. She then went to Luisita's, near the Salesians. The school was not very good and somewhat expensive, but it was in all ways better than the public school, to which she could not send Marcianita at any rate until she reached a certain age. Twenty-three children, eleven male and twelve female, were Luisita's quota. Number twenty-four was Marcianita. On the afternoon in February when she entered, holding her mother's hand, the rest of the children—who as usual had started in October—stood gazing at her. Manuela had not taken her in October because if the mothers of the others had found out, the school year would never have begun at Luisita's. In February, with only three-and-a-half months left to the school year, the reaction would not be very strong. No mother was going to have her child lose an entire year of school just for sharing the same room with the demon. That is what Doña Manuela thought and that is what she told Luisita, and in order to be sure the teacher would not protest, even when she was known to be very liberal and tolerant, Manuela assured her that for every child who left and did not return because of Marcianita, she would take over the payments as if all were attending.

With so many precautions, neither did Luisita anticipate any problems nor was Doña Manuela pessimistic, but in those days Tuluá had not forgotten the scandal Paulina Sarmiento had caused when Marcianita was born. The next day, after all the children had gone home to say that some Marcianita had begun to study with them, and of Marcianitas in Tuluá there was but one and she was the daughter of a sacrilege, eleven mothers rushed to Luisita's to protest and to threaten the withdrawal of their children if the daughter of Manuela Barona were not expelled at once.

Luisita held her ground, and six mothers held theirs, and the next morning Marcianita counted six fewer students in class, and her mother had to send the monthly tuition as if she had not one Marcianita but seven. The rest tolerated her the first few days, but as time passed and they got to know Marcianita and were guided by the venomous tongues of Tuluá, by the heirs of Paulina Sarmiento, and by the ladies of the Association who stood around the corner watching them pass in order to give them sweets and chant slogans against Marcianita, they too were turned against Father Tascón's daughter. No one evoked her origin or tried to ridicule her father, but they treated her like the devil, threw holy water on her, stopped playing with her, painted crosses on her desk, and blessed themselves every time they passed near her. When they ignored her in the classroom and Luisita wanted to prevent it by putting all the desks together with hers in the middle, they invented a way to isolate her completely. If they were obliged to be near her, they never allowed her to answer a single one of Luisita's questions, not even when she was specifically called on. All in unison, if possible, would drown out the voice of Marcianita, who timidly tried to respond to the teacher's questions.

They never touched her, much less attempted to strike her, but one afternoon Nina Pérez, a child with velvet tresses, a wiry figure, and the voice of a squealing rat, had it out with her, smashing all the defenses she had constructed. Marcianita did nothing to provoke her. Nina was just gamboling in from her house, and upon arriving and finding Marcianita dressed in the same white chintz that she wore, she could no longer restrain herself and flew into a rage at the devil reincarnate. The outfit, coincidentally, was just the same as Nina's, a sailor suit with blue fringes. The granddaughter of Doña Magdalena de Pérez grabbed hold of those fringes, trying to drag Marcianita down with them. Luisita could do nothing to halt the spectacle. The rest of the children, screaming together and in a circle that Luisita succeeded in breaking only with great effort, expedited the atrocity's consummation. Marcianita, with her diminutive figure, was easily thrown to the ground by the sinewy Nina, but from there, and in the midst of the astonishment of all—an astonishment they could never erase from their memories and which Nina has never been able to undo—Marcianita raised her right arm to the same height as her left, almost in the same position in which she attacked the in-habited brother, and instead of defending herself, shouted three times, very clearly, "Fat..., fat..., fat...," just when Luisita Tascón broke up the rout.

Marcianita did not return to school and never again knew a pupil's desk. Neither did she ever forget Nina or the other chums who formed the clique that had tormented her. From the depths of the house of jasmines, she remembered from one day to the next that not even at Luisita Tascón's had she been able to be a student. But she did not remain ignorant. Her mother hired Luisita to teach her for two hours every morning; Maestro Cedeño to give her the music lessons that united her with the piano in the parlor from the moment she was willing; and Don José María Tejada to provide her with a knowledge of polemics she could have used recently now to defend her sons. The rest she learned from life, from death (which always hovered about her without ever closing in), and from the malignant shadow that dramatically defined her destiny.

It was perhaps solitude that saved her. She could not honestly say she had a friend either in her childhood or during the many years thereafter. The only person who visited her, other than her teachers, was Blanquita Lozano, who during that period was infatuated with Don José María, her professor of rhetoric and an aspiring notary. Marcianita, nonetheless, never learned whether Blanquita visited her because of the boyfriend, because of her herself, or because of her mother. But in any case, Blanquita was the only other person she knew in the more than one thousand days between her departure from Luisita Tascón's school and the exorcism they performed on her from the pulpit for having run naked through the streets, chasing a pair of pampered armadillos.

Since she had no friends to visit her and Blanquita was too old for her, Marcianita devoted all the energy she had left over from her classes to cultivating the jasmines she inherited from her mother and to caring especially for the two armadillos she had bought, perhaps newly born, from a Barragán mountaineer who passed through selling them one Sunday. She spent time devising methods to graft, cultivate, and enhance the jasmines to such a point that when she needed to pick a blue one with red speckles in order to win first prize at her bazaar, she did no more than summon all the knowledge she had been accumulating from an early age with supremely intense organizational powers, synthesizing on one index card all the information and putting it into practice. She had done it very few times before; for years she would live obsessed with one single goal for her armadillos: their fecund reproduction. She was like that with almost everything; the more jasmines she produced on her patios, in her planters, and in her imagination, the more things she accumulated in her house. More decorated furniture, more armadillo food, and more gold thread for the ornaments that Luisita was teaching her to sew with incredible resourcefulness. Very soon the news reached the ears of Paulina Sarmiento, and instead of appearing as an exemplary seamstress, she was represented in Tuluá and its surroundings as Father Tascón's daughter, who made ornaments without ever having made her first communion.

And since it was true, because neither was Marcianita baptized nor did Miss Manuela go to mass or ever teach her anything about religion—although one could recognize in her a strange tendency toward the practice of the cult of San Bartolomé—Marcianita Barona had no choice but to make ornaments and save them. At first she saved them along with those that were in the great trunk, whose presence in the house was never explained to her, and later she hung them on nails, hooks, and tables, converting the room not into the dollhouse that all little girls of her age long for, but into the sacristy that her father could never make of his house. Nobody noticed that she raised armadillos, that she played the piano, that at the age of ten she was an expert cultivator of jasmines. Everyone did notice, though, that since she was seven, instead of making tablecloths with simple stitches or chain stitches that all the girls in the nuns' academy were sewing, she made ornaments that no priest would ever use because neither did she intend to sell them nor did anyone ever come to buy them. Despite all that, she felt more affection for the two armadillos than for the very jasmines, and logically more than for the ornaments, because only that pair of animals gave her the feeling that no one else offered, that nothing else provided her. In the back patio she made them a wooden house as if they were dogs, and instead of digging holes in the ground (which she later ordered made specifically so that they would breed), they got used to the brilliance of daylight. They found it cloying to enter the burrows and, as time passed, used them only for breeding. Doña Manuela never said a word but rather encouraged Marcianita's interest in the armadillos. That's why, the day that Tuluá was again shocked by Marcianita and her animals, Doña Manuela did not even bat an eye, giving her rousing approval to the scandal that her daughter had caused.

First she trained them. She spent days, entire weeks, teaching them to walk guided by a slender chain she tied around their scaly stomachs. It annoyed them to be directed, and every time she tugged at their chains they would immediately dig a hole. Finally they managed to walk with all the prosopopeia of dachshunds, and Tuluá was completely awash with comments, not to the effect that the demon's daughter was directing her first slaves, but that Doña Manuela must be suffering terribly with a daughter who walked armadillos instead of dogs. She took them only once around the park (and that took hours because of the pokiness of those little critters), but strangely the strolls made the tongues of Tuluá wag at her mother, and, even stranger, with a compassionate air. Miss Paulina said nothing or at least did not speak against them. Doña Manuela could not understand it. To her, what her nine-year-old daughter was doing was a typical scandal, and Manuela had always handled scandals in the same way. As soon as Marcianita came through the gate and her two armadillos entered with the speed of centenarian tortoises, a door slammed in the faces of the scores of onlookers, leaving Tuluá quaking. Not even after that did anyone claim that Doña Manuela was hurt or paying the price for having been Father Tascón's mistress. Miraculously, Tuluá had forgotten that detail, perhaps because Marcianita was so devoid of rhyme or reason. Her wickedness went beyond walking a pair of armadillos or chasing after them naked when they escaped. Instead of suggesting the excuse that she was an incorrigible child or the demon's daughter, they went so far as to feel unanimous pity for her mother.

Which was no mean feat. Marcianita, tolerated or encouraged by her mother, came very close to unhinging the most tolerant of mothers. She would eat only strained soup. Her milk could not have the tiniest trace of cream, for if it did she would scream insanely and go to the linen-covered urn that contained the rest, which, with or without the cream, she would sprinkle on the jasmines. Neither the pillowcases nor the sheets could be starched. If the maid made a mistake and gave her one belonging to her mother (who preferred them stiffly starched), she would carry them to the center of the yard and set them ablaze in front of her armadillos. Her clothes had to be old fashioned, of a style found in a magazine she discovered in one of the trunks of ornaments that Father Tascón had left behind, like the dresses worn by French nuns and not those which her obliging dressmaker in vain tried to propose. Perhaps she was the one who made Tuluá aware of the many misfortunes that Doña Manuela experienced with that child. One afternoon when she had come to measure her for her long dark-colored gowns, she found Marcianita collecting china in a basket. Doña Manuela, terrified, watched from her chair in the dining room. She murmured not a word. She said nothing to the dressmaker. If she had, the china would have been broken over her head, as she had verified one time when, upset, she had called attention to Marcianita's setting some curtains on fire because they had tripped her upon entering the dining room. That day she did not break the china but left it packed in the basket. And while the dressmaker measured her for her gowns, Marcianita managed to comment that her mother had no time for either helping raise the jasmines or walking the armadillos because she spent all her time cleaning china.

And it was true, but not because of the china. Upon reaching the age of fifty, Manuela Barona began to feel a growing malaise in one leg, either because of some curse or because of one of those cycles she claimed to be completing in her world. Sometimes it was a sharp pain, other times a temporary and momentary paralysis. Because of it, she had no choice but to carry on and experiment with various remedies on her leg, unguents on the joint, and exercises to keep it from growing useless. She often neglected the housework, but never did she forget Marcianita. Self-involved as she was, Marcianita still noticed that her mother no longer had so much time to care for her. Since her only possessiveness pertained to her mother, she reacted by putting away the china or hiding the wicker chairs from the gallery so that her mother would not sit down for so long. Manuela Barona had to use her cane so that Marcianita would understand, but it was already too late; her mother would remain lame for life. Her bed worsened her condition, and Marcianita had not left her a single chair. Doña Manuela then accompanied her on her walk every day after five o'clock, through the park and along the river bank, in a desperate attempt at what she termed the remote possibility of not becoming completely paralyzed. Tuluá thus could get to know her and show the pity it finally felt for her, accompanying her at every moment with sympathy that not even her accursed habit of clearing her throat every twenty meters, every ten seconds, could undermine.

Marcianita, as the years passed, began to abandon her infantile demands and to replace them with others, less annoying to her dressmaker and Blanquita Lozano, who continued visiting her, but more burdensome to her mother. Manuela, with a thousand and one gambits, supported her like a princess by selling jasmines and making candy, in addition to receiving in the mail every month a money order that sometimes bore the return address of S. Pérez and sometimes of F. Tobar, but without any doubt was sent by Father Severo Tascón, who was responsible for the child.

He never saw her or mailed her a single letter. Only the monthly money order from the day he must have arrived in Cartagena. It was not much, but together with the jasmines and the occasional box of candy she made and sold to the very demanding clients at prices no one else could afford, it was enough to maintain the house and satisfy Marcianita's endless caprices.

Only once, during the days when they varied their stroll through the park and took another route along Sarmiento Street past the railway station, could the mother not accommodate the daughter. Marcianita decided to fall in love with every hat she saw on the ladies on the train. For the first one, Doña Manuela took the bills from her wallet, and through the train window she bought a leghorn of Italian rattan from someone who would not sell it unless she was paid double what it had cost her. If her Marcianita wanted it, she was prepared to work to get it for her. What Doña Manuela did not foresee was that Marcianita's desires were inexhaustible. A week later, it was a pocketbook; a few days later, some shoes; and on Sunday, a suitcase. Doña Manuela could take no more, and in the middle of the platform she left Marcianita throwing a tantrum because she refused to buy her the suitcase. She suspended the walks to the station, returned to the park and its surroundings, and so distanced herself from Marcianita, and for so long, that many believed that Marcianita would eventually have to enter a convent. At least that was what in her bravado she had threatened to do on the station platform that Sunday when her mother refused to buy her the crocodile-skin suitcase. But since Marcianita had neither been baptized nor had her first communion, her confinement was not mystical but commercial, and along with the jasmines and the armadillo raising she combined the ability to make ornaments bearing unusual embroidery. Tuluá learned that there was no such convent, although she continued to announce it, and by the time she was fourteen, one by one, and almost always by means of a maid (because dignity, decorum, and what "they" would say dictated such measures), the ladies of Tuluá passed by Marcianita Barona's to have her fashion them a tablecloth, a shawl, or an embroidered skirt. She increased the sale of jasmines by offering them to each one of the embroidery clients, but did not sell armadillos because there was no demand for them in Tuluá. If she could have started a new fad, she would have done it with pleasure and grace. Her astounding ability to sell things would inspire envy from then on in Tuluá and would cause reactions from more Paulina Sarmientos than life had already provided. But it would also serve her as a fabulous vehicle for advertising.

With so much to do, she still managed to take classes from Luisita Tascón. She let the other professors go. She already knew how to do the four basic mathematical operations, was acquainted with Greece and the United States, recited the national capitals for all the continents except Africa, and was something of a prodigy at calculating square and cube roots. Luisita concentrated on teaching her the rules of etiquette, famous artists, and great novels. As the months passed, besides the embroidery needles, the multi-colored threads, and the tools for cultivating jasmines, Marcianita succeeded in making herself a picture collection so extraordinary that not even Don Marcial, the bookbinder who sold artwork, could equal it. She saved every one of the pictures in the trunks where she kept the sample ornaments that her Father Tascón had left, but she did not put them on display. She preferred to go to the window or the doorway just when school was letting out and watch those who had been her tormentors in Luisita's school walk past. Through her flattery, smiles, or persistence, they came to be the most assiduous clients for her jasmines. Every morning she would sell jasmines for the Virgin's altar, or for Saint Joseph's, or for the Christ. The ones for the Virgin were white; those for Saint Joseph were yellow. They all had the eternal fragrance of Marcianita Barona's jasmines, and as days and years passed, that fragrance and her ability to embroider came to endow her with untouchability, in a town that never thought it possible to forget her as the demon's daughter, the incarnation of destruction.

It was during those days that she made friends with Toño and Inesita González. It began each Saturday when they, holding hands and dressed in tulle and organdy, and topped off with little straw hats, came by the house to buy flowers for the altar of Our Lady of Perpetual Help. They were accompanied by Aminta, who was something like the matron of the house. First they approached timidly. As the days passed, their affection grew for the *señorita* who sold them flowers. And since Blanquita Lozano's visits became less and less frequent because matrimony had converted her into a lady who could not waste time on someone who was not her only child, Toño and Inesita came to provide the friendship Marcianita never had had with her companions. For them she saved the best jasmines; for them the strangest and most exotic products of her garden. She saw them only at the door, because Aminta, with the immense face of a scolding nun, would not allow them to enter. But from there, every Saturday, Marcianita made contact with the child's world that circumstances had denied her.

One Saturday they arrived alone to buy jasmines, saying that Aminta was very busy packing suitcases to leave for vacation in Madrevieja. Then Marcianita finally opened the doors of her house, produced the supernatural wind that has accompanied her at the peak moments of her existence, and in the midst of the endless fragrance of her flowers, took them along the ancient galleries, and picked the jasmines they wanted. Just when she was about to show them the ornaments in Father Tascón's trunks, Aminta arrived.

It was an outrage perhaps equal to the one that Paulina Sarmiento had wanted to commit with Marcianita's mother, a silent witness during those days. Aminta was not so dangerous as Doña Manuela's old neighbor. But she represented something so threatening to Marcianita that no sooner had she spied her with her confident and daring gaze than she made use of the power which she never planned to use on anyone else, and which in truth she should only now be using for indiscriminate revenge. Inesita's expression of fear was so great and Toño's frightened warning was of such magnitude that Marcianita was deeply impressed and decided to punish for always whoever might come to snatch away her happiness. "You will fall to your knees, uncomprehending," she said, raising her arms and making her voice resound like that of the prophet Isaiah. Aminta looked the way the inhabited brother or Nina Pérez must have looked, never again saying a word to the pair of children When they came back from Madrevieja in December they no longer felt constrained from entering.

Years later when Toño decided to study in Switzerland, he came back only once, to serve expressly as best man at Marcianita's wedding. It was not an unconditional friendship; it was only on Saturdays. And when it was no longer just Saturdays, it was occasionally for a glass of wine or *aguardiente*. In any case, it was a friendship for one who had no other social contact in the world, though as years passed it became common knowledge to all who bought jasmines, ordered embroidery, or requested armadillo ointments, which she decided to manufacture after discovering the benefits of such medication in a book of Danish witchcraft. She herself never used the emollient for anything, and the people who bought it did not say what it was for. But one day Toño González ordered some from Europe, and the whole world suspected why, knowing his penchant for fifteen-year-old girls. In any case, the armadillo ointment was sold, though not in such quantities as the jasmines or the gold thread embroidery or the fringed shawls. Nonetheless, it was sold, and Marcianita could then approach economic security as she approached both her fifteenth birthday and her goal for that day, the bazaar in the sacristy of San Bartolomé.

IV

There is no one in Tuluá who has not been to Salón Eva. No one who has not bought underpants, fabrics, brassieres, handkerchiefs, who has not obtained razor blades, nightlights, citronella candles, and condoms, who has not passed through its doorway and peered into its depths and recognized there amidst some ancient carved-wood display cases owner, Isaac Nessim Dayan, a Dutch Jew who arrived in Tuluá one day many years ago, rented the locale he has occupied ever since, filled the shelves with a dazzling array of wares, and gradually began to supply everyone with everything needed for daily use or with unnecessary trinkets in return for hard-earned wages. Thin, sallow, and emaciated, only with difficulty would he smile or rehearse a pleasant expression on his bony face. A consummate salesman in the early years (he would not allow a client to escape empty handed), he had now grown tired of selling, leaving that chore and others in the hands of his associates. These were young boys whom, according to the tongues that first reported it as gossip and later as history, he picked up at train stations, washed, fixed up, dressed in finery, and ended up using every night to satisfy his carnal cravings. Extremely affected, his everyday Spanish was filled with mispronounced flourishes. He moved his hands like a *femme fatale* and refrained from smoking; most of the time he dressed in a multicolored short-sleeved shirt, perhaps to emphasize his hairy arms and feign a masculinity that no one in Tuluá believed in during the days of the idiots.

Ever since he arrived, before the Second World War, and rented the site of his Salón Eva, it was a mystery in Tuluá from where or why Nessim the Jew had come. He never went anywhere on vacation, and his longest journeys were to Cali to stock up on merchandise. Although he did not open his shop on New Year's Day or Passover but put up a sign in Hebrew saying that it was Passover or New Year's or Purim, he was never seen speaking of religion, much less fulfilling the precepts with which the German Jews, who arrived with Ruta Knoenig and her parents during the Spanish Civil War, were acquainting Tuluá. He neither greeted nor acknowledged them or the many others who arrived and outfitted what was first a Jewish home and later a synagogue. When they brought in their first rabbi, a certain Efraím Cooperman, who cut his hair like the Nazis who, it is said, castrated him in a concentration camp, all of Tuluá expected that Isaac Nessim would attend the synagogue. But instead of that he decided to close his shop for two days and go to Cali to buy goods. He had no dealings with the

Jewish community or with anyone else. The boys who accompanied him from then on, until the one who lasted four long years and abandoned him when Nessim came down with a case of bishop's gonorrhea which the boy was absolutely certain he had not transmitted to him, arrived mysteriously and left town no less so. Although they often planned to stay after he threw them out, because they were convinced that in a place like Tuluá they were needed to sell merchandise (and he gave them a great enough portion of Salón Eva's earnings in order to establish a similar shop), Nessim, already coughing or gazing with depraved eyes, would persuade them that they could not remain in Tuluá and would send them packing with their belongings, their savings, and especially their skills in the art of selling.

Some who have visited coastal towns and others who have come from Pasto and points south say that Don Isaac's former salesmen own major department stores in those towns. Occasionally he would receive a letter from one of them, but none wrote with sufficient assiduity to make one believe that what over distance had languished for years could flourish anew. Not even for the one who had lasted four years and who, it is said, now had a store with incredible ornaments in Ipiales and who seems to have been the only one that was not thrown out but rather left *him*, and for whom he sobbed for almost nine straight months, every night, publicly and privately, sitting and drinking *aguardiente* in the Central Bar or leaning against the pillow in his room in Nina Pérez's boarding house (where he went to live during those painful days, incapable of setting foot in his own home)—not even for him did Isaac Nessim Dayan try to rebuild something of what he had already lived. Perhaps for that reason or maybe because of his obscure past, happiness was never plain on the face of the Dutch Jew, who outfitted half the town and without a doubt controlled the birthrate with the condoms which, in boxes of medallions or in gold buttons resembling chocolate coins, he sold every afternoon before closing. No one worried about understanding him, and not even Nina Pérez, who could bear witness to his tears during the months when he was left alone, nursing the gonorrhea that he'd really caught, was capable of approaching intimacy with perhaps the richest man in town. They never found any explanation for his glum look, his boys, the name of his shop, or his affectations. Tuluá did not know and could not know that Isaac Nessim was an orphan and only child with distant relatives who were finally swallowed up by the war, and that his sadness was due not only to his solitude but also to the homosexuality they did not understand and he made not the slightest attempt to explain.

Raised in an orphanage in Amsterdam, he reached twenty-one years of age acquainted only with the buttocks of his companions in the orphanage and the lashings of the directors of what, as the days passed, turned for him into a whore house and not a home. This, at least, was what the distant relatives had claimed who picked him up when the cholera of 1917 killed his whole family while traveling from Venice to Tangiers. Leaving the orphanage, he carried the order that his father had left to reclaim the family savings from a Zurich bank. He was already old enough and the war had not yet started. He reclaimed what turned out to be millions, and by traveling via England he reached the United States. He spent more than half of the fortune he had inherited visiting male brothels and regaling with clothes, food, lotions, and trips the boyfriends he picked up on the docks in New York and who accompanied him as he traveled to and from San Francisco in search of a distant relative he never found. Seeing that the stock market reached unexpected levels and that the more he continued to live at that pace, the less he was going to find the happiness he had never known, he took a boat southward, surveyed all the ports of call, and only upon arriving at Buenaventura did he decide to disembark. He did not remain there because the atmosphere of ports disgusted him and reminded him of the smell of the Amsterdam orphanage; he decided to go inland in search of a place to anchor his tragedy. A few months before the Second World War was declared, his belly girdled with dollars, Isaac Nessim arrived in Tuluá on a train that was headed for Cartago. He stuck his head out the train window and, as if impelled by a covert millennial force, decided to alight at the train station.

The next day Don Jesús Sarmiento accepted five thousand of the dollars he carried in a leather case tied around his belly, and Nessim rented the place where one month later, his shelves lined with merchandise, he hung his sign fashioned from an immense piece of brass with red letters on a black background: Salón Eva. He bought a house diagonally across the street from the store, hired a black maid, and daily, with bows that seemed like an invitation to a nuptial dance, Isaac Nessim began to become a character necessary in a Tuluá that was scarcely noticing that it was being inundated by progress.

The first sign of his unhappiness appeared during Carnival, when Princess Ruth was chosen as queen. Instead of donning a costume or going about drinking or dancing like the other men town, the surrounding areas, and the bordering regions, Isaac Nessim closed his shop and impassively watched without seeing from the balcony of his tiny house, his gaze set far off. The girls passed by to invite him, the other shopkeepers almost dragged him out, but he refused to accompany them. He gave money to the two political candidates who requested it, and today Tuluá enjoys the paved streets of the Boyacá Park thanks to his generous support. He was the only person the two candidates invited some time later, when Tuluá had forgotten its unrepeatable carnivalesque bustle, to serve as godfather for some of their sons. The church would not permit it because in spite of his having Jewish parents he belonged to no religion, but the two children received the grandest gifts any godfather could have given.

But his magnanimity did not stop there. Many people in Tuluá have said that Don Isaac Nessim was the personification of avarice, but the truth is that his generosity bordered on the quixotic. He practiced it secretively. Zabulón Zorilla's daughter, who had cancer of the blood, was able to travel to the United States, to the astonishment of their neighbors. They did not understand where the employee of the Colombia Drugstore could have raised the money, since he charged scarcely two pesos for an injection. The Franciscan Mothers, who saw their heavy iron tabernacle come tumbling down in the December earthquake, rebuilt the chapel either out of nothing or out of the treasure that Tuluá was said to have buried under it, and with the leftover money, they were able to buy a hundred new desks for the academy. Tránsito Girón, who subsisted for years bent over a cane begging for alms from friends and enemies alike, vanished overnight, and his straw shack was suddenly equipped with electricity, plumbing, and running water. On the day he died, his casket and flowers were almost equal to those of Don Jesús Sarmiento.

Be that as it may, either the people of Tuluá did not suspect or they chose not to recognize their occult benefactor. They only noticed the boys who worked for him. They always looked for a way to stigmatize him even more, to cast him as sinning against nature, doing wrong, and not playing by the rules. Obsessed with ridiculing Isaac Nessim Dayan's attitude to the maximum, they refused to consider a sign of generosity the fact that each one of the boys who lasted a few months came to own a shop or to dress as few people did on Sundays in the Boyacá Park. Many times they mocked him so severely that if it had not been for his incredible ability to endure reproaches and offenses, he would have killed either himself or everyone else.

During the days of the Violence, when almost as many dead people were collected every dawn as there were ants devouring them while they were being picked up, Isaac Nessim, who as a foreigner was neither a liberal nor a conservative, stayed out of the fray.

When the "Condor" León María's lackeys came to collect the necessary "contribution" that supported them, he gave them as much money as he had given Ansermanuevo's liberal guerillas. They both used the same method of persuasion: if you don't help us buy weapons, we will burn down your store. In the end, as was the case with many others in Tuluá, his payment became a monthly installment. But although many knew that Isaac Nessim was gay, no one was clever enough to extort money from him for that reason. Alvaro Henao, who, before obtaining the van in which he now carts pilgrims, lived off the thin air of the Boyacá Park, tried to blackmail him one night. The Dutch Jew grew furious. Bellowing, Nessim threw Alvaro Henao naked from his house, his rod in his hand. He barely let him carry his clothes. "Nobody get money from me! All Tuluá know I queeerr, queeerr." And Alvaro Henao, like so many others who thought to blackmail him, found Nessim's indiscretion to be a barrier. But Tuluá, which did not wish to blackmail but rather to degrade him, to ridicule his flightiness, and to embitter even more a life that had been acrimonious since his infancy in Amsterdam, wanted to grasp him in its clutches.

There was no gang in the Boyacá Park—and they changed every two years—that did not try to buy something at Salón Eva in order to deceive the Jew. Many times they sought to mock him, but his sixth sense always anticipated their ruses, and by one trick or another, feigning ignorance, he managed to evade their pranks.

Except for the case of Alvaro Henao, only once was Isaac Nessim known to be the victim of a practical joke. Oscar Arias, whose gay condition was entirely unsuspected by conventional wisdom, succeeded in getting Nessim alone by pretending to look at fabrics and, playing dirty, by supplying Don Isaac's Lubyn with a little action in Buga. Oscar sent the boy off on the first bus to Buga; a skirt and a bottle of perfume served to liberate him from Salón Eva's proprietor. He made a date with Nessim for the riverbank at eight o'clock, and instead of suggesting that they go to the house diagonally across the street from the store, Oscar convinced the finicky Nessim to go to the apartment of Campo the odontologist, a comrade in arms.

Isaac Nessim smelled something rotten when he entered and saw one of the doors of the apartment stir, but he quickly dismissed it, thinking it had been only the wind. Eyes like those of Oscar Arias could not be found any more, much less a hairy chest of that sort. When it was time to hit the sack, Oscar and Isaac undressed. The fear he felt every time he was going to fulfill his role, the unhappiness that overtook him at every turn, came strangely over him at that moment that should have spelled rapture. His sixth sense—he said many days later, still seeing red—told him it was a trap. They had just gotten into bed when, like a battalion, through doors and windows, armoires and closets, curtains and tables, the gang of intruders from the Boyacá Park burst in. "I am queeerr, queeerr," and he reinforced the r's with a grimace as he got dressed in the midst of a mockery that reached Tuluá's farthest confines and spread from mouth to mouth for days. He dressed with haughty patience and went out into the street almost as exercised as if he were the perpetrator of a most nefarious crime. Few people shopped in his store during the following days, and from then on there was no mother who would send her son alone to Salón Eva. Isaac Nessim, disowned by a town that exploited him but would not tolerate him, had been marked for life. Shame seemed to combine with the gloom on his face. As the years passed, his unrequited love for the boy who left him because of his bishop's gonorrhea finished him off.

During four long years Nessim had kept him with unequaled indulgence. They traveled to San Andrés several times. Nessim sent him to Miami twice. The boy's clothes were made in Cali, his shoes brought from Medellín. He even bought him a car for their third anniversary. Lubyn González was the young man's name. He handled clients with as much grace as his genitals at bedtime. He came to be so much a part of his life that Isaac Nessim may have almost managed a faint smile on his face during that time. But in the face of temptation he forgot the jealousy his Lubyn harbored, and he caught infidelity and a case of bishop's gonorrhea from the buttocks of Fernando Uribe, a medical student with a moustache and a year of rural service in Tuluá. He did not find out until the fourth day, when he awoke to find his underwear stained and Lubyn screaming because his behind was infected. The lad grabbed his suitcases, threw them into the car, cashed two huge checks, and without sighing an explanation or allowing for a truce, he abandoned the orphan of Amsterdam.

It took Isaac Nessim a long time to get over him; he sustained that memory in spite of all the hands and sheets that passed by in the meantime. The look of tragedy again swept over his face, and unhappiness haunted his figure. As the years went by, his spirits sank to the point where he hardly left the store to go home and back. He continued selling because he owed it to himself, it was a habit as strong as life itself, but he was no longer the diligent salesman or the conversationalist with the ladies and gentlemen of Tuluá of three years before.

The spiritual malaise that afflicted him seemed to have no cure. People sensed that, and although they still recounted anecdotes and gossiped about his little adventures, they no longer considered him the young queer to be feared, but rather the old male whore who deserved their pity.

Every morning he would open the window of his room in hopes of living no longer than that day. Every night he would close it certain of never again seeing the morning light. But since in his depths he still harbored the slightest illusion of becoming straight, and with that he replaced the long-standing illusion of finding the perfect Adonis and then of reclaiming his Lubyn, he lingered on for quite a few years in spite of the fact that every morning and every evening were torture for the formerly powerful Dutch Jew.

As a distraction, he finally attracted—as if with a magnet— Lieutenant Caravalí, a recent graduate of the police academy. Since he could not rent him a room in his house because the populace would lose respect for the agent of law and order, he bought one of the houses on the other side of the block, whose patio was adjacent to his, and rented it very inexpensively to the lieutenant. He built a special gate between the yards, and every night since then he consorted with the armed gentleman, who still continued to visit young girls and take maids to bed. He had as much trust in him as love for him, but never so much of either as he had for the one who fled the bishop's gonorrhea that he finally cured as easily as if it were a case of seminarian's V. D. The nights when the lieutenant was on duty, melancholy enveloped the Jew's body and soul, and on many other nights while lying at his side his boundless self-loathing made of Nessim a dejected lover.

It was during those days that he began to think of going to see the idiots.

V

The look of satisfaction on Marcianita Barona's face when Nemesio Rodríguez, army captain, engineer from the Medellín School of Mines, and builder of the Pacific Railroad, passed by and stopped to stare at her on the station platform, was almost the same one she wore the day she decked out her first bazaar table in the doorway of the San Bartolomé sacristy.

Unbaptized and personally unacquainted with any church, because the few times that Doña Manuela had entered any temple she had done so alone, Marcianita suddenly decided that the bazaar would be her means of communion with that church and those saints she had never known. Her solitary nature kept her from putting the table in the vestibule. She did not think of her uninitiated status, because neither she nor the priest nor many Tuluans (who had forgotten) knew of it; she assumed that only those who truly wanted to support the congregation would approach the sacristy to buy from her, and not those who were after her fifteen-year-old body.

She sent Blanquita Lozano to intercede with the parish priest, and the father, unaware that he was giving free entry to one of his predecessors' daughters, offered her carte blanche. Marcianita did not want to abuse her situation, so she brought her own table, tablecloth, and chairs from home. She simply placed the table on the sacristy walk and, seated in the chair or standing by the prizes, began to sell chances for the raffle. The first prizes she awarded were from her own pocket. As days passed, and she held the bazaar every Sunday except for Palm Sunday, the gifts eventually came from the ladies who ordered embroidery or bought jasmines. She would arrive at nine o'clock in the morning. The lottery tickets were always ready for those who went to High Mass. Nevertheless, she sold more at vespers than at the eleven o'clock mass. Her old companions from Luisita Tascón's school, Toño and Inesita González, with the ever-present Aminta, would buy from her, as would Nina, who had already begun to grow disproportionately fat; and many of Tuluá's men, aware of her origin and her mother's talents, bought tickets with libidinous intentions. She attended to all with the same amiability, and at twelve-fifteen, when only dogs and drunks remained on the streets of Tuluá, she gathered up her table and chair, stored the unawarded prizes in one of Father Tascón's trunks, and headed for her dining room table. There she would count the money that at eight o'clock Monday morning she would send in an envelope to the parish priest, labeled in large Gothic letters, "For the Reverend

Father Phanor Terán." There would go the revenues from the sale of the bazaar raffle tickets along with the donation she would personally add, secretly increasing the proceeds from her miniscule fundraising. She never stopped at the rectory and never said more to the parish priest than the four or five words they exchanged when he would enter the sacristy as she would go on busily selling her tickets or arranging prizes on the table. Since she did not attend mass, never went to confession, and never participated in processions (omissions the father finally took note of), Marcianita Barona was, in the eyes of Tuluá, a sort of blossoming nun who never looked at men or accepted a suitor, but who also dressed no saintly statues, no matter how long she held her bazaar in the doorway of the parish church sacristy.

Doña Manuela did not tell her who had been her father. When the last Tuesday of the month flowed into the first Tuesday of the next month, and the money order which without fail came from Cartagena—the final link with a man who built his life around a daughter he never knew or held—finally did not arrive, Manuela Barona, leaning on her cane and clearing her throat as much as on the night of the sulfurous air, dressed herself in severe black and appeared alone at the parish office to request the celebration of a requiem mass for the soul of Father Severo Tascón, the former parish priest of Tuluá, deceased in Cartagena de Indias a few days before his seventy-third birthday.

Had it remained strictly between the parish priest and herself, the matter would have gone no further. But since she made pompous ostentation of her black dresses, and since the mass was so full of the tolling of bells and the church adorned with so many jasmines (perhaps to remind the deceased of the fragrance that used to drive him crazy), old and new Tuluans alike learned of the circumstances of Marcianita's birth from the mouths of the elders. Doña Manuela was proud of everything, and although she did not take her daughter to church, because not even at that moment did Marcianita consider entering San Bartolomé, her dignity and self-esteem were so much those of an honorable widow that she ended up by collecting condolences. The next Sunday the bazaar in the sacristy could not keep pace with the demand for tickets and prizes. As the final compensation from a town that scorned one who was not guilty of having been born, the bazaar sales reached heights they would only attain again in the final days of its existence.

Because the plants were depleted from having so many flowers plucked for mass at San Bartolomé, no jasmines were sold for several weeks. The money order no longer came, and Doña Manuela viewed the horizon as somewhat bleak. She did not express this to Marcianita, but Marcianita noticed anyway, and on Monday when she sent the money to the parish priest, instead of adding her customary alms she removed them for her mother. Neither the parish priest nor anyone else was the wiser because so much money had been collected that even Marcianita, who had never been intimidated by anything in her life, felt palpitations that Sunday afternoon when she emptied her apron pockets and her jars of coins. The clock had struck six before she finished counting it all.

The money lasted four more weeks. In the fifth week they were able to sell three dozen jasmines. The sixth, they fashioned half a dozen boxes of candy. The seventh, Marcianita's hands almost dripped blood from trying so hard to embroider faster. Their finances were so precarious, accustomed as they were to the monthly money order and the daily sale of flowers, that when in the sixth week they grew hungry and Manuela Barona looked at her Marcianita, neither needed to say aloud what was happening. By making candy or sewing ceaselessly the two women survived for two more weeks when, at midday, with such parsimony that he scarcely dared leave the heat of the streets of Tuluá, the railway clerk came asking for Doña Manuela Barona. At the station platform, in her name, had arrived a shipment of ancient trunks from Cartagena. Also a letter. It explained no more than ever. In the trunks, more ornaments, more portraits, more old notebooks, but what redeemed them forever after was a coffer of gold coins with a handwritten note: the tremulous, perhaps repentant hand recognizable from afar as that of Marcianita's father.

Doña Manuela made no fuss over the trunks. Since the sender was unidentified and occasionally great shipments of merchandise or fabrics to embroider would arrive from Cartagena by way of Buenaventura, those who saw the trunks waiting on the platform before Doña Manuela had them picked up believed anything but that they were her inheritance from Father Tascón. That day Marcianita must have realized that she and the father shared some eternal bond. But since they did not talk about it yet in her house—what with their being so occupied with embroidery or cultivating jasmines—she made no comment, accepted life as it came, and did not even reduce the rhythm of her hustle. Doña Manuela sold some of the gold coins and bought in Marcianita's name the house at La Rivera, on the road to Picacho just beyond the curve by the Ruices' house. Six months later, so as to avoid arousing suspicion, she bought four-and-a-half hectares next to the house. She planted half the land with jasmines and proceeded to abandon her house near the

Boyacá Park. Marcianita completed the move. She transplanted the jasmines, dispatched many of the trunks, and finally moved herself there. They did not sell the house on the park until Nemesio Rodríguez arrived. They returned to Tuluá on Sundays for the bazaar in the sacristy and the stroll on the station platform while they waited for the noon train, which changed schedules during those years and would arrive every afternoon at three. The house was turned over to one of the servant girls for the sale of flowers. Supported in part by the vegetables they planted on the remaining land and by the sale of some gold coins once every six months, Marcianita was able to give up her embroidery (which she did very rarely and only when it was unavoidable). Completely encloistered in her suburban retreat, she adopted the behavior of the nun that Tuluá had predicted from an early age she would become. She dressed in bright colors and old-fashioned styles. She refused to receive any man, and the one who dared insist learned the hard way that Marcianita really meant what she said.

The adventurer was Bernardo Cardona. In the days of the purchase of La Rivera, he began to pass by the door of the house on the Boyacá Park. When Marcianita moved up to the other house and shut herself in to raise armadillos, plant vegetables, and dote on her jasmines, he stalked her on Sundays, following only four or five paces behind her on her journey to the station and while she strolled on the platform waiting for the train to pull in. He was always uneasy, for if they went to meet the train they must have been expecting something for which he ought to be prepared. But since several Sundays passed without anyone's arriving, and he was already losing hope of succeeding in his pursuit, he went ahead to wait for them at La Rivera, frustrated at not being able to shorten the distance between him and them to less than three paces. Carrying a bouquet of flowers, smelling of benzoin, his hair slicked with pomade, he was prepared to wait for three hours. The servants did not invite him in, nor did Marcianita. When she arrived she regarded him the way an aristocrat looks at a beggar and broke her mother's rapture by taking her arm. She then fed her armadillos the flowers that Bernardo Cardona had tremulously left at her door.

At midnight, after six continuous hours of drinking *aguardiente*, Bernardo Cardona, rising to his full height and feigning the dignity that perhaps he would have on the day of his marriage, appeared at the house at La Rivera commandeering a musical serenade. Marcianita must have smelled him or in some other way ingeniously sensed him, because when he was about to begin she opened the doors of the house, bade the musicians to enter, served them black coffee, and listened to their selections. Bernardo Cardona did not know if what was happening was real or an illusion inspired by the *aguardiente*. Seated on one of Manuela Barona's armchairs, he gazed and gazed and gazed. He uttered not a single word, nor did he proffer an idea. Perhaps that is why Marcianita's screams took him by surprise. He merely stared at her, and that was enough to trigger the tirade. Then he reached for her and touched her hand. Marcianita could not stand it, and with shouts of "You ill-born oaf, you've probably gone to bed with every whore in town, don't you dare touch my hand," she threw him out of the house. Pursued by the fragrance of jasmines, which hearing their mistress cry, hurried to her aid and kicked him out the door, and, drunk as he was, believing he saw ghosts in mid-air, he climbed the first tamarind tree he could find.

There he spent the night. The eleven ghosts did not move from the foot of the tree, but the musicians ran off abandoning him. He had no intentions of climbing down. Around two in the morning Marcianita turned off her light. For an hour she waited with a double-barreled shotgun, expecting the lout to try again. When she thought the bounder had suffered enough, she went to bed. Bernardo Cardona could not climb down from the tree until six the next morning, after his drunkenness had passed and the ghosts had fled with the light of day, inoffensive as everything is at dawn. His legs were wobbly, his hands were scratched and his back was so twisted that for several days he could not straighten up. For Marcianita there was no longer any doubt that the men of Tuluá pursued her only because they wanted to take her to bed. She lengthened her dresses ten more centimeters and dressed completely in white. She wore the headdress of a Persian empress and walked like the governess in some French movie. She continued selling lottery tickets at her bazaar, sending the money to Father Terán every Monday, cultivating jasmines to sell, armadillos to amuse herself, and vegetables to live on. She started an endless embroidery of a tablecloth for her grandchildren and ignored the urgent requests to return to her old profession, responding that she had made a contract with the Palmira cathedral to dress all the statues for Holy Week. She embroidered only the infinite tablecloth. She decorated her house, covering tables and filling showcases with the ornaments she had embroidered and no church had bought. She left only Father Tascón's things in mothballs in the trunks, even though it often seemed that she exchanged his for hers in the showcases and on the tables. She went about moving Doña Manuela from her chair in a forgotten corner, and only on Sunday afternoons, after the bazaar, would she go arm-in-arm with her to the station, strolling on the platform and waiting for the train. They were always hopeful as the locomotive thundered in, but when Nemesio Rodríguez, President Reyes's aide-de-camp, captain in the Thousand Days' War, engineer from the School of Mines, and builder of the Pacific Railroad arrived that Sunday, only Marcianita felt a trembling in her most intimate vitality.

Doña Manuela kept on waiting, watching passengers and suitcases descend. She did not notice her daughter's expression or the man who had gotten off the train. She was still hopeful. Marcianita was, too, but for some other reason now. The minutes between the time that Nemesio Rodríguez left the train and awaited his luggage at the car door and the time when he crossed in front of them and the fragrance of jasmines filled the station platform, seemed endless to her. Doña Manuela noticed the fragrance but immediately attributed it to her handbag, replete with aromatic essence. She could not accept or understand that her daughter Marcianita was enraptured. If she had done so, perhaps she would have understood her daughter's behavior from that moment on and would not have been so surprised by her absentmindedness. But since she made not the slightest effort to understand, from that day on, life at La Rivera and perhaps in Tuluá, which in its myopia failed to measure the consequences, changed radically, making a half turn, doubling back over the same route, and finally meeting up with Father Tascón, Doña Manuela, and the newborn Marcianita.

Because on the Sunday when he arrived in Tuluá he was tired of living and was looking to begin anew, Nemesio Rodríguez appeared unaffected that afternoon and during the many nights when he was smitten from ass to gills. On other days he attributed his strange infirmity to the endless sunny afternoons he had spent, theodolite in hand, laying out the tracks from Buenaventura to Cartago. He had come as a surveyor of irrigation ditches, having been hired by Don Jesús Sarmiento, Miss Paulina, and Toño and Inesita González's mama to measure and build them.

He did not manage to meet Marcianita until the day he went up to talk to Doña Manuela. That moment marked the end of the progressive endeavor Marcianita had been nurturing day after day, month after month, dressed in a long white gown, breaking traditions and customs, but looking like the nun that Tuluá expected her to be. Every morning at seven, bright and early, before Nemesio would go out to measure the Sarmientos' trenches and ditches, Marcianita would head for the Boyacá

Park. Sometimes she carried jasmines, other times not, but from Monday through Friday she was again seen on the streets of Tuluá. No one suspected or foresaw anything; Marcianita simply continued coming to town.

Nemesio Rodríguez did not go up to La Rivera to visit Manuela Barona's daughter. He went there because, as the builder of the great irrigation ditch from the mountains to the Cauca River, including the Tuluá River, he ought to speak to all the parties concerned, and La Rivera was very close to where the channel would lie. Only three blocks from Marcianita's jasmine plantings Nemesio Rodríguez was going to construct a dam which, until it was completed, would endanger Doña Manuela if the water rose. He explained it to her meticulously, with a certain malice that Doña Manuela, clearing her throat, recognized but did not acknowledge. She had decided to leave Tuluá in search of peace and quiet and was not going to put herself at the mercy of what those few construction workers might say, much less to live imploring the saints to keep the river from rising and flooding her house. Marcianita learned of the situation, understood it in the depths of her foolishness, and before Nemesio Rodríguez could leave, appeared with a tray of refreshments she had prepared. She made some raspberry-guava juice and a love potion, among other things, and offered him some English crumpets. Her heart began to pound again as it had the day at the station, but regardless of her emotional state, she drank raspberry juice along with the engineer. She did not take her eyes off him, tried to transmit her thoughts to him as she had always wanted to with the jasmine plants and the armadillos, and spoke to him of new friendships in Tuluá. Ten days later, in silence—because she answered to no one—she received the first letter, the first indication that the love potion had worked. She did not answer it. She incinerated it in the kitchen stove. She waited for the second, the third, the fourth, and when the fifth arrived, she again inflicted on him the same pain from ass to gills, writing him a short note. It said nothing, hardly a thank you. She handed it to him personally one morning when she went down to town laden with jasmines and he was heading out with his theodolite to measure ditches.

They made the dam three blocks farther up, on the property of Miss Paulina Sarmiento, who continued to be a neighbor even at La Rivera. He showed no feeling, and even when she recognized the onset of her palpitations, she did it in a manner so elegant and discreet that Tuluá could not imagine that between Doña Manuela Barona's nun and the railway construction engineer and captain of the liberal forces of

Palonegro, the most capricious and disconcerting love affair of all history was gestating.

Doña Manuela was also slow to notice. Marcianita, who preferred to confide in her pillow as to her adolescent problems, began to do so again with her first secrets of the heart. Weaving her long white gowns, cultivating the jasmines, or feeding the armadillos, she brooded and vacillated over what steps to take. She continued feigning her future religious vocation before Tuluá and, in passing, before Doña Manuela. She told no one of her loves and desires, and when, between expectorations, her mother noticed that something was stirring in her daughter's spirit, she easily cloaked it, attributing her mood to some old armadillos that had recently died. She continued to receive letters every Friday. She answered on Sundays. She saw him fleetingly on Wednesdays and Saturdays as she arrived with her load of jasmines. They gazed into one another's eyes and said not a word. There was no need to. Nemesio walked on the paths and plains of his measurements in perfect contact with his beloved. If he tried to forget her, the ache from ass to gills immediately reappeared. The itch brought him back to Marcianita's wavelength and set him aright. He never consciously attributed it to her, but when he thought a long time had passed, he returned to the house at La Rivera. With an almost trembling voice he asked Doña Manuela's consent to call on her daughter.

When he entered the parlor of the house of jasmines, two years and three months had elapsed since the day when Marcianita had given raspberry juice to Nemesio Rodríguez, the military captain. Marcianita knew it and expected the visit. At the end of twenty-seven months he would be driven to her. Upon the completion of thirty-nine, he would ask for her hand in marriage, Tuluá would laugh to learn of it, and she, whether justified or fiendish (she never knew), would demand special terms. She was brusque this time. "I've ordered the wedding cake from London," he told her, trembling and afraid that the cake, which had arrived the previous afternoon at the train station, would spoil. It was seven layers high with a little frosting doll holding the hand of a gallant gentleman on top. He described it in lavish detail, almost making her an intimate photograph of all its qualities, after its four-month journey. Marcianita was not impressed. For four long years beginning with that day, she always found an appropriate excuse as to why the wedding cake could not be cut. He continued measuring ditches, constructing channels, amassing a calculable but unseen fortune with the salary he received and his pension from the railroad. He ordered no more wedding cakes from London because the label said that it was guaranteed to last for seven years, nine months, and eleven days.

It almost came to that. In the meantime, Tuluá continued to make fun of Nemesio Rodríguez and to assume that Marcianita Barona would enter the Conceptionist Convent. She no longer came to town except on Saturdays, and that was to meet him for a scant ten minutes at nine in the morning in the house on the Boyacá Park. The letters continued coming and going, and their love survived on the basis of courtly epistles. Every Monday's letter dealt with the same theme: death. The Tuesday letter answered the one of the previous week. Wednesdays and Thursdays they would not write; Fridays they talked of the Saturday appointment, and on Sundays they talked of everything but matrimony. He never proposed to her face to face, using the letters for that purpose. She never answered in writing. During the ten minutes of each Saturday for the seven-and-a-half years of their courtship, she either answered negatively while he frowned, dropped a handkerchief, and left with his tail between his legs. Or she outlined for him the compelling need for a party replete with sweets and confections, like that of the first communion she had not been allowed to make.

And when Doña Manuela arrived at the Red Ball Restaurant, reserved a setting of sixty seats from Barbarita Lozano de Aramburu for luncheon the next day, and requested that Rosaurita Jiménez come up to La Rivera to cut selected jasmines, Tuluá wailed and whispered until midnight, speculating as to how Marcianita would defend herself at the hour of truth. With her long white gowns cut considerably below the knee, and her raffle-ticket sales every Sunday in the sacristy door, it had become impossible to imagine her any different. As for Nemesio Rodríguez, a stubborn old man like no other who had ever arrived in Tuluá, the people came to accept his mystery, always wondering where he kept the growing cache of money he earned for his work. No one believed that in the end he would marry Marcianita. Neither was she marriageable nor was he suited to be the husband of someone so nun-like. Paulina Sarmiento, far along in years but still delivering milk from her jeep starting at five in the morning, thought nothing of the matter except to begin to feel again the need which day after day she had been harboring in the immense repository of her memory, for twenty-five, almost thirty years. Hardly had Tuluá learned that afternoon that Marcianita Barona would be married the next day, that the cake had already arrived at the house on the Boyacá Park—the cake that Nemesio Rodríguez had saved for seven years, nine months, and three days— and that he, dressed as a captain, was being measured for new shoes at

Nessim's department store, than there was Paulina, going through all the notary's records and then those at the rectory. "I'm doing research," she told Aurita Arias, the priest's secretary, as she took down book after book without finding what she was searching for. She left at almost nightfall, went back home, and for the first time in many years did not sleep, waiting for eleven o'clock on the Sunday morning when Marcianita Barona would marry Captain Nemesio Rodríguez de León.

At dawn she was at the church of San Bartolomé. She went to nine o'clock mass and heard the blessing of the *aves* in order to maintain her privileged seat in the first pew. Since she did not know a single one of the many prayers the old pray-ers intoned from one mass to the next (because she had had no time in her life to learn anything other than how to earn money), she listened and listened. She remembered as best she could the phrases she had rehearsed for the moment when the father would ask the faithful if any impediment existed. If she forgot anything she would start over again; she would look carefully at the number on the notary's certificate and would begin anew.

Doña Manuela spent the eve very differently. The marriage itself meant very little to her. What was concrete and real for her revolved around giving a party for fifty guests, taking care of certain official details with notebook in hand, and finally getting even with Tuluá. She had seen plenty of years come and go, continued to cough up copious amounts of phlegm, and found the support of her cane absolutely essential. The lack of exercise, the sale of candies, and the manual dexterity of her Marcianita brought her peace of mind, but they detracted from the supreme confidence she had wanted desperately to maintain during the days in which Father Tascón abandoned her and left her expecting the damned childbirth.

She had the most splendid jasmines cut, arranged the house on the park with the meticulousness of a Vincentian nun, hung the ornamental runners that came in Father Tascón's trunks, burned incense in every corner of the house, placed the wicker chair of her transfigurations on the spot where she had suffered them, arranged the dining room furniture, rented forty chairs and six tables from the Central Bar, and awaited the next day as if what she was going to witness were an everyday occurrence and not the outrage it was for Tuluá. She had been faithful to nature's commands, meticulous as she was; not an evil idea crossed her mind, nor did she deliberately rehearse the vengeance toward which she was unconsciously impelled by extraterrestrial forces. If for Paulina Sarmiento every minute before eleven o'clock was a chance to review what she was going to recite in front of all of Tuluá in San Bartolomé, for Manuela every minute promised the arrival of that longed-for goal, distant so long ago, and discovered anew in the form of a wedding cake, saved for years and years, awaiting a knife that would cut it. That was the only thing that worried her: the knife. For the rest she was relying on Barbarita Lozano or Rosaurita Jiménez. The ceremony was not hers; it belonged to Captain Nemesio Rodríguez. Nor were the visitors her responsibility; the two brothers of the builder of the pacific Railroad were staying in Miss Benilda's hotel. They would be cared for there. Perhaps because of them Miss Paulina was apprised of the error she was committing, when the clock was about to strike eleven in the morning as she, with indecent rhythm, rehearsed word for word what she was going to respond before all of Tuluá, gathered in San Bartolomé, when Father Phanor would ceremoniously ask, "Is there anyone present who knows of any just reason why this couple cannot be united in the sacred bond of matrimony?"

The two brothers, dressed almost identically, strolling slowly, left Miss Benilda's hotel exuding elegance. Those who saw them pass were more terrified than Father Phanor Terán, seated in the parish office waiting for Marcianita Barona's long-announced visit for pre-nuptial instructions. Since they knew no one, they greeted no one. They crossed the park from Don Marcial's bookstore to the notary, but first they passed by the bride's house. There, in deepest black, starched collar, and silk bow-tie, was Nemesio Rodríguez de León, President Reyes's aide-de-camp, builder of the Pacific Railroad, and captain of the Palonegro liberal forces. In his hands was the only message that had arrived, one from General Uribe Uribe's widow, the only person he had informed of his wedding.

At the windows of the houses on the park, on Don Carlos Materón's corners, on Don Marcial's sidewalk, and as far as the town hall, Tuluá was gathered. San Bartolomé was filled to the rafters. In the first pew was Paulina Sarmiento, mentally rehearsing what she was going to decry before a town that had forgotten even its most minimal conscience, its eternal condemnation. On the paths of the square were the rest, those who, owing to youth or daring, wanted to see everything from as close as possible. Aurita Arias, who a half hour later tended to Father Phanor when he was taken ill, described it as something akin to the arrival of Dr. Tomás Uribe after he renounced the presidential candidacy in Ibagué. Everyone attentive but fearful. Nemesio Rodríguez perhaps more so than anyone else. With the file of official documents in his hand, his eyes fixed on Doña Manuela and her cane, he waited in the doorway of his mother-in-law's house for the minutes to pass. Exactly at eleven, when Paulina Sarmiento was already losing count of the minutes and starting to fall prey to the desperation that finally overtook her and spread to Father Phanor, he came through that door accompanied by his Marcianita Barona, dressed all in pink, as if at that age instead of going to a wedding she should have celebrated her sweet-sixteen party.

San Bartolomé's bells again chimed the hour a minute later. Nemesio Rodríguez's brothers looked at each other bewildered. Tuluá roared. Not because the clock repeated its chiming—perhaps in order to give them time to cross the park—but because the captain of the Palonegro liberal forces and his betrothed, the demon's daughter for Paulina Sarmiento and her contemporaries, headed not towards the parish church but towards the notary. Nacianceno and Aristóbulo Rodríguez de León, José Antonio González (who came expressly from Lausanne for the wedding), and Doña Luisa White de Uribe (perhaps a token), all of legal age, the first two neighbors in the capital, and the second two from the municipality of Tuluá, served as witnesses before José María Tejado, the area's only notary. He placed their names in the marriage registry as husband and wife after the one had demonstrated his having become a member of the Catholic church on the second of December in 1902 before the Bucaramanga circuit notary, and the other had certified that in some place there existed a notation of her having been baptized in that religion and had presented testimony of witnesses of never having been seen professing or practicing any other doctrine.

Father Phanor was left waiting. Tuluá breathed deeply, very deeply, so deeply that when its contained breath was released, the bells seemed to chime again. Miss Paulina's shouts seemed almost to come from the beyond, and through the door of the sacristy, where there was a bazaar table every Sunday, a misfortune began to hatch. Tuluá could not shed its astonishment for many days. The next Sunday that astonishment was converted into an impressive weapon.

Father Phanor initiated everything. During the honeymoon of the captain of the liberal forces and Father Severo Tascón's offspring, he spoke with the ladies of the Association, with Aurita Arias, and with the Blessed Sacrament of Christ. When they arrived on the next Saturday, many believed that if Marcianita Barona married, nullifying all the predictions that had been made about her calling as a nun, the bazaar would have been the first to suffer the consequences. But she returned as usual on Saturday in order to be present on Sunday in the doorway of the sacristy selling tickets for the bazaar. At nine in the morning, with the same chair and table that she kept in the sacristy, Marcianita Barona de Rodríguez began her daily work. Sales were incredible. Tuluá, upset at being mistaken and battered for counting among its citizens a pair of apostates who were married in a civil ceremony, decided to buy up every last ticket. By the eleven o'clock mass, the table was swept clean. The cracker tin in which she kept her receipts was so full it would not close. The funds for the Holy Week festival had grown overnight because of Marcianita's marriage. Father Phanor knew it, and before saying anything from the pulpit at the eleven o'clock mass (that mass at which a week earlier he had been taken ill because of a sin that his eyes were not capable of apprehending), he ordered the sacristan not to allow the bazaar table and chair to be kept in the sacristy any longer as soon as Marcianita finished. This was no problem for her, and her reaction could have been foreseen centuries before. She called two porters from the plaza and had her table and chair carried to the house on the park. The first thing Monday morning, she diligently sent Father Phanor an incredible sum of money from the day before, and by Tuesday she was already collecting more prizes and making more tickets.

From early in the morning she would sit at the dining room table. She cut up the slips of paper with a tiny pair of scissors, and with *biyuyo* paste and a porcelain brush she smeared the tickets. She made one hundred with numbers and two hundred blank ones. When she started the bazaar she thought that the most convenient price was ten centavos a ticket, and she left it that way for years and years. Not even when she got married, when the consequences of war and the scarcity of tires and spare parts were being felt and inflation was rampant, did she plan to change the price. Better times would come, she said with her apprentice-at-law's philosophy. For that reason, or because in truth she always believed that one should accept one's lot in life, she made no protest to the priest about having to keep the table and chair at her house and not in the San Bartolomé sacristy. Father Phanor was incapable of confronting her impassiveness and neither said anything from the pulpit nor succumbed to the incisive demonstrations of concern by Miss Paulina and the group of ladies from the congregation. He let Marcianita have her bazaar every Sunday, and although she had been married in a civil ceremony, he did not consider her a threat to his flock. No one knew if he did it out of condescension to the daughter of his predecessor, out of kindness, or out of physical cowardice and fear of confronting a problem as serious as Marcianita. If the truth be known, the last was the most likely. In any case, many years had to pass and many things had to happen in order for Tuluá to recreate the illusion that it had not been wrong about Marcianita. Sooner or later the marriage of Doña Manuela Barona's daughter and the construction engineer of the railroad would end sensationally and everything would be clarified.

It was during that time that the mother of Father Tascón's daughter became ill. The cane with which she supported herself no longer helped her as much as she would have liked, and she no longer went down to Tuluá. Marcianita moved definitively to La Rivera, and, with the same care she applied to her jasmines and armadillos during the eternal days of her maidenhood, watching her wedding cake become encrusted with a mold that prevented trying it and learning that it tasted like soapstone and was drier than a witch's tit, she carried her mother to the house on the park and cared for her around the clock. Nemesio Rodríguez was not absent from such ministrations. Every morning before leaving to take the ditch measurements that never seemed to cease, he would pass by his mother-in-law's room and, using the mellifluous genuflections of his days as General Reyes's secretary, would wish her good day and improved health. But actually neither Marcianita's care, the wishes of the son-in-law, nor the drugs that Dr. Tomás sent her daily made a dent in the illness that was consuming her. Every day that passed she had to clear her throat more and more. The first weeks she would daily fill a chamberpot with her phlegm. By the fifth week, the pains were stronger and the smell of death and the feeling of a journey flooded the house, obliging the servants to carry out three and four chamberpots absolutely overflowing with a sputum that came to acquire a color very much like that of a snake in heat.

The sixth week Marcianita saw the future darken. Her mother began to rant and rave, and every night before her fever rose, Father Tascón and the gray mare of better days began their funereal march through the rooms of the house. They conversed with their ghosts as if they were chatting with the living beings that affectionately surrounded them. For Father Severo those were the best moments. For his daughter, the same. Manuela's shouts marked the spot where the mare appeared. The first time the animal burst into the room, only Doña Manuela identified it. Marcianita, seated next to the bed with a bottle of alcohol in her hand, saw nothing. She had, of course, grown delirious. Nevertheless, because the dying woman reported to her daughter the next day all her memories of the previous night, Marcianita paid greater heed and waited—it was around five o'clock when the fever began—for the mare or Father Severo to appear. She armed herself with a whip like those used by Don Jesús Sarmiento's cowboys at the time of her birth. At eight o'clock in the evening Nemesio Rodríguez joined them. At nine-thirty, when the fever reached 104°, steps were heard as if coming from afar. Nemesio looked at Marcianita, Marcianita looked at her mother, confronting the celestial noise that was approaching her, and in half a minute the whip was on the floor and they were both looking intently at the sick woman. The footsteps were those of a mare, the stain was blackish, the smell, of sulfur. The sick woman cleared her throat, cleared her throat with gusto, with infinite gusto. The beast reared up; Nemesio and Marcianita saw it clearly; it seemed to climb up on the bed, and with a kick in the head it brought on the death that Father Tascón's concubine had been expecting for weeks. The mark of the horseshoe on her forehead refused to disappear no matter how Marcianita tried to erase it with muriatic acid. The skull was not fractured, the doctor said, and death had been caused by cardiac arrest. Throat and lung cancer finally took her life. They put a nun's wimple on her and closed the coffin so as to hide the scar on her forehead.

At first they were alone at the wake. As when Manuela Barona expired, the mare appeared in the Boyacá Park, running circles as it had done almost thirty years before in the first days of the Violence, when no one dared go out on the street. They did not tell a single soul. The bad news was learned only the following morning, when Blanquita Lozano de Tejada passed by on her way to five o'clock mass. She saw the open doors and the lighted candles near the coffin they had taken down from the ceiling where Doña Manuela, owing to some strange, undiscovered mania, had collected them. Word got out, and those who could attended the wake. From the group arose the religious fervor that was missing at the wake, and Blanquita herself took charge of a plan to have a mass sung for Manuela Barona at San Bartolomé. Since neither Captain Nemesio Rodríguez nor Doña Marcianita Barona de Rodríguez could enter the parish office, as the one was an apostate and the other had never wanted to go, she, notary's wife or not (but an exemplary Catholic all the same), would go to San Bartolomé to request a burial. Nemesio Rodríguez, with the prosopopoeia that had characterized him since the days of the Santander battles, and gazing with a depth that Marcianita seemed in her alienation to share, categorically opposed the idea. Doña Blanquita did not insist, for the wake was then disbanding. At ten in the morning—accompanied only by two of her maids, her daughter, her son-in-law, the notary, his wife, and Miss Paulina Sarmiento, who, repentant of all her guilt and persecutions, appeared grief-stricken when it was time to go—Manuela Barona made her last journey through the streets of Tuluá. The captain of the liberal forces of Palonegro and builder of the Pacific Railroad wanted to sing as they processed from the park to the cemetery, and the more Marcianita objected publicly, the more he obstreperously insisted on doing so.

The next day Tuluá commented at the top of its lungs not about the few people who had accompanied Father Tascón's concubine, but about the racket that Nemesio and Marcianita had made, thus confirming the conviction that she should never have married him and that sooner or later her error would be much more evident than it was on the day of the burial.

VI

Tille Uribe was Dr. Tomás's youngest daughter. She did not use the ear trumpet her father used when he saw his patients, but she talked as much as he, if not more, stressing final syllables and sing-songing everything as if her voice were an old flute and not that of a woman of thirty eternal years. She was tireless since birth and had little eyes lost in a white, almost albino face that as the years passed abounded in freckles. Tille Uribe's only friend was an Amazonian parrot that she had received back in the days when she was being treated for her incipient puberty by sitting on hot bricks before going to bed.

Since she was the youngest, her father spoiled her rotten. Instead of calling a midwife for his spouse, he hired one of the nurses from the hospital, and for years, for almost a decade, the same nurse served as nanny. For none of her nine brothers or sisters did Dr. Tomás take the same precautions to which Tille was subjected. The day she was born and he saw her as white as a tallow candle, the doctor took it into his head that his daughter was susceptible to a cancer which could be avoided only by giving her punctilious care. Her baby bottles became famous throughout Tuluá because of the exaggerated stories her brothers and sisters, who were especially prone to gossip, indiscriminately spread. The bottles were boiled for a half hour before they touched her lips. They were kept in an enameled pot that smelled of alcohol. The nipples were disinfected as if they were Dr. Tomás's surgical gloves. The diapers were not of that class of common gauze that everyone used but rather of an adhesive fabric that resembled carpeting. As a result, the little girl was so spoiled that when she finally confronted life it was already too late.

She topped off her coddled asininity with a flute-like voice and a demeanor that broadcast uselessness. She did not touch a pot without a servant at her side. She would not pick a rag up off the floor because it might injure her lower back. She could not cough without someone handing her a handkerchief. She was so finicky about food that when Dr. Tomás told her that at twenty years of age it was time she grew accustomed to a normal diet, she burst into a tearful tantrum which lasted for three days and nights, at the end of which her diminutive eyes were lost in an irritation that took months to heal. For the whole next week, out of anger—because that was what Dr. Uribe's freckled daughter felt—instead of eating what was served at the table she ate what she fed to Carlos, her parrot, which was the same food she used to have before her father obliged her to eat what was served to everyone else.

Perhaps that is what made her so angry with her parrot. He was the only joy left to her in her crisis, the last straw she could clutch at during the week when she was awash in tears. In the end she had to eat what her father ordered for her. She began to appear in public. Instead of the long flowered gowns that her sclerotic mother had made her wear, she dressed according to the latest fashion and ordered some embroidery from Marcianita Barona. In the eyes of Tuluá, Tille Uribe seemed to bring herself up to date.

But it was only an illusion. Tille Uribe, although she ate what was served to everyone else, although she dressed in Marcianita Barona's embroidery or showed her freckles off in public, was Dr. Tomás's indefatigable daughter, the parrot's mistress, the frightened member of an extraordinary family that had to include at least one fool. Although the doctor claimed to search out boyfriends for her who might entertain the prospect of matrimony, she always found her parrot Carlos and his antics more amicable, more obedient, more understanding, almost more desirable. At eight in the morning she would go to the coop where the Amazonian slept; she would sweep and clean the floor of his cage. She poured copious quantities of detergent on the spattered floor and would scrub the walls of the parrot's house with a rag. Whoever saw Carlos hanging on the shiny pipe that stretched from one wall to the other, did not believe that he was a real animal, much less the lousy parrot that Tille Uribe obtained when she began to feel sensations she had never felt before. A junk dealer from the south brought him to her. The bird was very young. He still had downy feathers. She picked him out amidst childish squeals. Her father bought him begrudgingly, and the girl held him in her hands as if she had been waiting for him since before her birth. The strange thing was that he was so tame that even the salesman was terrified. Tille took him home, found a plate to feed him with, and while her father had the cage built in which he later lived, she provided him with a branch in the dwarf apple tree her mother had planted the day Tille was born. From the first moment she called him Carlos. It was a name that had never existed in her family of Luises, Federicos, Alejandros, and Felipes. Neither was there any neighbor called Carlos. No one asked her reasons, and she never explained why she had so dubbed him.

As months and years passed, Carlos came to replace in Tille's thoughts the sweetheart her girlfriends acquired, the lover for which one girl or another shed tears in classes at the academy of the Franciscan mothers, where she studied until the third year of high school. She had to leave school because the nuns would not permit her to repeat a year for the fourth time. She knew nothing of mathematics, less of literature, but she kept such lovely notebooks and looked so wise with her freckles in the air and her little face of a fallen angel that they let her attempt her third year four times. Then, because her previous grades had been entirely unsatisfactory, everyone was finally convinced that she was never going to pass. Tille Uribe arrived at final exams during one of her menstrual periods, which to her seemed to last for months. She could not answer a single question. With the final report card that informed Dr. Uribe that his daughter had failed the year for the fourth time, they sent a letter informing him it was absolutely impossible for her to repeat again. The nuns must have been beside themselves. She was not only the daughter of Dr. Uribe, the official physician of the school, the nuns, and their order throughout the country. She was also the sister of five young women who had brought honor and glory to the academy. Three of them were among the first graduates of the academy, and one became the first woman lawyer in Colombia, and, as years passed, the first minister and first senator. To speak of the Uribes with the Franciscan mothers was like intoning canticles of praise to the gentleman who had been their great uncle, the army general. But Mother Delfina, displaying talons that no one suspected she possessed, signed that letter and caused the doctor's family the unspeakable distress that led him officially to resign his position as doctor of the academy, the nuns, and their order.

He never again addressed the nuns, much less provided them with the civic and political support that for years he had given them. But as days passed he became convinced that Tille would do better at home than as a student at the academy. Doting on her parrot from eight in the morning, when she cleaned his coop and first fed him, she checked his food three times a day and prepared him for what would happen at three in the afternoon. Then, with towels, mercurochrome, and salts from the Buga veterinary pharmacy, she would examine him from top to bottom and treat the eternal mange on Carlos's feet, a malady which has recently caused the ailments that have driven Tille nearly insane.

The parrot was so polite and so loved his mistress that many times he seemed not like an Amazonian mimic of the notes of the national anthem but rather like his mistress's peer. She would talk to him as she fed him, as she treated his sores, as she cleaned the floor of his cage, as she polished the walls. He looked at her like one hearing a confession, and at the end of each sentence he would invariably repeat "Well, that's life, child." No one knew who taught him that phrase, but he said it with such distinct conviction that there are those who have sworn he understood everything she told him.

As years passed he began to lose tone, and even when an approaching downpour made them remove him from his coop amidst songs he had learned in his first years in Tuluá, when Dr. Tomás's house bordered the Capuchin convent, the words Carlos spoke lacked quality and clarity. Tille noticed the difference but harbored the hope that her parrot's verbal skills would never be completely lost. His eternal molting encouraged her in that belief. The dead never grow ill, she thought, and like so many other things in her special life, this idea was not modified or abandoned. But the illness, caused perhaps by an excess of detergent used to clean the cage, came to vex Carlos so much that one day, at eight in the morning when she arrived to give him bread and milk, the parrot scarcely greeted her with the chirp of a soaked sparrow. My Carlos, my Carlos, my Carlos, Tille Uribe began to cry at the foot of the coop. The maid called one of the brothers, who called the doctor-sister in Bogotá and the other brothers and sisters. They called veterinarians in Barranquilla. They wrote to zootechnic experts in Boston. Her brothers and sisters had incredible connections. But they were to no avail. Carlos, her lover, was ill.

She herself treated him with linden blossom tea. Then, with an eyedropper, she gave him penicillin. As days passed, someone told her that the best remedy was cortisone, and she tried it. The veterinarian in Barranquilla ordered baths of salt water and hot magnesium. Practically all of the bird's old feathers fell out. The Boston man ordered a mixture of merthiolate and iodine prepared for the bare spots, magnesium salts for the swelling, and rhinophrenol drops for his throat. In his view, the illness that affected Tille Uribe's lover was in his throat, and the only remedy was to treat it as if it were sinusitis. The pains that must have afflicted the parrot were as severe as those of a person with an acute nasal infection. Tille and everyone at home thought so. The problem was giving Carlos the rhinophrenol drops. Not even Tille, who knew his most intimate parts, could get him to open his beak. The parrot defended himself with a shrill death-whistle that paralyzed everyone. Drops poured into his beak would be out a half second later, because he would stick out his tongue and spit them. Finally they had to administer them to him through the little holes at the base of his plumage. It worked for the first few days. The tone of his speech improved and the whistle disappeared. But Carlos must have been very ill indeed because only his voice improved. His long wings continued to lose luster and grew completely limp. The bald spots on his feet spread almost like a cancer and completely engulfed his talons. The iodine and merthiolate slowed the disease's growth but did not cure him. Tille was growing desperate.

On the twentieth day she remembered that Doña Laura de Garcés, the witch from the sugar mill who had prepared and supplied the unguent she had anointed Carlos with, should know the best way to treat him. She rushed again to her table, had her read the cards, look into the future, and prepare a balm similar to the one she had made twenty years before to help train Carlos. It was the witch who had deceived everyone into believing in the magical powers of Tille, who had domesticated Carlos, whereas before, among his many endearing qualities, he used to attack anyone who so much as approached his cage.

During the time when he was losing his last feathers, more or less at the end of the fifth year, Carlos began to hate Tille. He would not accept the bread and milk at eight in the morning; the cage cleaning was like a spat between cat and dog. She would pour the water and he would flap his wings to prevent it. She would scrub with the soap and he would peck at the cage's main support. Without a doubt, it was the lack of a mate that was responsible. Tille, in her spoiled adolescence, suspected as much and decided, perhaps from that moment on, to serve as the parrot's lover. Miss Laura gave her special ointments. She did no more than put a feather on her head and another at her tail, and the unguent took care of the rest. She smeared herself with it for nine days and nine nights, three times on the nape of the neck, three times on her behind, and three times on her bosom. On the tenth day, Carlos climbed onto Tille's shoulder and spoke in her ear as if she were on the honeymoon she had always been denied.

The day she returned, Miss Laura recognized her instantly, overturned the cards, and sent her for a goose feather. It did not take Tille long to find one. Her Aunt Ramona supplied her with one from the legendary Filopotes, famous from the days of the Violence. With the feather in her hand and facing north, her eyes closed for eleven minutes, and Laura de Garcés's final prayers on her lips, Tille tried to save her ailing parrot.

He was so doubled over on that twenty-seventh day that Tille smelled death on him. She stuck in the feather that she had brought, first in his beak and then up his rectum. Carlos was so sick, sprawled on the floor of his cage, that he did not even twitch. This time the unguent did not work. Tille Uribe's eyes were glazed with tears. She had been sure she could somehow revive Carlos, but when she pulled out the feather that she had stuck way up his ass and remembered the death rattle it had eliminated the first time she had used it, she felt death's presence at the door of the cage. It occurred to her to hurry over to Chuchú so that she, blessed by God, could provide her with a glimmer of hope, but the arrival of Brother Andrés for the benefit performance at the Marist Brothers' academy persuaded her to forego that option. If Brother Andrés knew about spiders, lizards and other animals, perhaps he would know about parrots too. Not long before she had read his articles in the *Press* about the Amazonian jungles. Carlos was from there, so Andrés could probably cure him.

She went to the academy. She bought five tickets for the performance, though she was certain not to attend. She appeared before Brother Andrés and with tears in her eyes convinced him to go home with her to diagnose the parrot's illness. Brother Andrés, considering the possibility of becoming an animal consultant so as to be known as the St. Francis of Assisi of the modern era, rushed over a half hour later. Carlos was still sprawled out over the straw on the coop floor. At another time, the mere presence of a stranger would have been enough to make him leap from his perch, raise a tremendous racket, and peck at the stranger. But when Brother Andrés approached, he scarcely whistled in agony. The brother examined him carefully. He put him in a box lined with gauze. He prescribed three spoonfuls of pure serum every hour. If the treatment did not work, he would return twenty-four hours later and give him a transfusion. Since it was a time-consuming procedure and he had to go prepare his spiders, toads, and lizards for the benefit show, it would be better to perform the transfusion the next day.

Tille agreed with raised hopes, but that night when she was told that the brother had been bitten by the poisonous spider and was in very serious condition in the hospital, her hopes were dashed. The serum she gave Carlos was helping a little. At least she sensed life in the parrot, but not much more. The transfusion might have worked the miracle, but Brother Andrés had no time to think of anything other than curing himself.

During the days of Brother Andrés's cataleptic coma, Tille stayed practically in a trance. Every hour her crumpled body would crouch to give the spoonfuls to Carlos. For five days he improved, but on the sixth, when it was said that Brother Andrés had no chance of salvation either, the parrot entered a slow but certain agony. He indifferently spread his wings, again clacked his beak, and threw himself on the gauze in the box. He refused to take the spoonfuls of serum, and in place of the death whistle he had made for days, for the first time he made a rasping noise that sounded more like that of a cat than a parrot. Tille looked in the mirror and, from the depths of her freckled face, emitted a cry as she had on that day long ago when she was twenty years old and Dr. Tomás had made her eat just like everybody else.

VII

The problems between Nemesio Rodríguez and Marcianita Barona were not limited to the day of the phlegm-hawker's burial. They had begun long before, the very day of the wedding, when Nemesio had refused to allow a photograph of the couple cutting the cake, which had waited for years for its moment of glory. He argued that one hour after making his first communion he had been forced to pose rigidly and look at the bald town photographer, only to learn a month later that the pictures had not come out. So if he did not have a picture of his first communion, what did he want a picture of his wedding for? He was so adamant, so inflexibly emphatic in his demand, that Marcianita had to appear alone, cutting the cake that had awaited her for seven long years and that no one ate for fear of food poisoning.

Doña Manuela served as a bridge in the quarrel between the newlyweds. It was because of her that Marcianita posed alone in front of the English cake. If she had not interceded, surely the marriage would have failed from the start, because neither of the couple was accustomed to giving in. For that same reason, they spent their honeymoon no farther away than the house at La Rivera. Nemesio said Cartago and Marcianita said Popayán. The one ranted against the city that had carried away his family in a malarial typhus epidemic still remembered by the evil tongues of the city where saints were dressed by elegant ladies; and Marcianita was not going to Cartago because she had learned that Father Tascón's two brothers lived there, and they had received none of the inheritance he had sent in his many-faceted trunks. Nemesio could not very well explain that the typhus had not only carried off his family but had snuffed out the life of his intended, Laurita Valencia; much less could Marcianita divulge (although Nemesio doubtless knew, since Tuluá repeated it every time a few drinks were taken) that she was the daughter of the San Bartolomé parish priest, deceased in a state of grace while gazing at the sea in Cartagena.

Doña Manuela's intervention saved them from the initial debacle. My house at La Rivera, was the energetic proposal of the lady of intermittent expectorations. Nemesio Rodríguez, arrogant as any untitled, army-less captain, and Marcianita, with the stubborn expression of a woman condemned to limbo from birth, assented. Breathing the scent of the jasmines she had raised with care, and evading the armadillos which, as homage to their beloved, emerged each day to lavish their caresses on her before dawn, they spent their brief honeymoon together.

Surely they argued, but the disputes must not have been very serious because Doña Manuela was not called upon to mediate. Convinced that her daughter would always argue with a man who tried to order her about, as if she were one of his remote subordinates in Peralonso, she tried from her invalid's couch to attenuate the hostilities which arose daily between them. If news of their problems had not reached the outside world—so that Tuluá would not have the pleasure of seeing so soon destroyed that which it had wanted to smash to smithereens since the beginning—these conflicts would have persisted for days and weeks between the couple, jealous in their immovable postures and longing for the freedom that each felt sacrificed in marriage.

The first public demonstration of their splitting was on the day of Doña Manuela's burial. Leading the wake, Marcianita opened doors and windows and planned to call on the nearest neighbors for company. The captain of the liberal forces, taking more to heart than his very wife the problem of ostracism with which Tuluá had punished and scorned Father Tascón's concubine, imposed his will upon his frightened, embittered, and grieving wife. Not until dawn, when Blanquita Lozano arrived, did anyone learn that Manuela Barona had died. Perhaps for that very reason, Nemesio Rodríguez tried to sing all the way from the Boyacá Park to the cemetery. Since Manuela Barona was not religious by nature, and since singing in San Bartolomé would ruffle many a feather (but neither were they going to bury her indifferently as if she were Tille Uribe's parrot), the most brilliant idea that occurred to the builder of the Pacific Railroad was to sing as he followed the bier. They knew no more of the Popayán Seminary canto than "furrowing the depraved sea of a treacherous world that will direct us...," and repeating it over and over again, before the lonely coffin left the house of jasmines in order to incite Miss Paulina's repentance, aroused Marcianita's anger.

When the clock struck ten in the morning and, borne by the four surveyors of ditches, the coffin containing the remains of Manuela Barona left for the Boyacá Park, and when in the house of jasmines resounded the furrowing of a treacherous world's depraved sea, Marcianita took up her mother's cane in order to deposit it in the tomb. Laying it on the floor, she discussed the silence at the burial with her domineering husband. Tuluá witnessed every single detail. Behind the windows or on the street corners they happily lived the moments they had been waiting for since the day when a luncheon at Barbarita

Lozano de Aramburu's had definitively sealed the first and perhaps the last civil matrimony the town had ever seen.

It was the same years later when Marcianita was expecting her first child and Nemesio Rodríguez enjoyed the caresses of Rocío Jojoa. The argument on the day of the burial was the noisiest perhaps because it was the first. Marcianita won a resounding victory. The silence interrupted by the argument came completely to overshadow the procession. All that was heard were the heavy footsteps of the four pallbearers, the elegant strides of Nemesio Rodríguez, captain of the liberal forces of Palonegro and President Reyes' aide-de-camp, those of his wife Marcianita Barona, of Doña Blanquita Lozano de Tejada and her husband the notary, and of the repentant Paulina Sarmiento. No one else. Tuluá would not allow anyone else to walk behind the casket of the woman who had expedited their curse, who unreservedly had confronted them with sacrilege. It was difficult to hear the murmur that Marcianita Barona believed she always noted at the peak moments of her life. The same one she must have sensed when she decided to be born that October thirty-first on which Tuluá howled with hatred. The same with which she eventually received Paulina Sarmiento when the clock struck eleven and no one entered the central nave of San Bartolomé to get married. It was not the murmur of market day, nor the murmur of Holy Week; it was, it had been, a special murmur, perhaps made only for Marcianita Barona. With the murmur, Tuluá identified in great detail what it still really thinks of Marcianita Barona, in spite of many years, defective memories, and waves of civilization; and even though the miracle working has recently made them forget everything the living history that overwhelmed the streets could explain to them.

Nemesio Rodríguez, who felt he did not have the supernatural mental powers necessary to identify many valuable details that controlled the lives of the jasmine cultivators, did not perceive the murmur his wife felt reverberating in her ears. He scarcely felt the logical discomfort of an insignificant, solitary, and, more than anything, ill regarded burial. Worn out as he was, he looked only at the ground from the Boyacá Park to the Palobonito Cemetery. When they crossed the train track before arriving, he looked both ways, expecting perhaps to hear the train that would squash him in his tracks. Then he quickly lowered his eyes again and did not raise them except at the instant when Manuela Barona's cadaver descended into the grave they had ordered dug at the foot of the wall that divided the Catholic cemetery from the so-called general cemetery, which was no more than a vulgar and disowned dung heap.

As the last shovelfuls fell on Father Tascón's hawking concubine and the gravedigger placed a cement slab marked with her initials in what would be the beginning of a great mausoleum that Marcianita would have built for her mother, Nemesio Rodríguez considered fulfilled the greatest obligation of his life. He had buried his mother-in-law in spite of so much prejudice. With her, he mistakenly believed, had also been buried his wife's strong, capricious, unyielding will, so that he could be the captain of his family, since he no longer was the captain of General Reyes's forces. If Marcianita was adamant before, however, with the death of her mother—Nemesio Rodríguez's illusions of her yielding notwithstanding—she tightened the screws even more, and from that moment on it was she who was the irreplaceable directrix of a world that challenged her ingenuity.

She gave the first demonstration of her power at midday, barely after returning from the burial. At the door of the house by the park they said good-bye to Blanquita Lozano and Paulina Sarmiento. They strolled past the jasmines in the garden. They looked affectionately into each other's eyes and gave the order not to be interrupted. They closed doors and windows, lit the copper pots of incense, and in the bed that may have served Manuela Barona and Father Severo Tascón in the conception of Marcianita, they performed a sexual act so prolonged, so expressly requested and directed by Marcianita in grief over her mother, that when days later she felt pregnant, she said nothing to her husband, arranged her things, designed new clothes, and then definitively forbade him to touch her again. It was exactly three months later that she broke the news to him of her pregnancy. She was dressed in a yellow tunic that she had at first explained as inherited from her mother. She did not tell him with the tenderness with which a woman informs her husband of the prospect of their first child. She told him with such obvious aggression and antipathy that Nemesio Rodríguez perhaps thought he had married Paulina Sarmiento, the vendor of milk bottles, cows by the kilo, and plots of grassland. It was not the simplicity and courtesy one would expect of the most expert and delicate cultivator of jasmines in the whole region. "Starting today I have to sleep in a separate bed," she told him, cut and dry, at lunch time. "Not only am I no longer in mourning, but I forbid you to touch me; I'm expecting." And if Nemesio Rodríguez thought he would faint or fall in a swoon because he was going to be a father, Marcianita immediately convinced him that none of that was necessary. Rather than rejoicing over what she was creating, he should feel unfortunate. She did not tell him that, but he understood. He did not know if it was due to that strange mental communication between them or if it was rather the result of the way they both had to behave from that day on. Regardless, Marcianita no longer allowed him his connubial lodging and he, teeming with a sexual vigor that he had suppressed for so many years of measuring highways and ditches, fell straight into the arms of Rocío Jojoa.

The first days, he did so with reticence, enveloped in abashed modesty, in a feigned lassitude that he had inherited from his elders. No one in Tuluá, not even Marcianita, who could read minds, managed to untangle the snarl that he had been fashioning for months. Rocío Jojoa was the daughter of some Putumayan Indians who had built a fireworks factory in Tuluá. With the alluring features of an Indian and the stature of a Greek goddess, Rocío, gazing every morning at the sextant wielder, came to be the girl who satisfied his repressed impulses and who curdled in his wife the desperation with which she implemented her premature delivery, spouting curses and enduring labor pains.

Nemesio Rodríguez visited Rocío Jojoa, bathed since dawn, bursting with vitality, every morning as he went with his surveyors and his sextants to take measurements. Since her house was on the outskirts of Tuluá on the road to Las Playas, he had only to pause in his daily travels. As months passed and their passion grew, the visits began to last longer. But later, in order not to lose surveying time, he began to delay his return home at night. At first, Marcianita, beset by her bursting belly, paid little attention to the early rising or the late arrival home. But since the pregnancy occasioned in her some strange caprices, in satisfying them she discovered the scaffolding of infidelity that her husband had been erecting. Her first fancies were simple. Instead of drinking orange juice, she asked for grapefruit. Instead of cow's milk, she demanded mare's. Before lunch she would bathe in cold water for half an hour. She went to sleep at eight o'clock at night, hermetically sealed in her room in order to prevent her husband's intrusion. She got up at five, bustled about, picking jasmines and arranging the things that she would take when, at eight o'clock, she would head for the house at La Rivera to cultivate more jasmines, contemplate her armadillos, and let life pass by as she sat in her mother's wicker chair.

Later her prenatal manias became more complicated; she began to loathe people. Her first victim was Don Telesforo Lozano, the telegrapher. His moustache, his precise gaze, his elegantly repeated formalities, his motiveless courtesy, his constant willingness to serve exasperated Marcianita. She did not send a single telegram. But every morning at almost eight o'clock when she was already putting her things in one of the cars from the plaza to go up to La Rivera, Don Telesforo would pass by and greet her, offering her a thousand congratulations and shouting at her—because that was the only way that Don Télez, who was on the run, could make himself heard—saying that her belly was getting riper and riper, more full of life, more special...

She moved her trips up to seven-thirty. Either Don Télez spotted her or else his telegraphic service somehow managed to be wireless before Marconi. At six in the afternoon, the moment of her return, he was passing by to add to his morning bouquet a sonorous "What an early riser, Doña Marcianita." It almost produced a hecatomb. Don Telesforo could not be pressured, but Marcianita could find some relief. For five days she did not go to La Rivera, and on the sixth, when she went, she left at ten in the morning and returned at four in the afternoon. The next day, Don Télez passed by at ten in the morning. Marcianita could not stand it, and like a crazy woman, she went in search of one of the Putumayan witches who hung around Las Playas.

It is not known if it was pure coincidence or her sixth sense that carried her there in search of a Putumayan Indian, but in any case she went there not to free herself from Don Télez but to follow her fancy and to discover what eventually became her tragedy. The Indian woman read her future, grimaced when asked about the husband, gave her some black pebbles to throw in Don Telesforo's path, and warned her of the fatal discovery, indicating that the only salvation could be a purgative of *mamatolina*. Marcianita did not know that not only was Rocío Jojoa taking away her own husband but she had also lured away the Putumayan woman's Cayetano Achicanoy. For the black pebbles to achieve the desired effect, she told her—her thoughts lost in the moment when Cayetano Achicanoy left, never to return again—you have to get some sand from the Jojoa's, the powder makers. You can only get it at six-thirty in the morning, when Old Man Jojoa has finished throwing out the first calcium sulfide. Marcianita believed it, and an irate Nemesio Rodríguez crossed paths with her. Arriving at six-thirty and crouched in front of Rocío Jojoa's house picking up sand, she recognized her husband's bay mare tied by the door of the house. She was not angry; she patted her belly lightly, gave half a turn, and waited until seven in the evening, seated on the same wicker chair where her mother had awaited the arrival of that fateful hour during the days of the gray mare at the Boyacá Park.

All day long she rehearsed what she was going to say; so much so that she almost turned into the Paulina Sarmiento of her own wedding day. She had wanted to put his clothes in order, but she decided instead to make tickets for the bazaar while she waited. When he arrived she was still making them. Without raising her eyes, as if she were going to say something trivial, Marcianita confronted her husband with the name of Rocío Jojoa. He did not bat an eye. He never let himself be embarrassed by what he did; he admitted the affair with tremendous awe, justified it as a consequence of her not allowing him to lay a finger on her, and continued on to his room. He won the battle, but Marcianita, distraught in her anger, set in motion the plan for vengeance that ultimately led to her tragedy. She scattered the black pebbles in the direction of Don Télez, gave Rocío Jojoa's sand to her husband in his coffee, and served the purgative of *mamitolina* in his soup at mealtime. Nothing had any effect on him. Immune to all witchcraft, he simply complained of the soup's rancid flavor. She continued giving him the *mamitolina* every day, encouraged by something she had read in the past about poisoning by arsenic. But when, after thirty-seven doses, the purgative still had no effect on her unfaithful husband, she decided, unthinking or upset, to try it herself to measure its effects.

The *mamitolina* had the effect that a potent bovine purgative would have on any human. At four in the afternoon, worn out from sitting on the toilet seat in a cold sweat and smelling like a stable, she started to swell up. At first she did not notice it, since her belly of seven months hid the swelling. When her husband arrived to find her face down on the bed in the throes of unbearable cramps, the swelling had gone beyond her breasts, bursting with milk. They called the doctor; they called the midwife. Dr. Tomás sent her to the hospital, and in the operating room of the recently founded San Antonio Hospital in Tuluá, staring at the white of the lamp and writhing in relentless pain, Marcianita Barona realized that the creature in her belly had also felt the effects of the *mamitolina* purgative and had converted her cavities into the toilet that she so craved at the very moment. The nurses who spread the news through Tuluá vomited in telling of the miscreation that had been removed from Marcianita Barona's womb. The operating room in the hospital had to be washed with disinfectant to counter the odor that gushed from the uterus of Nemesio Rodríguez's wife. Finally, Dr. Tomás, anointed to the gills with shit, was able to extract from that diarrheic tempest a creature of masculine gender, resembling more a rat than the son that Nemesio Rodríguez had hoped for. Father Phanor tried to baptize him, but no one, not even Dr. Uribe, would allow him to.

At the notary—the only place they registered him—they recorded the name of Bartolomé Rodríguez Barona. For days and days the fever consumed Marcianita in the hospital. The baths in boric acid, rubbing alcohol, rosewater, benzoic acid, and whatever else occurred to the doctor, seemed to have no effect. The odor disappeared, the swelling diminished, but Marcianita remained enveloped in a stupor. She drank twenty-three glasses of water daily, and the nurses used up five gallons of alcohol dampening the sheets that covered her to counteract the effect of the heat that already fogged the window panes. For a while they thought she was going to burn up. The sheets dampened with alcohol sizzled when they touched her body. On the seventh day, already enveloped in the prospect of death, delirious as no one else had ever been, she asked for jasmine water. Nemesio Rodríguez, terrified upon contemplating the lamentable portrait of his rat-son and his agonizing wife, had fifty dozen jamines cut. They were put in an immense pot with hot water; they turned out to be just what Marcianita needed. Instead of alcohol, they dampened the sheets in this infusion. Two hours later, Marcianita was immersed in the lethargy that some nurses identified with death but that Dr. Tomás called a marvelous recovery.

Within the next month the little rat-like creature they called Bartolomé grew almost an inch, gained a couple of pounds, and began to show in his movements and in his bewildering cries the inevitable signs of idiocy. Marcianita got up during that time, and before asking to see the child she sat down to organize the lottery tickets. Perhaps that moment marked the origin of Nemesio's hatred for the bazaar, but he said nothing. Marcianita's condition was so wretched—she had lost forty pounds, her face was drawn, her eyes were sunken into her head, her skin was as waxen as an Easter candle, and her hands quivered when she touched them to her head—that Nemesio held his tongue when he saw her making out the tickets for the bazaar in the San Bartolomé sacristy. He hired a servant to help her, another to sell the tickets every Sunday, and then and there he decided to drop Rocío Jojoa. Marcianita did not say a word about it to him. Such a childbirth had presumably made her forget even his infidelity. But since he had used Rocío only to replace the caresses that his wife denied him, and since the day of their renewal was approaching, he decided to sever all ties with the Indian woman.

Marcianita knew things had changed because her husband no longer got up before dawn and he came home earlier than before. Bartolomé too almost understood the change because before getting to know his mother he had grown accustomed to spending the whole night lying on his father's chest. He was still the little rat that had emerged in the diarrheic tempest. His little hands were like a sigh, and his breathing was only the slightest palpitation. He did not laugh as other children do at that age but only opened those eyes of a new-born calf that made one suspect the evil that afflicted him. He sucked like mad on the bottle and often kept suckling the air that no one could see after the nipple was removed. He could not distinguish between the real and the imaginary. He stared at bright colors and showed definite signs of deafness. He did not respond to the loud noises or the guttural sounds his father would make to attract his attention. He simply grew, as Marcianita learned soon enough. For some reason she preferred not to touch him, but when she did she felt the internal trembling of all the strange power she had inherited from her father. She did not cry; she had not even done that on the day of the *mamitolina* swelling. She lowered her eyes and took care of her idiot.

It was something like a punishment for her. At Marcianita's request, Dr. Tomás examined him the day he turned three months old. Nemesio Rodríguez, either because he was always out measuring ditches or because he must, after all, have felt some pride in having a son, did not detect what Marcianita had known for an entire month. Her son was deaf and wet his diapers with astonishing alacrity, much more often than any normal child. The changing of diapers reached such an extreme that there were as many diapers hanging on the line as there were jasmines on the patio. At first she thought it was an excess of food combined with the boy's mythological ingestive capacity, but one day when she did not feed him and he practically peed himself dry, she was convinced that there was something wrong. She dressed him in her brightest silks in hopes he would notice the color, but the diaper's limpid color was the same to the child as the scarlet robe she donned once a year. The final indication was that she found an improbable slowness in his reflex movements that month. Most of the time when she tried to stimulate them, she encountered a rigid mummy who would rather let his bib cover him and the box of rattles and toys bury his face than even raise his arms. It was no longer just that the child was deaf. Not only did he not flinch or show fear of anything; her child was an imbecile, and Dr. Tomás was the only person who could officially say so.

In order for him to do that, there was no need for the thousand and one examinations that psychiatrists give to drive normal people crazy. He timidly held out his osculator, his little silver mallet, and the wisdom of his years. He gave Bartolomé a tap on each knee with the hammer. He put the stethoscope on his chest and back, gave him aromatic salts to smell, shouted in each ear, and peered into his eyes. It took scarcely five minutes. It looked more like the visit of a social services paramedic than that of the family's private Galen. In the doorway, Marcianita Barona was confronting an objective. At that moment, Nemesio Rodríguez must have been marking a line or looking through his theodolite. At six-thirty in the evening, when he arrived home, he found a note from Dr. Tomás. It must have been premonitory or very compelling because he did not even take the time to change his clothes. Wearing his muddy boots and smelling of sweat from a day in the sun, he rushed to the doctor's home. Neither the doctor's wife nor Marcianita, who had said something earlier about the visit, found out what the captain of the liberal forces of Palonegro had discussed with the general's doctor-brother. Surely they spoke in tones that the brother used with his captain. When Nemesio Rodríguez, dragging his feet as if the mud of all the ditches he had measured in his life were clinging to them, or as if he were tied to the tracks of the infinite Pacific Railway line that he had laid, told Marcianita that her vision of reality was not hers alone and that the idiot they had created they would have to tolerate together, the house lit up as if struck by lightning.

Nemesio Rodríguez entertained no thoughts of submission. His utilitarian and mathematical engineer's mind disposed him to act differently. He took off his heavy, muddy boots, washed away the sweat in a long bath, closed the doors and windows, turned out the lights, and accompanied Marcianita as she gave the idiot Bartolomé his bottle. Then, almost as if it were the ultimate military command, he forced his wife to copulate with him, and they conceived their second child. If the first had been an idiot, the second would not. If the illness had not abandoned Marcianita's belly, his masculinity, which cured all, would eradicate it. She could not utter a peep. All the force he withheld in the wartime defeat that was not released with the construction of the Pacific Railway or in measuring the Sarmiento's irrigation ditches was revitalized by the defeat incarnate in his idiot son and materialized in Father Tascón's daugther's plump arms. He lay her on the bed, mute, resigned to a truth that crushed and frightened her. She enjoyed it until she was seized by the premonition that they were banging out another idiot. She tensed her weak arms of a jasmine cultivator and ornament embroiderer and stoically withstood what Rocío Jojoa had been taking for months.

The next day she ran to Dr. Tomás and told him in detail what had happened. The doctor perhaps felt guilty for having incited the engineer of the School of Mines to go to such extremes, and he cared for Marcianita the way he never before or never after cared for an invalid. He sent her to bed for eleven days and eleven nights, and twice a day, at dawn, when Nemesio Rodríguez left with his theodolite on his shoulder, and at dusk, as the lights were coming on, Dr. Tomás visited Marcianita. On the twelfth day, the symptoms of pregnancy they both feared were evident, and then the life of the armadillos' mistress became as methodical as her animals' and as protected as her jasmines'.

The initial instructions were prohibitive. "Marcianita, you may not bathe except in warm water at noon," roared Dr. Uribe. She could not eat spicy foods and should vary her diet to include all the nourishment and vitamins her organism and that of the gestating child needed. Strenuous exercise was eliminated. She had to find someone who would come to Tuluá to care for the jasmines there, as the sons of Florentino Pastaz, the Indian from Chachagüí, were doing in La Rivera. The armadillos that were left, which could not even walk on the pavement in the park, she cared for by remote control. She no longer sat in the rocker where her mother had awaited the appearance of the mare and she herself had awaited the arrival of her idiot, but preferred to recline on the hard dining room chair where she had been making tickets for the bazaar, the only exercise the doctor did not forbid.

She continued to care for her idiot, changing his wet diapers fifteen or twenty times a day, wiping the shit that flowed from him like an uncontrollable fountain, feeding him when he demanded it with irksome tears every ninety minutes. As she did all this and her belly steadily grew, she also balanced her meals, read the books on nutrition she believed she should read, and even measured, ounce for ounce, the water she drank. She was enclosing herself in a cage so incredibly well wrought that there seemed to be no exit.

She had everything at her disposal: her husband good and early, her food, her jasmines, her armadillos. She made no effort at anything, and as in the days when she had to leave Luisita Tascón's school, she shut herself in so as to see no one. Only on Sundays, and almost as if under guard, she would sit in the chair at the foot of the sacristy door to sell bazaar tickets. That was her chief entertainment all week long. Mondays she counted the money to send to Father Phanor; Tuesdays she cut up the little pieces of paper for the tickets or made the numbers, from one to one hundred, so that on Wednesdays she could put them with the two hundred blanks that were ready from the day before. On

Thursdays she sent for the raffle prizes; she was already buying or ordering them from one store after another with a card that she, systematically, sent each month to a different person in order not to wear out her welcome. In a school assignment book she recorded whom she had written to in order not to request from them again. She classified the prizes and readied everything so that on Fridays she could stick a number onto each one. She gathered the ones left over from the previous Sunday, recorded the numbers, destroyed the extra tickets from that Sunday, and confirmed that the tickets from Tuesday included those numbers. On Saturday she packed her French wicker trunks and left everything ready so that on Sunday at eight-thirty in the morning, the bazaar would arrive at the sacristy door in Chucho Zafra's cart. It was driven by two servants who acted as bodyguards and heralded by a boy who in another age would have served as a standard bearer, but who only rang insistently on a nun's little prayer bell. Bartolomé stayed with Nemesio or with one of the other three servants. He was really no problem. He did not cry, other than every ninety minutes for food; his movements were growing little by little clumsier; his silence was sometimes terrifying, yet almost no one noticed him. Only Marcianita, tending to her idiot infant, was aware of him in the grand jasmine-scented house, vitiated by silence and solitude.

When the clock struck nine in the morning at San Bartolomé, the bazaar promptly opened. Two servants sold tickets and handed out the prizes. She, seated in her chair, watched, controlled the money, conversed with the clients, and presided over the activities as if they were of supreme importance, an act of solidarity with what she was bound to by centuries and centuries of heredity and promise.

As the months passed, her belly became more noticeable and her care more extreme. But when Inesita González became the beauty queen that Tuluá chose for the national beauty contest in Cartagena, and Dr. González's money was not enough for a town that idolized his daughter, Marcianita Barona made her presence known to her oldest client. Not because the child Inesita had been the buyer of at least twenty bazaar tickets every Sunday, but because it had been she, together with her brother, who at a time when no one would even look at Marcianita, defied the ire of Aminta and offered her the minimum that she incessantly searched for among the human beings she saw from the door of her house. Compelled by a force of gratitude as strong as what she felt when she screamed "fat" at Nina Pérez that day at Luisita Tascón's school, she bounced up from her pregnant confinement and, directing her armadillos, participated in a costume ball that was held to raise money for Inesita's trip from Tuluá to Cartagena. Marcianita did not reserve a space for fear of disobeying Dr. Uribe. The pregnancy would not have mattered to her; for Inesita she was capable of forgetting that her first child was an idiot and if she did not take the precautions she had perhaps not taken for Bartolomé, her second could be the same.

Not content with that donation, she contributed to the fund drive by organizing a bazaar so gigantic, so boundless, that perhaps Tuluá had that day the most comparable example of what has been happening around here lately. She did not scrimp on the slightest detail. She set thirty children from Father Phanor's catechism class to cutting paper and gluing blank tickets for the bazaar. She obtained prizes from merchants, housewives, and rich farmers. Those that seemed too small for the table she envisioned—a forty-meter-long gangplank that she'd had custom made—she put away for the Sunday bazaar. She coordinated the cash baskets with ten girls from the support committee, whose help she solicited without really expecting a response. In order for her to be able to carry out this project, it was necessary to empty four of the seven rooms of her house, to send Nemesio to sleep in Bartolomé's room, and to stow away the chairs and the plants from the breezeway in the dining room. There were so many prizes on the infinite table that Marcianita had to get up at four in the morning on that Sunday when the streets of the Boyacá Park saw the largest bazaar in their history. Right alongside, the miniscule bazaar was in the sacristy doorway. When Inesita González arrived at the table, the sales reached such a pitch that the ten girls, Marcianita, and the three servants were not able to keep up with all the work that had to be done. At three in the afternoon, because the endless table was empty, the bazaar closed.

Marcianita turned over to the support committee one thousand one hundred twenty-three times what she turned over to Father Phanor every Monday. But at midnight, when she had just finished tallying the extraordinary yield, she felt a fever coming on. At dawn Nemesio Rodríguez had to call for Dr. Tomás. The next day, Inesita González, dressed all in white and with a broad-brimmed hat that would have caused an uproar in Cartagena, appeared in Marcianita's room. On other days, in view of the doctor's prohibition of the slightest contact, Inesita limited herself to sending sweets and flowers to the great organizer of the festivities. Around seven in the evening that Monday, a gloomy day for Nemesio Rodríguez, Dr. Tomás gave his diagnosis. He did it not with the dumbfounding ease he had for announcing to Tuluá or to any of the relatives of his patients that the ailing one had ceased to live or was condemned to die very soon. His eyes brimmed in front of Nemesio Rodríguez—paled by the memories of his weakness as a captain in the war as he awaited the doctor's diagnosis—and with a voice that is still crying out for compassion, he blurted out that Marcianita had contracted German measles.

An engineer by all accounts and absolutely ignorant of medicine, Nemesio did not understand the gravity of the situation that Dr. Tomás had sadly hurled at him. In order for him to comprehend, the doctor had to look at him with the expression with which General Uribe perhaps looked at him upon giving the word of his final defeat at the hands of General Reyes. German measles?, queried the anxious captain of the liberal forces. Yes, was all Dr. Uribe responded, looking at the floor. Marcianita was in the third month of her pregnancy, and it seemed more than likely that the child would be born deformed. The present tragedy was nothing compared with the tragedy of the future. Marcianita knew it, and on the third day, when the fever had broken and the rash consumed her with profound itching, she called Dr. Tomás and suggested an abortion. The doctor almost dropped. Although he was the brother of the general of the liberal forces and, besides that, a radical liberal and no friend to priests, he opened his eyes wider than a white whale's and from his mouth issued a rotund NO. Months later, neither Nemesio Rodríguez nor Marcianita Barona would be able to forget that refusal. When everything unraveled and Dr. Uribe tried to act as intermediary in a lost cause, Marcianita had the fortitude to scream in the doctor's face and never to speak to him again from that day on. During the whole pregnancy, he continued to see her every morning, and at some moment she contracted the Christian hope that the doctor, with his monotonous voice and ancestral foolishness, conveyed with each examination. She was put with her belly between a pillow and a hot water bottle, and as the days passed, she took on the pallor of Holy-Week virgins. Nemesio Rodríguez, surveying land and toting theodolites, returned then to the arms of Rocío Jojoa. Bartolomé, bellowing every ninety minutes, spent most of his time in the care of one of the servants. He had turned into such a handy, manageable idiot that his existence was hardly noticed. Marcianita did not forget him, but neither did she want to look upon him again. She did not want any of the horrible defects that were gaining prominence in the idiot Bartolomé to be reflected in the new child that was gestating. His eyes were slanting to the sides; his ears stood up like a donkey's; his head, which tried to be round the first few days, looked with each passing day more like a pointed egg. His hands were always still and the drool dribbling from the seldom-closed lips became one of the most notable traits of the Rodríguez Barona's elder son.

During the sixth month, Marcianita began to dream of the mare. Since her mother had never told her of its existence, she scarcely remembered that something similar had been seen or dreamed of during her mother's agony. She was filled with dread. As days passed, the mare's nocturnal visits became so frequent that she grew accustomed to them, and if the animal was late in entering her dreams, she was almost certain to wake up. Like her mother, she told no one of that nightly visitation, but in the seventh month, when some annoying pains appeared at the height of her navel, her concern looked like fear to her husband, who at that time was bursting with optimism. He could do no less; Nemesio Rodríguez had been convinced by Dr. Tomás's angelic smile and firmly believed that the new child would be absolutely normal. He did not oppose Marcianita, but it was in his confronting her pessimism that the tragedy began.

He became stricter than ever, and Marcianita had to tolerate all his manias, intended to protect her as if in a crystal cage. Completely forgetting that his wife had had German measles and confusing exercise with illness, he believed that if she bent down to pick something up or moved from the bed to the dining room, it would occasion a miscarriage. He obliged the maids to serve her breakfast in bed. He permitted her to get up only for lunch, and then enveloped in veils and seated on feather pillows. He made Dr. Tomás come twice a day to osculate that deformed belly she was acquiring, and when he took even a few extra minutes to examine her or came only once, Nemesio would run through the galleries as if possessed, anticipating the tragic final moment. In the last month, he stopped measuring ditches. He awaited the child's arrival with such intensity that many were saying it was he that was expecting and not Marcianita. Since he continued to restrict her, and she to resist him, one day in the eighth month the catastrophe occurred. Marcianita, who could no longer stand the constraints, got up for breakfast, went to the jasmines, fed her armadillos, and even gave orders about the management of the house. Nemesio could not control himself and stood in the door of the room screaming like a banshee. Marcianita did not understand him, but he screamed so loud and in such an unpleasant tone that she raced like a runaway horse through the corridors of her house. He did not stop screaming even upon seeing her run. He did not moderate the tone of his voice at seeing her weakened and on the verge of insanity. He kept ranting at her, and then Marcianita, who could take no more, fell to the floor half dead and with such contractions that they took her to the hospital a half hour later. Dr. Tomás had to put Nemesio to sleep; Marcianita, on the other hand, behaved stoically. She did not groan or grimace from the pain she must have been feeling. But when they showed her the boy-child that she had borne and she recognized Bartolomé's egg-head and the sick-frog face of the mentally retarded, she let loose with a shriek that those who heard must still be hearing, cursing to the very end her husband's name. No sooner had he arrived and, still half asleep, heard the bad news, than she made him swear before Dr. Tomás, the hospital nurse, and the memory of Manuela Barona, that they would never have another child.

Nemesio did so in the midst of the commotion, but a couple of months later he forgot, and at midnight entered Marcianita's room. If he is still alive, on one buttock he must have a burn that she inflicted with the glass chimney of the kerosene lamp that always lit her room. He may have forgotten the prohibition, but not she. He returned to Rocío Jojoa and awaited the Putumayan Indian's pregnancy. It was his last hope; he made love to her twice a day, ate quantities of agave, and bellowed like a bull at stud when he came in the belly of the woman who *would* have him. But if Marcianita could get pregnant at the drop of a hat, Rocío had no idea of what it even meant. Nemesio Rodríguez had her examined at the medical center, but since they found nothing wrong and he wanted her to have his children, he dared take her to Dr. Tomás. It was no problem for the doctor, but for Marcianita it was something more than a confirmation of her incapacity. And for Tuluá it was perhaps the opportunity it had been waiting for since that day on which she married him despite all predictions: the chance to prove there had been no error and that this marriage would not last a day longer.

Nina Pérez, fat but good for a story, was the one who told her. She had never before visited the house. Marcianita did not forget that day in Luisita Tascón's school, and Nina, preoccupied with her obesity, had never had time to visit a woman as problematical and isolated as Marcianita. Bartolomé, dragging his imbecility around a wooden pen at the entrance to the house, was the first thing that fat, prodigiously fat Nina encountered. She needed a dozen jasmines in order to initiate her explosive attack. She bought them as an excuse, made small talk, asked about the children, the armadillos, the plants, and, with the dissimulation of a fine lady, admitted that a while back she had seen Marcianita's husband entering Dr. Tomás's office in the company of the powder-maker's Indian daughter. The captain had seemed rejuvenated at the side of that woman who, it is said, anointed herself with eggplant to preserve her youth.

That was sufficient to plant in Marcianita the germ of an idea. When at seven in the evening, carrying the theodolites he perhaps did not use that day, Nemesio Rodríguez, captain of the liberal forces of Palonegro, President Reyes's aide-de-camp, and builder of the Pacific Railroad, arrived home, they did not exchange a single word. They would not for many months to come. Bartolomé walked a little; his imbecility was evident not only in the drivel that dripped from his mouth, but also in his lizard-like eyes and puny hands. She continued making tickets for the bazaar and caring for her idiots. They called the second son Ramón Lucio. He cried much less than Bartolomé had done at that age. There was no doubt that he was even stupider than his brother. When he was hungry he produced a guttural sound that only remotely resembled a cry. The low, lost tone which he emitted was so difficult for the servants to recognize that they almost always let him go hungry. His mother neglected herself somewhat for him, was obsessed by the bazaar, and treated her husband like just another creature, like an armadillo that had to be fed, clothed, and housed. When at seven in the morning he went out to take his measurements and to see Rocío Jojoa, whom he was still trying to impregnate, she was busy watering her jasmines or packing the bags for a whole day at La Rivera. When he returned from his work, drunk, theodolite on his shoulder, and smelling of Rocío Jojoa, she was already ensconced in her rooms, giving the idiots their bottles or glued to the radio listening to stories of Oscar and Amanda. If they met in the hallways they ignored each other. The captain passed by as stiff as in those distant days of war, and she as if what had passed her were Father Tascón's ghost. He knew very well that she would never speak to him again, and she expected the same of him. They were not too mistaken, but they had not taken into account a new factor that began to play a part in their relationship. Nemesio Rodríguez, tired perhaps of living, of trying to produce a normal child in Rocío Jojoa, and of having to live in a house where he was almost a free lodger because his wife would not take a cent from him, turned to drink.

Instead of coming home at seven in the evening, as had been his custom when their marriage was stable, he would arrive at nine or ten, dead drunk. He would trip through the door; sometimes he managed to go directly to his room, but other times he fell asleep in the first chair he saw. He did not get sick or bother anyone. With the immense hangover that accosted him, so great was his fear of his wife that he preferred holding in his vomit to countenancing a scathing word the next day from that ogre who was shut up with the pair of idiots. He drank in the Central Bar or at Rocío Jojoa's house. He drank *aguardiente* because it was cheapest. But he could just as well have drunk whiskey because the Sarmientos continued to pay him royally for surveying their ditches, and he had nothing to spend his money on. Marcianita bought everything for the house, paid the jasmine gardeners, the servants, and even indulged her husband's gastronomic whims. Only once did he try to bring something home. Marcianita said nothing to him, but her reaction was so strong that Nemesio Rodríguez de León saw his days numbered.

He was coming back from surveying the new diagonals that would come down to the Burrigá ditch, which surrounded the Sarmientos' cane fields, when a black woman offered him some avocados. Probably he forgot that his house was no longer his, or maybe the woman struck the same chords in him as Rocío Jojoa; in any case, he bought a half dozen. They seemed to him just the thing to have with the stew, and so he turned them over to the servant that night. She looked at her master trying to warn him, but he did it with such amazing naturalness, as if everything were once again back to normal, that she had no choice but to take them to the kitchen. She put them in the urn where they were usually stored when Señora Marcianita bought them. In her encloistered rooms Marcianita was giving bottles to her pair of idiots. Bartolomé already ate stewed fruit and even soup by himself. What he lacked in speech, expression of desires, and movement of his head, he made up for in manual dexterity. He ate with outrageous speed and dressed like a cat in pattens, but he was incapable of peering in at Ramón Lucio's cradle to get to know him. His small motor movements were utterly awkward, he urinated with the same assiduity, and he could not learn to say that he had to go. He hardly recognized his father because Nemesio every morning, with the tragic expression he had worn since his first communion, drew together his handlebar moustache, his sardonic eyes, and his *aguardiente*-ridden breath in order to confront or torment himself looking at his own twisted countenance.

The night of the avocados he went to bed early. Perhaps Rocío Jojoa had left him exhausted. He sat down to read in one of the chairs in the parlor and before the clock in San Bartolomé had struck nine, he fell asleep. The next day he had the courage to respond to his wife's attack. As soon as she saw the avocados, she surmised who had brought them. She stared at the servant but said nothing. She took one of the ripest avocados and with it in her hand searched through the house for her husband. She found him about to leave, carting his theodolites. The avocado was soon smeared over one of them. "No one is going to bring me food anointed with Putumayan witchcraft. Do what you want with that Indian but you're not going to cheat on me again." And then Nemesio Rodríguez screwed up his courage. Tuluá almost got to see what it had expected for so long. He raised his theodolite and it seemed as though he was going to strike Marcianita. By a strange coincidence, a long, harsh roar, stronger than ever before, halted the captain of the liberal forces of Palonegro. Ramón Lucio, who now had the energy to ask for a bottle, set his father on the right path. He lowered the theodolite and climbed onto one of Chucho Zafra's twisted-footed beasts. That day's surveying would be 'way up in the hills where no jeep could reach. He hung his head as if convincing himself of a reality as cruel and abysmal as death; he did not go to Rocío Jojoa's that morning, and of the eleven measurements he had to take, only the last one came out right. He did not return to his house for three days, and when he did he came drunk out of his mind, knocking into furniture and planters, but in absolute silence. Marcianita said nothing. Flatly ignoring him, she continued to make tickets for her bazaar, to feed her idiots, and to wash the dirty and wet diapers with which Bartolomé and Ramón Lucio regaled her at least three times each morning. She had his clothes and bed linen washed separately and in hot water and continued to have him taken care of as in the best years of their marriage, but never again deigned to glance at him for so much as an instant. Sooner or later he would grow desperate and leave the house. She grasped only the view of the outsiders who had no knowledge of the crisis they were undergoing. But Marcianita, endowed with the strange powers that had made Nina Pérez grow fat and had halted the in-habited brother, was mistaken. Because she was busy making bazaar tickets, caring for her idiots and her flowers, or because in truth she never had the slightest capacity for understanding men, she forgot what was fundamental in someone who had been a captain in the war and builder of the Pacific Railroad.

VIII

Perhaps the only opportunity that Tuluá has had to feel unified, capable of overcoming the obstacles before it and moving forward, was in the days of the reign of Inesita González.

Never before had Tuluá participated in those crownings. From the Department of the Valle they would send a Cali girl chosen in a simulated competition from among the prettiest girls of well situated families. The story would appear in the newspapers, and when she arrived in Cartagena to participate in the national beauty contest, the Valle, which had hardly seen her in the papers and had no idea who the girl was, because she was one of those rich ones the poor people are forbidden to look at, would tremble as if she had embraced them all before leaving. But that year it occurred to someone that in the other Valle towns there must be at least one pretty girl who could compete with the Cali girls. One weekend, going through the mayor's offices and social clubs, that person managed to find six more girls than usual to send to Cali for the competition. The jury was composed of as many outsiders as possible so that no one could claim the title was sold to a *caleña*. Such an apparatus was devised so that everyone in the Valle would believe that there was as much a chance for the candidates from Cartago, La Unión, Zarzal, Buga, Palmira, and Tuluá as for the Cali representative.

That impression was not unfamiliar to Tuluá, and ever since they decided that the representative to the contest would be Inesita González, all forces, dead and alive, those who had never thought to cooperate in anything civic and those who always did; in short, everyone lent their support so that Inesita could show up in Cali accompanied by an incredible retinue and would have as her goal in Cartagena not the title of the Valle del Cauca, but that of all Colombia.

Because Inesita was the daughter of Dr. González, Tuluá's historic doctor-senator who had died leaving a substantial inheritance, they did not organize a single benefit. But they did produce elaborate shows to pay for buses and bands to go to Cali on the night of the competition. Aware that she was reaping a popularity that her father had sown five years before with his congressional labors and his constructive efforts on behalf of the region's development, she greeted all her admirers, paraded through the streets bestowing smiles, and addressed any audience they could assemble together during those days. Tuluá then grew concerned, and those who did not travel to the coliseum in Cali the night of the competition followed the events on the radio. *The Press,* which has typically been conservative in the Valle, could not deny the importance of the daughter of one who had been a Senator on the national level, Governor of the Department, Minister of State for the Conservative party, and even its founder; so for the whole department the undisputed favorite was Inesita González. And with good reason. Not just because she was Dr. González's daughter and all of Tuluá was agog over her. Her beauty was dazzling. More than one person stood with his mouth agape when her beauty mark sauntered by, peeping out from the low back of her dress. Her brother Toño cared for her as though she were a piece of Bavarian porcelain rescued from the bombings of the Second World War. Her measurements, as Nina Pérez shouted from the balcony of the San Fernando Club, where the girls were measured like cattle before an auction, were perfect, those of Miss Universe. She had no chance of losing. The other candidates were just filler. All of them, except for the one from Cali, considered themselves as such. They kept the appointment just to show departmental unity, rather than expecting to make off with the crown for their villages.

The night of the pageant the fans were almost all from Tuluá, and when Inesita paraded down the runway in the middle of the coliseum, all one could feel was an earth tremor. Her gown, full-length and bedecked with sequins, was as dazzling as her beauty. The judges could not deny that reality, and although the girl was not from Cali, she had to be the winner. It must have taken great effort for them to pronounce her name, but when they did, Tuluá seemed to rise from its foundations, the coliseum shook to the rafters, and a single cry rang out that night along the highway from Cali to Tuluá. She went ahead, the queen, prepared to carry to Cartagena not only the name of the Valle del Cauca but also her *tulueña* heritage and love. That is what was broadcast over the radio when she was crowned, and instead of going to the dance that the Cali oligarchy had organized, she preferred to mount the Tuluá firetruck and lead the parade that arrived in the wee hours, waking those who were already asleep, and turning a night that should have been a peaceful Saturday into a veritable carnival.

Cali and its power brokers managed to forgive her extraordinary beauty, to yield the sceptre that was traditionally for the rich daughters of the capital of the Valle, but they did not forget the offense of not attending the dance they had planned in her honor. Every time she went for departmental assistance or to Cali companies for support, the doors were closed with bureaucratic excuses. Either she paid her own expenses or she did not go to Cartagena. Cali was not going to open its coffers for a girl who had snubbed them.

Tuluá learned of it the afternoon when she arrived disconsolate with her brother Toño and her mother, ready to renounce the crown and all it meant. Although Dr. González had left them a large enough fortune, a trip to the national beauty contest cost two years' worth of the income they had been receiving since the death of the conservative senator. They could do without many luxuries on the journey to Cartagena, but if she wanted to make a good impression, she had to show up with money to burn, and Dr. González's fortune could not endure such extravagance.

So Tuluá turned on itself like a serpent smitten with ire, and in order to demonstrate to Cali that it had no need of their money, which actually was not theirs but that of the Department treasury, it organized a committee that set itself the task of raising funds to send Inesita González to Cartagena. It was then that Tuluá saw the possibility of unity, and even the most silent of inhabitants deposited his grain of sand. The firemen held a grand raffle. They hired Lucho Bermúdez's orchestra for the price of Maestro Cedeño's. One of the honorary lieutenants was the brother of one of the orchestra conductor's lovers. Don Alfredo Garrido lent his airplane to bring them, and between the two of them, with the help of many others, they succeeded in making a reality the sound of Lucho Bermúdez's trumpet the night of October twenty-fourth at the immense site of the Antonia Santos School. Not many *tulueños* attended because Tuluá's population was small, and too many came from Buga. In the end, half the revenues went to purchase a new fire engine and the other half to pay for three evening gowns for the queen and twenty tickets on a chartered plane. Inesita González accepted that money with a blush, her mother's heart began to palpitate, and beginning at that moment an inaudible obsession overtook the house.

On the first of November writers from the Bogotá dailies arrived. The beauty of the queen of the Valle, the queen from Tuluá, was such that it had transcended all boundaries, and if a few weeks earlier she had been the favorite for the Cali competition, now she was the favorite to take Cartagena as well. They took a thousand pictures of her in a thousand different poses. She could not attend to all of her admirers because the next day, All Souls' Day, was to be—taking advantage of its being a Sunday—the grand bazaar that the citizenry of Tuluá held in order to give her three more evening gowns and to pay for three buses and the hotels and meals of the one hundred twenty people who would accompany her to Cartagena. The departure of the queen and the buses was set for the eighth of November. The selection and coronation would be on the eleventh, and the whole country was already counting on the triumph of the beautiful girl from Tuluá, whom the Valle, the seedbed of beauty queens, was sending. An atmosphere of excitement reigned in the streets. Pennants were peddled door to door. The newspapers sold out. Every time pictures of candidates from other departments appeared, they were compared with the fixed image they all had of Inesita, and the result could not have been more favorable. Inesita's measurements, as Nina Pérez shouted on the day of the Cali election, were those of Miss Universe. She had to be the queen; she could not lose.

On the day of the grand bazaar even Marcianita, forever sealed in her house of jasmines, came out to help. They held it in the Boyacá Park. La Chapeta provided the *empanada* table. Matilde Uribe, the spectacle of trained animals. Her parrot, leaping through rings of fire made of crêpe paper, drinking wine, eating grapes, walking like Mélida Palomeque (the wooden-legged teacher at the Antonia Santos School), and in particular reciting entire passages of the Apocalypse, was the main attraction. The punchbowl that was placed at the entrance was soon filled with twenty-*centavo* coins. Ignacio Cruz Roldán, who was studying bacteriology, offered to examine the urine of anyone who was so inclined. Often he played practical jokes on his clients. As if he were the great Wizard of Oz, by using special reagents he created in their urine multi-colored layers, spirals that looked like worms, or clouds of smoke so horrible that they led him to shout at the top of his lungs from the top of one of the tables in the Central Bar that the person who had pissed in that tube had every possibility of perforating the spot where he would next pee. Many believed him, and the next day the doctors' offices were full, perhaps in anticipation of the congestion that would develop four days later. The market vendors set up a fruit stand; the butchers sold fried pork. Plantain vendors, members of the Santander Cyclist Club, the Lions Club, the Ladies of Charity, the Rotary Club Masons, the bootblacks, and even the hacks from the park took part in the grand bazaar. And over it all presided Marcianita Barona, her table replete with gifts and her servants selling lottery chances.

The yield could not have had a greater impact. At midnight, the treasurer general of the grand bazaar, who was the secretary of the mayor's office, was still counting coins and making separate accounts with the members of the support committee in order to post them on the town hall door the next day. Few people noticed. Marcianita, who would have been the most interested, decided in her pregnancy to come down with German measles in order to infect Inesita. The rest had to buy up copies of the Bogotá papers that dedicated half a page daily to the Valle queen, who according to the writers had all the attributes necessary to win. There were many who memorized entire paragraphs the reporters wrote about Inesita. The pictures in *The Spectator* were clearer, but the copy in *The Times* was better. All of Colombia knew of the beautiful queen from Tuluá who had daringly posed in a skimpy bathing suit—a bathing suit that her brother had brought her from Europe and that she, although the daughter of the most pious woman in Tuluá, considered absolutely normal to don because it represented no indiscretion.

Many of Colombia's bishops and thousands of parish priests thought different, and the next Sunday, when the whole Cartagena pageant was popping, they seized upon those photographs and the scandalous stories in the papers for their sermons. The sin of nudity, the lack of modesty, would be castigated by the Lord who commands all, condemning entire cities to eternal fire. The Valle's queen had sinned, and the all-powerful Lord would have to punish her.

And perhaps as oracles they were right. On the seventh, when Tuluá was abuzz with the preparations for Inesita González's departure for Cartagena; when Maestro Cedeño's band played fanfares to bid farewell to the caravan of buses which, after seventy-two uncomfortable hours, would flood Cartagena with *tulueños*; when everything was ready and waiting for the midnight chimes to signal the departure of the chain of buses, as if sent from seventh heaven or expressly from the pulpits by the Holy Spirit, the news hit like a bucket of ice water. Inesita González had just suffered a strange attack. A half hour later, as people milled about in front of her house, the doctors who entered and exited declared themselves unable to contain the evil that afflicted the most beautiful woman in Colombia, the aspiring national beauty queen. What had begun as an incredible pain in one of her hands and then one of her legs had developed into total paralysis. No one was able to identify the exact nature of the problem, but Toño, her brother, who had studied in Switzerland, reported it with a transparent face and a shaken heart as they moved her to the hospital. Without a doubt, Inesita had suffered a slipped disk of the spinal column, and at that time with the backward state of medicine in the country, all treatment would be futile. Bedrest and tranquilizing waters were the only thing that could be prescribed for the future national beauty queen.

Tuluá could not believe it. The people howled. They had to elbow their way in to see her leave for the hospital in an ambulance—her one hand numb and completely paralyzed—in order for their last hopes to be dashed. All the next day's newspapers spoke of the evil that afflicted the pageant favorite, and some columnists clarined it was the effect of witchcraft performed by the followers of the contestant from the new Department of Guajira.

Inesita canceled her trip, and the hopes of a proud town were dashed in frustration. She gave the surplus money to charity and took to a bed and a wheelchair that would keep her for years and years. This was the fate to which was finally relegated the most beautiful specimen that Colombia has managed to produce. The legend of her name, of her tragedy, surpassed all bounds. There was not a single Colombian who did not know what had happened to the daughter of the late Dr. González, the Valle's beauty queen, the great frontrunner for the pageant in Cartagena that year. Her photos in miniature, her shining home, the legend of her bathing suit, summarized and amplified by bootleg booksellers, were engraved in the minds of a whole generation.

In April, facing the futility of the treatments of laying her down, raising her to a vertical position, and making her suffer a pain that distorted her perfect face, the family decided to take her for therapy to a hospital in Boston. Tuluá, which understood the significance of that queen and valued all that had been done for her, silently watched Her Highness leave for the Cali airport in an ambulance. The reports coming in were sketchy. The doctors did not have much hope; the illness, as her brother had diagnosed, although he did not practice the medical profession, had no cure. For three months, they had her hanging in traction with horrible weights at hand and neck, with nothing to look at but the blank wall of her hospital room. When they raised her up and traded her bed for a wheelchair, the pain had disappeared, but the paralysis was eternal.

Terrified, her face hidden behind dark glasses, her beauty only slightly more restored than when she had left for Boston, Inesita González returned to Tuluá. For years and years the neighbors saw her leave every morning in her wheelchair, completely immobile, pushed by her mother, or her brother, or one of the maids. Little by little she was regaining the kindness that had made her famous and endeared her to all the townspeople, but of her beauty, of her Miss Universe measurements—as Nina Pérez had proclaimed at that magnificent moment—there was but the memory in the minds of *tulueños* who saved the newspaper clippings from those days of glory.

Almost fifteen years later, her elegant legend already fading under an avalanche of many other fables that were born or fabricated in a nation that went in that time from the mule to the jet, from partisan violence to bureaucratic arrangements among contenders, Inesita González, still without having lost her benevolence, had a rebirth of hope: Marcianita Barona, the same one who since childhood had sold her jasmines to carry to the May altar of the Franciscan Mothers' Academy, familiar with her sorrows and aware of the powers growing manifest about her, invited her to the house at La Rivera. Inesita, in her wheelchair, then appeared before the idiots.

IX

The infinite fear Tuluá felt that Wednesday noon when Nemesio Rodríguez publicly forbade his wife to hold the bazaar in the sacristy doorway was almost as great as what she felt two hours later, when all that had identified her for so many years, along with her aching body, came undone.

Bright and early, and in keeping with her maniacal habit of planning something specific for each day, Marcianita announced that it was maintenance day. Since she had not spoken to her husband for many months, and neither of them relented in their respective positions, she completely ignored him in calling for repairs. They started out by taking down the curtains in the living room where he was reading *The Press*. Then they rolled up the rug. He did not open his mouth, but the dark glance he cast at his theodolite indicated to the servant women that the captain was irked. For about two months he had not worked on Wednesdays or Saturdays. On Tuesday nights he drank aguardiente until he could not even open the front door. He never came home later than ten o'clock or woke up later than eight. It seemed as though the only remaining vestige of his past was his work ethic. He had bought five hundred hectares of land from the Sarmientos for livestock, and with what that produced he justified taking Wednesdays and Saturdays off. He continued to dress just as elegantly on town days as when he first arrived in Tuluá on the train from which Marcianita saw him alight. Although he was well into his fifties, with wrinkles already enveloping his face, he felt as captivating as when he had undressed daily before Rocío Jojoa in search of a pregnancy that never materialized. He scarcely remembered his two idiots even though day after day he saw them taking feeble steps around their playpens or about their cloistered rooms. He no longer carried Bartolomé as he had in the beginning, nor did he stop at Ramón Lucio's cradle to curse the moment of the boy's conception. He only watched, watched, and kept on watching, and that is what falsely reassured Marcianita.

It annoyed him to see light shining through the living room windows and to be incapable of preventing the rug's removal. He took his hat and cane and, fixing his eyes on the luster of his patent leather shoes, strolled through the streets of Tuluá. His face was still wrinkled. If it did not get that way every time he drank aguardiente, Tuluá, believing its time was nigh, probably would have been more frightened than it was. A half hour later Marcianita left the house, crossed the park with one of her servants, stopped in the courtyard to converse with

Blanquita Lozano, approached Isaac Nessim's department store, looked at the boy he was keeping, tolerated his faggy chit-chat, bought a yard of lace and three of taffeta, wished him a wheedling good-bye and good luck, and went to stand in the sacristy doorway. There she waited for her employee to pick up the bazaar table which, because one of its legs was loose, had been left in Father Phanor's sacristy. It was repair day and the carpenter should also take care of Sunday matters. The bazaar continued to be her passion. The fashioning of tickets, the acquisition of gifts, entire mornings spent pasting tags on the new gifts, eleven o'clock Sunday mornings: all parts of a solemn ceremony for one whose only contact with a town that did not want to see her born was in selling those insignificant tickets. She attended no meetings, joined no societies, no associations. She neither went to mass nor paraded in any processions. She had no friends other than Blanquita Lozano and Inesita González. Miss Paulina Sarmiento, who attended her mother's burial, did not even pay her a condolence visit. Every December Father Phanor sent her a card of thanks and a basket of fruit. Dr. Tomás, tired of practicing, opened his office only from four to six every afternoon, and she, because of her many premonitions, would not let him examine her after noon. So the bazaar became for her the essential breath of life, and she defended it as such. That is why on repair day she had thought of the table in the sacristy and had gone for it. She carried in her hand the satchel from Isaac Nessim's store, and in her heart the hope of repairing the keys to the garden of jasmines when she again passed through the courtyard.

What happened was so simple that, perhaps because of the very simplicity, Tuluá remained completely submerged in fearful silence, reaffirming a notion already forgotten but at bottom long awaited. Nemesio Rodríguez, leaning on his walking stick like any decadent dandy, conversed with his friends in the San Bartolomé courtyard. Because Maricanita's servants seemed mute, neither his friends nor anyone in Tuluá knew that it had been months since the couple had exchanged words. One of his friends must have said something, or perhaps Captain Uribe Gaviria chided him for his discourtesy. He raised his cane a bit, looked to the end of the courtyard where his wife was passing through with her bag from Nessim's store, and with a certainty that he neither felt in any other moment of his life nor ever expected to feel when he built the Pacific Railway through the rocky thickets of the Dagua Canyon, Nemesio Rodríguez, captain of the liberal forces of Palonegro and President Reyes's aide-de-camp, brought his wife, Marcianita Barona, up short with a call from beyond the tomb.

"Until today, Madame, you have thought only about your bazaar. Next Sunday there will be no bazaar in this town. My life (and at this moment his friends and Tuluá learned their marital relationship was on the rocks) will not be controlled by that infernal bazaar. Since the table is already being carried home, leave it there and don't bring it back. This is a non-negotiable ultimatum." And Marcianita, who had paused in the courtyard to listen to the absolute drivel, could hardly suppress a smile and, looking at him the way one watches a lunatic reciting unspeakable offenses in public, she continued on her way. Captain Uribe Gaviria said, two days later when he explained to Tuluá the result of an encounter unlikely though brief, that Nemesio Rodríguez had been deeply offended when his wife paid no more attention to him than she would to a stray mutt. A little while later, and it was not yet eleven o'clock, Nemesio Rodríguez was drinking as he had never drunk before. Seated at a table in the Central Bar, first with Captain Uribe Gaviria, and later with Chava, the one-armed lottery-ticket vendor, and still later alone, he drank the aguardiente that soothed his pain and allayed his propensity for tragedy.

At two p.m., having paid twenty Colombian pesos more than he was charged, absolutely upright, without wrinkling his clothes or fumbling his cane, he left the Central Bar and headed for the corner of the park. Nina Pérez, who was there, later said in reconstructing those moments that Tuluá was submerged in absolute silence, pained from knowing that Marcianita Barona's marriage, which everyone had considered impossible and whose dissolution everyone had foreseen almost from the start, was really and truly over. Surely the fright could have come from the dramatic scene that a solitary Marcianita would create with her pair of idiots. Actually, neither Captain Uribe Gaviria nor Nina Pérez nor anyone in Tuluá was really capable of disentangling the meaning of that afternoon's events. Nemesio Rodríguez must have thought a great deal before striding out the door of his house. After standing at the corner of the park, staring at a beyond that the liquor rendered unrecognizable to him, he hurried to enter the house of jasmines, with a determination similar to that of his nights of drunkenness.

The clock in San Bartolomé had just struck two-thirty. Marcianita was seated in the dining room cutting up slips of paper for the bazaar. She did not stir when he opened the door and strutted in along the corridor, tapping his stick and stomping his patent leather shoes. Although he must have drunk a lot of aguardiente, he did not stumble or stray from his course. He entered the dining room and, breathing heavily, like a male manatee in heat, stopped at Marcianita's side. She went on as if everything were normal; she had ignored him for months and saw no reason to acknowledge him at that moment. One of the servants who was seated at her side fathomed the captain's intentions. She warned Doña Marcianita with a call of "Señora," but Marcianita, trusting with ancestral pride in her mental capacity, was incapable of avoiding the full thrust of what came crashing down on her. Nemesio Rodríguez, confusing her with the Palonegro conservatives, beat her with his cane, which turned out to be made of platinum through and through. Marcianita could not flash her dark eyes to ward off the attack as on that day in Luisita Tascón's school. She hardly managed to raise her arms and tumble with chair, bazaar tickets, and paste onto the floor. "Never again, damn you, woman, will you hold a bazaar in this town! You're married, do you hear, married!" And he continued to beat her like a coach horse that would not budge. All the blows fell upon the same place, the nape of her neck at the top of the spinal column. He did not quit until she stopped crying and ceased all movement. Then, composing himself as if nothing had transpired, he left as he had entered and strolled about the streets with the tranquility of one who laid to rest a debt that had tormented him for years.

Tuluá, nevertheless, knew that something was wrong because, although Marcianita screamed silently in order not to be heard, at that very moment a thick, annoying rumor gnawed away at many people's innards. Everyone rushed to the park, compelled by a supernatural force. There they saw Nemesio Rodríguez strolling; he seemed so cool, so calm that in truth, looking at one another, none of them could understand why they were there. The marriage of the captain of the liberal forces and Father Tascón's daughter had to end. They knew it; they had awaited that end for so many years that they almost forgot it when they hurried to the park and came upon Nemesio Rodríguez. Marcianita, in the meantime, had been carried to bed by her servants. She was completely unconscious. They rubbed her with alcohol, gave her smelling salts, and put iodine on the nape of her neck where a lump had begun to form.

When the clock at San Bartolomé was striking four and those who had rushed to the park continued to follow the satisfied husband about, Marcianita awoke. Her order was peremptory. She remembered nothing, neither her idiots, nor Dr. Uribe, nor the magical drugs in her secret locker. "Close that door with the double lock; bar the windows." And she fell again into a deep stupor, moaning erratically. The servants put hot salt-water compresses on her, again gave her smelling salts, propped her up with three pillows, and brought her Bartolomé, who babbled with his guttural sounds, and Ramón Lucio, who breathed heavily near her. None of these measures helped her regain consciousness. At eight in the evening she asked for water, and they gave her sugar water in a crystal chamber pot, along with some soda crackers. It was a terrible chore to get her to take nourishment. She could not raise her head, so it was necessary to use two more pillows. The nape of her neck had swollen so that the lump of the first few hours was almost like a zebu's hump. Some purple streaks descended from the top of the inflammation to her shoulders. "The doors, are they securely locked?" was the only thing she asked before returning to her stupor. The servants wanted to call Dr. Uribe, but she, anticipating the events, must have given them some mental command, because not one was capable of even thinking of crossing the park.

At nine-thirty, when the clock in San Bartolomé had already stopped chiming the hour, Nemesio Rodríguez, much drunker than at noon but with a voice as crystal-clear as in his best days as engineer of the Pacific Railroad, knocked at the door. His key could not open the lock. "Marcianita, Marcianita, Marcianita..." echoed throughout Tuluá, which was still awake with anxiety. He again knocked at the door, clenched his fists, and pounded more forcefully. No one answered. He shouted, filling his lungs and revealing a tone vibrant with emotion. "Marcianita, Marcianita, Marcianita..." and he again beat at the door. From the depths of her room, at a distance from the door he was pounding, and with a voice that the servants swear was exaggeratedly weak but which all of Tuluá could clearly discern, she placed the final period at the end of their marriage. "Why don't you go see Rocío Jojoa? Tomorrow before six a.m. you will find all your clothes and your papers at Captain Uribe Gaviria's house. I'm not going to open that door for you now or ever." And that was that. Tuluá sensed the completion of the cycle that began the day Paulina Sarmiento was left waiting in San Bartolomé. If it were not for the fact that everyone had heard that voice without physically perceiving it, surely they would have danced through the streets as at the height of Carnival. Marcianita did not say another word, not even to her servants, but at five the next day, after packing all night long, they left with Nemesio Rodríguez's trunks—loaded with uniforms wrapped in naphthaline, theodolites, maps, plans, and measuring chains—and placed them one by one at the door of Captain Uribe Gaviria's house. They overlooked nothing, they damaged nothing, and Marcianita did not even open her eyes. Her coma lasted until noon, when Dr. Uribe entered the house through Paulina Sarmiento's adobe wall in spite of the servants' refusals to unlock the door. He examined her from top to bottom and found her so unfit that he prescribed bed rest for a month. Her spine was not broken, but she was so bent over that out of pity for the pain she must have felt, he gave her morphine. Before he administered it to her, through the door that the doctor had opened came Captain Uribe Gaviria. He came to request in every possible way that she forgive Nemesio. She was so emphatic, so energetic in her refusal that Blanquita Lozano, who came for the same reason, did no more than look at her with pity from the edge of the bed. "That accursed man will never again set foot in this house. I have been raising my idiots without his help and I'll go on doing so." That was her only response to his emissaries. Nemesio Rodríguez knew her so well that that afternoon, without a thought for the five-hundred-hectare farm he had bought, without finishing the maps he owed the Sarmientos, and without collecting on his various debts, he caught the train for Buenaventura. The freight car carried all the trunks that the servants had transported to Captain Uribe Gaviria's house at dawn. His face deadened and perhaps tearful, that was his only farewell. He did not even tell Rocío Jojoa he was departing. After his messengers gave him the definitive news, he seemed to accept his destiny, and without a word he left for the station with all his belongings. Captain Uribe Gaviria went silently at his side. A few minutes after the train had pulled out, blown its whistle around the curve by the cemetery, and disappeared down the track, Dr. Tomás opened his office to examine Rocío Jojoa and diagnose her pregnancy.

Nemesio Rodríguez left no trace of his whereabouts. No one knew anything of him even after the Putumayan had read her cards, smoked tobacco, and made contact with her ancestors. The last one to see him—boarding a Norwegian ship in Buenaventura—described him as withered, gray, and bowed with immense sorrow. Since then no one has heard of him, in spite of the many who—remembering those days— claim to expect that amidst so many miracles he will appear now as if by magic. They forget, perhaps, who Marcianita is. They had already forgotten in the days following his departure. Since that time she has grown profoundly stooped. At the site of the blows arose a hump so phenomenal and of such rapid growth that a year later, going down to Tuluá to pick up some jasmine seeds that were arriving by train, she was recognized by only a few people. Only with great difficulty could she look at anything but the ground.

The day she got up, exactly one month after the doctor had seen her, there was nothing in her house. Even the jasmines had been transplanted to La Rivera. Perhaps in acquiescence to what Nemesio

Rodríguez had tried to accomplish with the blows of his cane and his prohibitions, she never again held a bazaar. To Bartolomé, who was the first to begin to talk, she taught, with much repetition, a few phrases that the poor idiot used in every conversation. Five or six years later, Ramón Lucio combined them into his first coherent sounds and repeated incessantly: "The world is a bazaar." But Father Phanor no longer received on Mondays any "assistance" from the raffles, and Tuluá never again saw Marcianita seated in the sacristy on Sundays.

Caring for the jasmines that she now not only sold to the ladies of Tuluá but sent as far as Buga every day, and teaching her idiots, step by step, with infinite patience, all the necessary gestures and expressions: that is how Marcianita has spent the years ever since. She shut herself in at La Rivera much as her mother had secluded herself in the house on the Boyacá Park. Many men attempted to encroach upon her domain, but either the idiots or she herself repulsed their efforts. Once again she wove ornaments as she had done during her maidenhood, and she embroidered Bartolomé's suits with brocade. She entertained the remote illusion that her idiots were a pair of princes from another world and that Bartolomé was the heir apparent. As a symbol of his royal blood, she dressed Ramón Lucio in bright colors and velvets. She devoted herself to them and to creating every means of maintaining that illusion, and she almost managed to invent a pedagogical method for the education of her young under-endowlings. Since Bartolomé did not hear well, she concentrated on sensitizing him. She tried every method: she tested him with fire, with acid, with needles, with nettles, and with the bark of the mango tree and ammonia. At last, in the midst of a vomiting spell that the poor child suffered for days, she found he responded to mare's milk. She had only to give him a few drops of equine milk in his cow's milk to make him hear, respond, and behave with perhaps the same facility he had with his hands. Without the drops, Bartolomé was like an adobe wall. He could not hear, but he could take the chinaware and smash it to bits only to glue it back together, making it impossible to tell that it had been shattered. He did nothing more, he could do no more, and only mare's milk had any effect on him.

Even so, his idiocy was obvious enough. His gaping lips, the slobber almost always running down his jaw, his drooping eyes, his protruding ears, and his unruly hair manifested the impossibility of civilizing him. Marcianita put astrakhan hats with luminous, deformed, triangular embroidery on him in order to camouflage all those defects. While he spent entire hours gluing dishes together, she taught him to produce the movements of opening and closing his mouth in order to avoid the noisy drip of his drool. The first days the results were satisfactory, but as months and years passed, instead of helping, the movements became so methodical that he, endowed with an incredible capacity for destruction, came to damage his mouth. Where before there trickled a stream of drool, there now flowed a cascade. Marcianita had to try again to correct the damage. She put court plaster on him and had an odontologist come from Buga to reconstruct his mouth. Finally, when she was about to lose hope in her heir attired in embroidered fabric and an astrakhan cap, what did the trick was alum. Taking mouthfuls of alum water every day made his mouth pucker and brought his drooling to a halt. His lower lip did not raise but rather hung limply down, like a prostitute's vulva, but at least the foaming stopped. It was one of the many things that Marcianita had to devise in order to modify her sons' external appearance. She not only embroidered the suits she made for Bartolomé and bought velvet to cover Ramón Lucio, but by having them imitate expressions, gestures, positions, and attitudes, she succeeded in creating in them a behavior that was often nearly normal. But they were parrot-like attitudes, and if they deceived the few people who saw them for ten minutes, they could not do so for any longer. The result was something like a movie that repeated itself every ten minutes. Tille Uribe's parrot might have done it better, or at least more naturally. If robots had existed in those days, the competition would have been phenomenal. The pair of idiots ended up ordering their life as a series of movements, sounds, and poses, to the point where, if one thing was lacking, the whole process went awry. They practically came to be marionettes. At meal time the dining room bell rang, and, like ever-faithful slaves, they would hasten from wherever they were to their places. They would drape over their clothes white tunics that she had made and would sit again at the table. After a hand clap that cued them to start their meal, they would not stop until a servant put a glass of water in front of their plates. If she came quickly, they ate little; if she was slow, they ate and ate, not only until they cleaned their plates and the platters but also after they managed to smash them, thinking they too were edible. If the water did not come in time, a catastrophe could befall Marcianita's house.

She had them trained to bathe in the same way. They could not do it before ten in the morning because the mare's milk did not arrive until then, and trying to give Bartolomé an order without his magic drops was as useless as toothpaste for Ramón Lucio. He could not see it. Despite the brush passing once or twice over his teeth and gums, no foam at all came from his mouth. At ten or ten-thirty, Marcianita would play "Frère Jacques" on the piano. That was the order that set the pair of idiots into motion. Bartolomé left his brocade pajamas and royal ruffles on the bed. Ramón Lucio, standing by the bathroom door where he waited for Bartolomé, was already undressed. Since it took tremendous effort for him to walk in any case, the majority of his movements were within a very limited range. He had only one testicle, but it was so large that it surpassed the two that Bartolomé displayed visibly from an early age. Dr. Tomás had circumcised him the day he was born, but such bulk seemed so strange to him that he confused the skin which covered his monotesticular endowment with that which covered his masculinity.

As soon as Marcianita or one of the maids would turn on the shower, Bartolomé, as the eldest heir, would enter first and soak himself for as long as his custodian allowed, but never more than three minutes. When the water stopped, Bartolomé would take the soap, and Ramón Lucio would clamber in to get wet. He could not last long in the same position because his weak legs would buckle and then the water would have to be quickly turned off. To dry the boys the production was similar. Bartolomé took the towel in his hands and with unusual swiftness, possible only with his hands, dried himself in the time that Ramón Lucio hardly finished soaping himself. Bartolomé's clothes were in his room; Ramón Lucio's were on a chair near the bathroom. At first, Marcianita would dress him, but—with exquisite effort—she finally succeeded in teaching Ramón Lucio to do it for himself. To facilitate his task the velvet robes that he wore were designed something like Roman tunics. Instead of pants (it would be impossible for the poor idiot to stuff his weak legs into them), he used a skirt a little narrower and much shorter than the velvet. Since he really had no feeling, the warmth of his apparel amounted to no inconvenience. They had similar problems with colors.

Neither of the two could tell them apart. In that regard, they committed an error that almost cost them their lives. It was actually a smaller error than the one they committed the day they became entangled in the machinery of perfection for which Marcianita had them trained, but it still could have been fatal.

She had made a tremendous effort to teach them the colors, but neither Bartolomé nor Ramón Lucio could recognize a single one. For them, the world must have passed by in black and white; there was no way they could distinguish the green of the meadow from the white of the jasmines. The red of Ramón Lucio's velvet skirts must have seemed the same to them as the black of Bartolomé's brocades. Nevertheless, she suspected that as the years passed, and with the mare's milk, Bartolomé had been acquiring the possibility of rudimentarily discerning between red and green, black and red. Some days before they dressed him he would try to choose his own outfit, pointing with a finger. He did not know the names of the colors because his vocabulary scarcely consisted of a hundred words, but in order to indicate one and not another he must have been able to distinguish some shades.

Ramón Lucio, on the other hand, was an adobe wall; too heavy to move about, he also had difficulty in expressing himself or differentiating colors. Marcianita either forgot this one day or, thinking her idiots were fooling her, she took a chance. She boiled the milk in the kitchen. The pot handle was red hot. It was a large pot, big enough to store all the milk the pair of idiots would drink, the curds the armadillos demanded, and the liquid the jasmines needed for their whiteness. The servants were on the patio; the burner was low to the ground. Bartolomé could reach the pot. Ramón Lucio, always bringing up the rear with the pokiness of a dromedary, watched everything. Bartolomé approached; she handed him the stick they used to unhook the pot, but since he could not tell the difference between red and black, when the stick did not fit well into the handle Bartolomé grabbed that red-hot loop.

There was a smell of burning flesh. He neither screamed nor howled, nor did the poor idiot feel a thing; but Ramón Lucio, who was nearby and saw everything, almost dropped dead from the bath of hot milk that Marcianita gave him when, looking as she was at her son's seared hand, she could not avoid tipping the pot. It was at that moment when Marcianita saw in Ramón Lucio the same powers that she had possessed in her childhood. The milk jumped over him without touching or marking him. He simply looked at it, moaning as he had always moaned since birth.

The next day, what should have been an incredible lesion needing medical attention, parboiled plantain leaves, and even hospitalization, was scarcely a trivial scrape on Bartolomé's hand. His hand possessed not only splendorous dexterity but even the power to cure itself. Neither that day nor ever after did he distinguish colors, but Marcianita began to inform him of a truth that would eventually destroy her. She continued to train them with the same robot-like methodology that had brought such good results. She converted Bartolomé into the helper for her embroidered ornaments and Ramón Lucio into the perpetual aide-de-camp of the armadillos. Since he could stay on his feet only for as long as it took an armadillo to waddle two meters—he was almost that slow—no one was better at caring for those animals. The litters increased, and Marcianita, who had previously sold only jasmines and embroidery, ended up selling armadillos as if they were chickens. Don Diego Hayer, representing a Swiss drug company, came to buy them. He bought ten or twenty on each trip. He did not say—and they did not ask—what they were used for. He learned of their existence from fat Nina Pérez, who had as many friends as kilos, and for months that grew into years he was an assiduous client at La Rivera and a friend to Ramón Lucio, who saved the best armadillos for him.

Bartolomé was not attracted to him. He felt a definite repulsion toward persons who were not like him—large, with agile hands, drooping eyes, and protruding ears. He accepted only his brother because he adored him so but could not tolerate the existence of other such persons. Don Diego Hayer did not resemble Ramón Lucio in the least, although he was short, fat, and wall-eyed like his brother. Deep down, though, there was something more than that; it was a question of jealousy. Bartolomé, who did not see anything except through his brother's eyes, who did everything with him or waiting for him, could not stand the fact that when Don Diego Hayer arrived, Ramón Lucio abandoned him. What's more, for two or three days afterwards he would be in the clouds remembering the stout Swissman's figure.

It became such a regular monthly visit that when he traveled to Switzerland for two months and sent his chauffeur with the little pick-up truck for the armadillos, Ramón Lucio stood in the animals' den and would not permit a single one to be removed, emitting such moans that Marcianita came to believe that the chauffeur would immediately denounce her son as the abominable snowman.

Bartolomé, unable to shake his brother out of the self-absorption in which he remained after that day, because he was scarcely able to do anything except with his hands or in robot-like compliance with commands, followed suit. Marcianita found him refusing to get out of bed the day after the arrival of Don Diego's chauffeur. She almost went crazy. Her two idiots were sick. She could not diagnose the problem. As if manipulated by invisible strings, she fearfully mounted her bicycle and rode to downtown Tuluá in search of a doctor. The town, which seldom saw her, almost shook to its foundations. Her hump had grown so large that on top of the bicycle she resembled a circus monkey. Dr. Uribe had for years been ensconced in his old age and she had no car in which to take a doctor, but she remembered Inesita González and her infirmity.

She knocked at the door and went in to where Inesita lay, suspended in her bed with weights on her hands and feet; she told her of the tragedy, and ten minutes later, with Aminta, she left for La Rivera, taking Dr. Fajardo with her. "What is your name?" was all the idiot Bartolomé said when he saw the doctor with his black bag. "Diego, Diego Fajardo," said the doctor, frightened to verify what they said in Tuluá about the idiots. Ramón Lucio leaped as if transported; the name Diego was a magical word. He allowed himself to be examined and returned to good spirits. Bartolomé did not fuss either; since the doctor was the same as he, tall and thin with a pianist's hands, he removed the sheet that covered him, and as Ramón Lucio watched, he too allowed himself to be examined. Massive doses of vitamins was the only prescription. "Diego..." was the response of Bartolomé, who could understand and speak with his brother. A smile crossed the idiots' faces and Marcianita, perhaps stupefied, paid the doctor, gave two dozen jasmines to Aminta, and promised her an armadillo. She had not finished uttering those promissory words when Ramón Lucio, with his methodical gait, appeared carrying an armadillo by the tail. He gave it to the doctor who, in order not to offend, but more flustered than anyone, put it in the back of the car.

The day that Don Diego Hayer returned, Marcianita understood the significance of the whole process her sons had undergone. He brought them a book of armadillo pictures. Bartolomé accepted it on behalf of his brother, who was in those days incapable of receiving anything, and every day the two of them would spend hours looking at the armadillo album as if they had never seen it before. They spent years doing that same thing. The norms of training persisted; neither they nor Marcianita tired of the same routine. Although they had not been born on the same day, they celebrated their birthdays together. The day they turned fourteen and thirteen, Marcianita expressly invited Don Diego. It proved to be a memorable day.

Bartolomé, as if compelled by a strange force, locked the door to their room. Marcianita had to knock to waken them. They were already wide awake, since more than an hour before they had discovered the outrageous, the glorious—and they felt powerful. They had almost crossed over the threshold where they had been waiting for millennia before starting their earthly task.

Bartolomé had arisen at dawn. An unfamiliar numbness surprised him. In the first few moments he could not tell where it stemmed from, but when his eyes had become accustomed to the light and his fine, sensitive hands had passed over his whole body, Bartolomé discovered something he had never before noticed. He wanted to believe that it had disappeared and became as frightened as a normal person would, jumped out of bed, and turned on the light. Ramón Lucio, with a smile and a whisper so as not to wake Marcianita, was the one to discover the truth about his brother. Although he was younger, he had been undergoing the same process for months. Since he had only one testicle, he had been afraid to fondle himself or investigate what was happening to him. His manual clumsiness was extreme, his incapacity for comprehension unequaled. He pointed with his finger at the promontory that had formed inside his brother's pajamas and as Bartolomé opened his immense eyes, he pulled away the covers and showed him his own unicorn in that same position.

For Bartolomé it was like the trumpet that announced entrance into the promised land. Impelled by the same force that had driven him forth many a time, he undressed completely; he must have heard the "Frère Jacques" of Marcianita's piano or succumbed before a reality that sometimes oppressed him, bringing him to the brink of normality. Ramón Lucio did almost the same thing. He undressed with his habitual clumsiness and, directed by Bartolomé's gaze, began to raise and lower his hand on the previously untouched masculinity. The facility with which the one did it was a far cry from the awkwardness with which the other practically tortured himself. Bartolomé opened his legs, but Ramón Lucio, impeded by his weakness, hunted for his bed, and there, moaning as in his finest moments, producing that sound that no other human could hear (but all the dogs in the neighborhood of La Rivera and of Tuluá heard it and set to barking immediately), he noticed that an infinitely restorative white liquid flowed from his unicorn and that the power that had prevented the spilling of the pot of milk had been invoked. Bartolomé felt his hands pierced, lifted them in their stickiness, and saw an infra-red light block out the rays of the room's lamp. Ramón Lucio opened his eyes, ceased the guttural sound that alerted all the dogs in the district (waking more than one landowner), and tried to run his rough hand over the same place, but Bartolomé's eyes stopped him. Isaac Nessim, who pretended to be well versed in such matters, opened his terrified eyes, aware that it was not only his dog that was barking, but all the dogs of Tuluá. He woke the boy he had with him, turned on the lights, and remembered that immediately before the Tokyo earthquake all the dogs had barked like that. He stood in the doorway and waited for dawn. Bartolomé did practically the same thing. Frightened by the newly discovered power, the glory that for centuries and centuries had been imprisoned in their bodies, and still enveloped in the infinite light that blanketed them, seated on the bed of his brother, who was still excited without understanding a thing that was going on, he waited for the dawn that for them was a birthday and for Diego Hayer, the Swiss armadillo man, would be his last journey.

Bartolomé opened the door at Marcianita's knocking. They were already dressed and ready to take on something more than the robot movements to which they had been limited. Nevertheless, they were unable to do so because their nature was still greatly inferior to the power they had discovered. They got dressed a little earlier than usual because the house had to be put in order for the birthday luncheon. Ramón Lucio did not understand the reason for the big fuss, and the change in routine along with the early morning fright combined to upset him. But when Bartolomé sensed what might be happening to his brother, he whispered "Diego" in his ear. It was similar to the howling at dawn. The sparkle returned to his eyes and the armadillos again felt stirrings of their coupling instinct, only three weeks after the previous time. He chose the best ones, as he did every month. He left them in the wire pen and went to be dressed, in a crimson tunic of brilliant velvet and leaden shoes so that he would not tip over.

At about noon, the table already pompously set with cakes of fourteen and thirteen candles, and with Bartolomé beaming in his best brocades and the astrakhan hat of the imaginary coronation, Marcianita raised her eyes as much as she could under the immense weight of her hump and stood at the door to receive her guest.

With the precision of a Swiss watch, Diego Hayer arrived at La Rivera. Bartolomé was horrified. In place of the Diego Hayer they had known, cheerful, smiling, with a robustness about his diminutive stature, the Diego Hayer who came had his hand in a cast, blackened eyes, and a cut on his cheek that was barely starting to heal.

No sooner had he shown up than Marcianita let out a cry. Bartolomé went back to the room and brought Ramón Lucio. Standing in the door to the dining room, they awaited the arrival of what was left of Diego Hayer, he who had cheered them so. They looked at each other and interrupted the greeting. Before he could explain the reason for such repair work—the circumstances that had turned him into a patchwork quilt—Bartolomé opened his palms, the infinite glow filling the dining room, and Ramón Lucio moaned. At first they heard him but later they only saw his gestures. The dogs again raised a din and Diego Hayer froze as if transported to the beyond. Marcianita felt compelled to do the same. She remembered only the day at Luisita Tascón's school when she had fallen to the floor and Nina Pérez had looked at her with terror. The spectacle lasted no more than a minute, at the end of which Diego Hayer felt his eyes relieved; the swelling and the purpleness disappeared.

The cast on his hand was loose and the inflammation no longer existed. The violet color of the scar on his cheek faded. Seeing himself miraculously healed, the Swissman almost cried. Bartolomé and Ramón Lucio puffed with joy. Dr. Fajardo, who coincidentally had treated him in the Tuluá hospital that afternoon, asked him why he had a cast on his hand if the x-rays showed no break or any sign of splintering.

Since he was a foreigner, the other doctors who examined him along with Dr. Fajardo supposed that the scar on his face, with its strange color, was the result of some marvelous plastic surgery. That night, Don Diego's wife almost lost her mind. She invoked all her Catalonian ancestors, requested a phone call to Tarragona and, screaming like a lunatic escaped from an asylum, told one of her frightened relatives that Diego was not only safe and sound after so many days of suffering, but that he had been miraculously cured by a pair of idiots who raised armadillos and had a hump-backed mother.

X

Tuluá had in Nina Pérez, until silence invaded her, the most aggressive and cordial advocate for its interests. Without the slightest thought for her obesity, without even considering that her dangerous tongue and her mania for considering already done what had hardly commenced might be tiresome, Nina Pérez, Tuluá's frank, loyal, and passionate defender, made a career of public service that began with Luisita Tascón's school and was interrupted only by the silence that eventually invaded her pores and left her motionless, as if the weight she carried about were not sufficient in itself.

Fatter than anyone else since the days of Luisita Tascón's school, Nina Pérez was born almost fated to be so. Actually she ate very little, no more than those around her in her mother's boarding house, but she assimilated it as if instead of one bowl of soup she had eaten five, instead of one plate of rice she had been served half a dozen. So fat that she had lost the notion of her own perimeter, she reached the extreme of not being able to use a brassiere to support her monumental tits because nowhere did they sell her size. On one occasion, when Isaac Nessim had written to various underwear salesmen, Nina Pérez's measurements were so monstrously great that the brassiere distributors themselves asked Nessim to put them in touch with her for advertising purposes. Incomparably rotund, she could fit in no chair, and perhaps that is why she never visited a house which did not have a sofa. Her buttocks were of such volume and extension that many people, upon seeing her walk from afar, did not think of the elephant with which fat women are always compared but rather of the prehistoric seal that appears in geography books. She moved them as if they were two masses of calves' foot jelly, and although they more than once knocked the bottom out of seats and their imprint was irreparably felt by more than one couch, they neither changed their way of being nor ceased hunting for accommodation wherever their owner went. For Nina Pérez was so fat but so active, even when sitting, so slow-moving but so mentally agile, that many came to believe she stored her intelligence and vivacity in those improbable masses that accompanied her from waist to legs. Knees together and feet apart, her strides were like those of somnolent giants, tremulous on some occasions, rudimentary the rest of the time, to the point that when she walked, Nina Pérez seemed always to be about to tip over. Her whole structure quaked; her arms, which resembled giant mallets, swung forward heavily and avoided catastrophe by counterbalancing her.

But replete with adiposity as she was, no one has been or will be able for many years, even centuries, to equal her capacity for civil service to Tuluá. As a student in the last years at Luisita Tascón's school, she organized the benefit festival in order to bestow upon her teacher a wheelchair in which to spend the last years of her paralytic existence. Since then, Nina Pérez has organized bazaars, dances, crownings, carnivals, collections, shows, trips to the Department of the Interior, to the Mayor's Office, to the Town Council, to the Departmental Assembly. One day she managed to reach the National Capital in Bogotá, where she introduced herself to the Fourth Commission of the National Senate to defend with her monumental fatness—which could not squeeze into any of the dumbstruck senator's chairs—a bill which would grant to Tuluá a covered gymnasium for the officers' training academy. Whether she was presiding from a built-in bench or walking with her gait of a tectonic tremor, she would try one means or another, move heaven and earth, and obtain for her town what innocuous mayors and councilors and members of their sclerotic public works societies and municipal enterprises could never obtain. Tuluá, nevertheless, although well it knows of these things, does not like to admit them, preferring to remember her only as the great heroine of the days of Inesita González's reign. The most emotional news for Tuluá was not that Inesita would be selected queen of the Valle del Cauca that memorable night in Cali, nor that she would travel by firetruck to Tuluá in the wee hours, but that Nina Pérez, from the balcony of the San Fernando Club, where the queens were measured and paraded in bathing suits, had screamed that Inesita had the measurements of Miss Universe. Those who were waiting below for the appearance of the woman who, according to prognostications, would be Colombia's next beauty queen, felt an infinite heat, and in less than ten minutes a hopeful Tuluá already knew via the grapevine that its queen was one of a kind. Nina had said so, and impressions of that magnitude are not forgotten.

If that were the extent of things, they would pass, but Nina, fat and civic minded, possessed a frightful tongue. Tuluá had always feared it, even during the years when silence invaded her and she was obliged to remain mute. It is not that she invents; Nina does not have that creative capacity. She stretches, disfigures, recreates reality, which begins to live as though she had special powers to see it take place beforehand. She has embroiled many people in messes; some married couples (it has never been determined which or how many), it is said, have failed in the management of their domestic lives, and there are those who accuse her of improper intrusion in the rearing of their children. Since she was unable to marry because of the fantastic unapproachability of her fatness, but has always wanted to have children, she scolds, cajoles, and even advises the children of others as if they were her own, causing on more than one occasion the protest of the displaced head of the household. But since it mattered little to her that they might look on her as fat, that many might mock her clumsy gait, or that someone could protest her earthquake tread, and since when she was left mired in silence many said that it was punishment for her venomous tongue, she neither spoke nor wrote on the little slate she used to manage with when she stopped talking; she was simply never heard from again.

She was endowed with the health of a Lebanese cedar; obesity, which in many people leads to heart attacks, diabetes or palpitations, was in Nina Pérez a symptom of unquestionable hardiness. In spite of having been born to be fat, she spent the first years of her childhood and the first years of school in a preamble to her fatness. Skeletal at birth, almost like a transparent toothpick, Nina arrived at school the first year weighing forty pounds more than her companions. Her mother, as long as she lived, blamed the fatness on a jar of vitamins that Dr. Uribe had prescribed. Nina, more certain of her actions, said that it was due to the soy milk she drank before entering Luisita Tascón's. Marcianita Barona, on the other hand, has firmly believed that it was the curse she cast on Nina, when Marcianita fell while being tormented by her schoolmates, that caused that accretion of gelatinous flesh. In any case, Nina's fatness increased with the years, and until the arrival of the silence her health was as robust as her weight gain was prodigious.

But one day, just after returning from the Departmental Assembly to solicit something for Tuluá, Nina Pérez felt the moment upon her. She had applied to the third commission of the douma in search of a budgetary item that would guarantee the Girls' Normal School the pair of buses it needed in order to be able to shuttle the girls from the Farfán airport, where the Normal School was built, to Tuluá. She was in fine form. Her fatness, in those days truly implausible, stunned the deputies, and they held three debates before her so that the item could be included in the budget. Perhaps she became overheated with so much talking, or maybe it was the crowd of bystanders watching her in action in the commission hall. In any event, upon leaving, she felt the coldness of the street, and for the first time in her life she smelled what she was sure death would smell like on the day it arrived. She climbed into one of the cars that had brought her and sat alone in the back seat. When she arrived in Buga she felt her entrails boiling. Instead of going home, she checked into the hospital. Since in addition to being the leading advocate for progress, she was a charitable member of the Lady Volunteers, the Gray Ladies, and the Ladies of Charity, the hospital went out of its way to take care of her. Her fever rose alarmingly and around midnight, bathed in gallons of alcohol and stabbed more than three times with *conmel* injections to lower her temperature, Nina Pérez felt the end of the world in her cerebral cavity.

Until that moment none of the doctors attending her had been able to diagnose the illness that afflicted her. The fever was not viral as they had first said, much less bacterial as they later asserted. She, who as a hospital volunteer had seen so many ill people from a distance, was scarcely able to say that there was something within her that was about to burst. The news reached all corners of Tuluá before midnight, and by three in the morning, when more than a hundred persons who truly loved her were spending the night near her room, an explosion that she alone seems to have heard put the final touches on her illness. From that moment on, perhaps forever, she was plunged into an absolute silence she shared only with her emptiness.

The first days the doctors thought they could treat her for a burst abscess in her ear. They examined her with otoscopes and one of those gadgets that squirts bitter water through the ear to the throat when it is deep inside, but nowhere did they detect inflammation or anything similar. She continued to say, in a voice so loud that they had to shut the door to her hospital room, that she was completely deaf and they ought to take care of her. She heard nothing from anyone. Perhaps starting at the very moment when she stopped communicating with the outside world, that late night on which something burst in the depths of her cerebrum, she began to read, as best she could, other people's lips in order to see what they were saying to her.

It was a tenacious struggle that fat Nina had to wage in order to understand everyone else. She had neither instructors nor teachers but just a book that Isaac Nessim had brought her all the way from Miami. With it and her cunning, Nina Pérez came to be such an expert lip reader that only those who knew of her absolute deafness could imagine the mental energy she expended in order to understand them.

What she could not do, because it was totally impossible for her, was to control the tone of her own voice. Two weeks after leaving the hospital she began to grow mute. Her words came out sluggish, simple, frightened to death. Since she could not hear, she did not know what she was saying. Although she controlled her head with astonishing ease in spite of the impact of the explosion, she started to abandon speech and to use a blackboard to communicate with others. Only after going to Bogotá and Medellín, sent by the hospital volunteers and tended to by those in the other hospitals in the country, did Nina again speak, but never so much nor so freely as in her days of glory. When she does speak, and as years pass she does it less and less, she speaks so loudly that one would rather keep silent than get in her way. In order not to become totally mute and thus to allow her vocal cords to atrophy, Nina sings three hours a day and raises her voice, toneless and with practically no rhythm, until she shatters glass and china for twenty yards around. Many neighbors abandon their houses around nine o'clock in the morning, when she begins her first cantata. She has bought the sheet music to many monorhythmic medieval songs, and taking advantage of her vague acquaintance with music, she chants in consonance with the markings of the score. Often, a sustained *do* ends up as a *fa*, but since she cannot hear and no one dares approach her cavernous voice, it is all the same if she comes out with one note as with another. She sings from nine until ten-thirty and from three until four-thirty. She drives crazy anyone who stays nearby; hearing her voice at high volume and with broken rhythm for an hour and a half every day leads to inevitable disorientation. The rental of neighboring houses has dropped radically, and those who live there out of necessity have been unable to protest that incessant spectacle. She sings and sings as if she were the frog who wanted to be an ox; she never grows tired or bored. She has stopped helping out with the Lady Volunteers and the Gray Ladies because her deafness might cause problems with the sick. She only goes on Tuesdays to distribute goods for the Ladies of Charity and on Fridays to the meetings of the Association, at which she does not say a single word, fearful as she is of stunning those who might be in her proximity.

Once during a stupid argument, which not even in her state was she capable of abiding, she lost control; her tone and volume were such that she broke all the china in the parlor where they were meeting, and the one who had made the absurd proposal came unhinged and collapsed with a broken eardrum. The meeting was immediately adjourned and Nina shut herself in her room awash in limitless tears. The next day she sang so loudly but with such a melancholy tone that the neighbors who had not left terrified before nine in the morning, because they were accustomed to the songstress's absolute volume, had to abandon their homes and keep their distance from the epicenter of the conflagration. She did not go out again for months. She stopped attending the Tuesday handouts and the Friday meetings and had to pay a courtesy visit to the woman whose eardrum she had broken before she—totally mute, and with a supreme capacity for self-abnegation—could return to her activities.

This was several years ago. Nina Pérez, fat, perhaps fatter every day, completely deaf, mute in the company of others, but vigorous in her matinal and vesperal vocalization, seems to have lost all hope of a cure. The doctors in the Bogotá and Medellín hospitals agree in their diagnoses. The exploded inner ear is irreparable. There is no way to operate, much less to restore it. In truth, what she ought to have felt was an explosion similar to that of a hand grenade. The x-rays they took came out like wartime photographs of bomb craters. What they could not explain was why it did not cause more problems in the cerebral cavity. But hopeless and unable to communicate, Nina did not stop thinking of Tuluá. Although she has not been aloof from the uproar that has accompanied this miracle working, only yesterday, foreseeing that all could end tomorrow, did she appear before the idiots.

XI

Marcianita had no need to ask any doctor, much less go to Europe as Diego Hayer did, because she saw immediately that the idiots' radiance had cured him. She was precisely aware of what was happening. Sure it was her sons who had acquired the august power that had been accumulating in their ancestors for centuries and centuries, she did no less than revere the pair of idiots like gods. She stopped directing them as the pair of automatons she had created, and even when they continued to behave as such, she no longer resorted to blows on the table or monorhythmic handclaps to have them perform their tricks in the house at La Rivera. She opened the trunks Father Tascón had left her and skimmed through such books as she could find in those dilapidated bins. Finding nothing that enlightened her as to the exact site wherein resided her sons' power, she decided to remain silent and wait for a new development before breaking the news. She had seen nothing during the cure of the Swissman's broken arm and wounds. She accepted it as one of the many truths that life had accorded her, and she acceded to it with the same serenity with which she had submitted to the hump that had almost completely doubled her over for years. Trying to exact the maximum from her new prospect, she measured the mental strength of her idiots with special exercises, invoked the memory of her mother, sat in the chair in the gallery, and waited for the idea to come to her in a flash.

She was certain of only one thing. She could not force her sons. If they told her, she would know where the miraculous power in the form of brilliant light came from. If they did not, there would be some other way of finding out. So she sat in the chair in the gallery to wait for the moment of enlightenment. Her hump no longer permitted her to rock with the same ease she enjoyed in the days when she was married, much less in the days of the idiots' births. One afternoon, nevertheless, the cadence of her rocking accelerated. She received a letter from Señor Hayer in Lausanne telling her that the doctors who examined him in the hospital had found him so completely cured of his ailments that in order to be convinced, they had to compare feature for feature the x-rays he brought from the hospital in Cali with the new ones they took there. He considered it miraculous and asked her politely to care for her sons as if they were the most precious jewels in the universe. He was trying to convince some eminent doctors from the clinic in Lausanne to undertake the trip to Colombia. If he succeeded, he would let her know beforehand so that she could attend to them.

This last sentence was the one that surely sounded harshest to Marcianita. Since the time when Dr. Uribe had said her sons were a pair of incurable idiots and she was able to direct them by treating them like robots, she had called upon Dr. Fajardo only the day when they were pining over the Swissman's absence. To bring more doctors—strangers—to disturb the peace with which through the years she had surrounded her jasmines, armadillos, and estate gave her pause. If the doctors turned out to be some know-it-alls babbling in unheard-of languages, she was prepared to throw them out the window. And if they happened to be some snobs who mishandled her sons, treating them like idiots, she would draw strength from her hump, and with a double-barreled shotgun, or whatever, she would blow the imbeciles' brains out. In no way was she going to allow her calm to be shattered for the sake of an armadillo salesman. The Swissman had said nothing about the cure, and since the doctors in the Tuluá hospital did not know of the incident, and since those in the Cali hospital, where he had first been treated, were too busy to investigate the cause of the Swissman Hayer's recovery, the news went no farther than his wife's family in Catalonian Tarragona. But since she had to respond to him in some way or be prepared to turn away the intruders, Marcianita sat down in the chair to contemplate the letter's contents. She found no way to answer him brusquely because the income from the sale of the armadillos was growing. And if she riddled her letter with prudish admonitions, it would probably sound too much like Juan de Urbina, Bishop of Salamanca, who had sent cards to Father Tascón. The solution would lie in the way she accepted those Lausanne doctors. They had not said they were coming; Hayer simply announced he was trying to convince them. Marcianita saw them virtually as knocking at the door.

Thinking about all this, she was bent over in the chair in the gallery, counteracting the effect of the prominent hump that prevented her from sitting up straight, when it came to her. Toño González had studied in Switzerland and would inform her of the quality and character of the doctors with the frankness and honesty of a best man. She sent one of her servants for a cab from the plaza, dressed up just as she had on the day she planned to attend the baptism of Blanquita Lozano's son, and with lapidary certainty drove up to the house of the paralytic queen.

She had not thought to visit since the day they had brought Inesita from Boston and pushed her about in a wheelchair. Inesita no longer bought jasmines from her, but every week, as a fulfillment of what she must have inherited from Father Tascón, Marcianita sent Inesita a dozen of her whitest jasmines. At Christmas time Inesita sent gifts to her two idiots, but neither party visited the other. Marcianita forgot neither Aminta's tiger-face nor the invalid queen, who, although she did not regret her life, tried to avoid doing anything that might put her handicap on display. Not being able to run through the green fields of the house at La Rivera would make her tremble with rage.

Marcianita knocked at the door with a dignity that she was incapable of mustering on the occasion of her desperate search for a doctor for her sons. Haloed by that strange fate she bore with her, she sensed the solution to her problems. For an hour she chatted about past details with Aminta and found that in front of Toño she could only stammer. No one understood the motive of Marcianita's questions, and Toño believed they were inspired by the remote possibility of a cure for her idiots. He did not completely discourage her but insinuated the unlikelihood of any doctor's being capable of curing her sons. They could come from Switzerland (and he spoke of his professors of medicine as of some awesome sages) or from anywhere else, and neither of her sons would be cured. Marcianita then insisted on dignity and respect for the medical profession. And Toño was more bewildered. It did not matter to Marcianita whether or not the doctors knew how to cure the infirmities that afflicted her sons; she believed in prodigious respect for them. Nothing else mattered. Believing that Marcianita was crazy, Toño González humored her. Suddenly, as if transported to the beyond, Marcianita changed the subject and looked deliberately at Inesita in her wheelchair. With utter clarity, the same aura that had illuminated her sons now enveloped her. She started by trying to convince Inesita to come visit the jasmines and offered her a special luncheon. When she had succeeded in convincing her to come to her house the next day, she terminated the visit.

At that moment, and not before or after, Marcianita understood her sons' power. Inesita, a despairing paralytic, would be the test case.

Marcianita and Inesita spent the whole night thinking; the one because it seemed essential to her to find a way to convince her idiots that Inesita, a person they did not know, was a being worthy of consideration in their robot lives; and the other because a strange sensation of emptiness was filling her stomach. Marcianita, nevertheless, turned out to be much more practical than Inesita. She, consumed by insomnia, believed it was not only fear of going to the house of Father Tascón's daughter, but an actual illness that would render her indisposed before her hostess. As soon as Marcianita got home, she checked the clothes her sons would wear the next day, convoked them with her mental powers, and, with a lot of fussing, gestures, and characteristic signs, prepared them for tomorrow's important visit. She spoke to them of the jasmines they saw packed in cellophane for Inesita every week; she succeeded in warning them about the exemplary behavior they ought to display for the visitor, since she was an ailing woman (and she was very insistent upon the point of Inesita's infirmity), creating an attitude of sympathy they seldom felt; and finally, showing them the clothes they would wear, she conveyed to them that the visit was so important that they had to use the brocades they wore only on the days the Swissman visited them.

In this way, Marcianita succeeded in converting her idiots into two gentlemen in waiting. If they had to put on the clothes of the Hayer days, it was because the person who was coming was like him, and the truth was that Marcianita had every reason to believe it would be so. Inesita, ever since the days when she bought jasmines, and later when she was queen, inspired in her an affection so profound that many people in Tuluá were terrified upon seeing Marcianita Barona de Rodríguez at one of the tables of the multitudinous bazaar in the Boyacá Park a few days before tragedy had ravaged the queen.

Father Tascón's daughter could not sleep. She was pacing, thinking about how to inspire in her idiots more intense feelings for Inesita. At dawn, when she believed she had the whole problem solved, she came back to the same place she had left on that bright day when she managed to devise the perfect pretext upon seeing Inesita in her wheelchair. She was as worried about identifying the site of the idiots' miraculous power as about convincing them. If it turned out to be something she could not control, everything would lapse into nameless frustration, and she would have to start over again. She was obsessed only by the possibility of controlling the cure of so many people, dominating with a smile or a dazzling idea those who had brought about her emptiness. Because of this potential reversal, and not because it was her sons who were gifted with the miraculous power, she waited for Inesita González the next day.

At five in the morning she was feeding the armadillos. She considered invaluable the spiritual depth she acquired through the elemental contact she maintained with those little animals at certain peak moments in her life. After the Swissman had stopped coming, the truck from his factory would pick up five to ten armadillos every month, each time for a higher price. Her ability to keep them constantly breeding and in superb condition proved to be hereditary. Bartolomé had inherited from her the same capacity. Ramón Lucio, although clumsier, was no laggard. The armadillos seemed almost directed by remote control as soon as one of the boys entered their mesh corral. They did not need blows on the ground or hand claps where the two robot idiots were concerned. They obeyed a tender impulse and proved to be all the more manageable. On that morning, Marcianita almost spoke to them, apprising them of Inesita's visit. Surely one of them answered her in the language in which she had communicated to all beings, and certainty radiated from this moment on in Marcianita's house. She went out to the garden at about six o'clock and picked the morning's most beautiful blossoms. She arranged them in a vase in the dining room and in one in the parlor, where she planned to place the wheelchair. All the maids received the order to sweep and mop as they had never done before (and they already did it three times daily). At about seven she woke her sons, who, directed since the day of brilliance by their own impulses, behaved appropriately. "You have to be really ready because Inesita will arrive before too long," she seemed to tell them with every gesture, with every telepathic message she sent them; and they, obedient to her commands, awaited Inesita, if not with the same expectation of glee they felt the mornings when Hayer arrived, then certainly with a growing curiosity, inexplicable to their obtuse minds. And when at ten a.m. the González car beeped at the curve by the Ruices' and from the window Marcianita contemplated the entrance to her yard, awaiting the moment the automobile would pass through, an irreverent clamor filled the expanse of her gardens, upsetting the armadillos and sending the idiots into a trance that for unknown reasons they allowed in order to receive their mother's commands. They were dressed in unsurpassable brocades, resembling the dauphins she wanted them to emulate, anxious to meet Inesita González, insistently evoked in their limited world since the day before.

They must have thought she would be like Hayer or Dr. Fajardo. They never expected to encounter the angelic face that was emerging in a wheelchair from the specially equipped car with ramps in the back. Marcianita looked at them with an expression of sorrow that not even her extraordinary powers were capable of masking, and her sons rapidly understood. Sluggish in movement, straining to make it from one end of the house to the other, they understood what it meant to be able to walk when they saw someone who could not, who had to be pushed about in a chair; they looked at their mama, exchanged glances, and prepared to go into action. Marcianita restrained them or they automatically braked themselves with an elegance and knowledge of what was to come. Inesita, overflowing with beauty, perhaps as she was in the best days of her frustrated reign, looked at them warmly and caressed them gently before giving them packets of sweets from an almost bottomless bag she had brought. They bowed in homage as they put the first candies in their mouths, walked at her side to the parlor where Marcianita had planned to seat her, and spent the half hour visit sitting on their chairs, admirably in their places. Inesita, although she had arrived in a car from her house, had sent the car home with the order not to return until four p.m. It was a full day's outing, and she was going to enjoy it as if she could walk.

Bartolomé and Ramón Lucio were the first to arouse her. Dressed as they were, they thought the paralytic ought to meet the armadillos. Marcianita almost jumped for joy at this first sign of sympathy. Inesita understood about half of what they said because their vocabulary was very scanty and full of screeches and wails, but Marcianita quickly translated. Radiant with happiness and as genteel as on the first days of her visits to the house on the Boyacá Park, Inesita accepted their invitation.

At the door to the patio, the breeze brought her the aroma of jasmines from all corners of the garden. She moved away in her chair and, in unimaginable bits and pieces, saw a reconstruction of her past. Paralyzed for years and years, she had been growing a scab over her internal world so as not to think about it and feel her grief. Practically speaking, her life had almost begun anew the instant she sat in the wheelchair to live her death. A queen in memory, beautiful in photographs, when facing the mirror she had no alternative but to devise ways to conserve that beauty as much as her infirmity would allow. Only that way could she survive the death wish she harbored ever since she had left the hospital in Boston, sure of never being able to walk again. Unable to marry, after having imagined herself the wife of a golden cavalier. Useless for performing any task, while having had the same abilities that made her father a great doctor. Incapable of committing suicide, for having been brought up to respect natural law, Inesita endured her life, spending each day trundled about by a maid, by Aminta, by her mother, or by her brother Toño.

The day before, upon receiving Marcianita's invitation, she was about to say no, to refuse, as she had done during all the years of her invalid uselessness; but an I-don't-know-what—which as the days passed she began to call hope, presentiment, premonition—led her to assent. Already many years had passed since that day in her youth when Aminta scolded her in her mother's name for having visited the house of sin. The world had already changed so much that women had stopped wearing shawls to mass; they even took communion dressed in pants. To visit someone who was not guilty of having been born, it turned out, was a simple act of charity rather than an invitation to sin. No one in her house opposed a whole day's visit to Marcianita's. Although Inesita did not abandon any of her activities (she was always a quiet woman who sewed, embroidered, read, or played solitaire), this obsession was viewed as the stuff of everyday life: amusement for the child-queen. Going to the country and breathing fresh, unpolluted air was big news. Everyone accommodated her plans for the next day. They organized the schedule of the visit, took charge of the coming and going for her, and procured sweets for Marcianita's idiot sons; they even polished the special wheelchair. Inesita, in contrast, did not even give a thought to her wardrobe, the wheelchair, the candies for the children, or any other normal matters. She thought of her past, looked in the mirror, set her face for sleeping, and every minute of the night, with a strange premonition that she did not even try to identify, gazed at her reflection in the mirror into which her room had finally been converted. Concerned about the slightest wrinkle on her face, she used ever so many creams to conserve her youth. Early on in her paralysis she had learned to smile so as not to lose her elegance or gentility, much less to wrinkle her expression.

In the morning, upon going to bathe in the special tub fashioned so she would not need anyone else's help, Inesita let the soap drop, wet the towel, and for the first time in her life did not look at her reflection in the water. After filling the bathtub with suds, she emptied it and re-filled it with crystal-clear water, turned on the shower, and finally dried herself, thinking of her arrival at Marcianita's, almost believing that she was about to return to the hospital in Boston. She called her maids, who helped her dress, and when all was ready and the clock was striking nine, she requested a delay in order to contemplate her journey. A Dionysiac terror seemed to seize the paralyzed woman. The very thought of confronting the past in Father Tascón's daughter—in the woman who before had been the child of the jasmines—filled the paraplegic queen to the core with dread. She used her pencils, her paints, her brushes, her creams. When she finished it was already ten o'clock, and without dwelling more on the matter, denying it as if she were about to relapse into the idea of suicide from the frustration she had repressed with mirrors, solitaire, books, embroidery, and knitting, she allowed herself to be put into the car and driven to Marcianita's.

Inhaling the fragrance of the jasmines in the doorway of the armadillo patio, Inesita relived in miniscule fragments the whole past she had succeeded so often in evading, but curiously she was not filled with the terror of the previous day as she had expected. She reviewed her life the way she used to look back in her wheelchair. She smiled at the idiots, and Bartolomé pushed her chair forward. Ramón Lucio looked at his handicapped brother. Perhaps at that moment, compassion filled the spirits of the pair of idiots, and Marcianita achieved the triumph she had been nurturing since the day before. They looked at the armadillos. Bartolomé chose the prettiest ones to place on the paralytic's lap. Ramón Lucio picked the best jasmines. Marcianita did not conceal her elation. Inesita caught it and did not cry because even that emotion was forgotten in her desire not to look at the past. She arrived at lunch exhilarated by the sun, the breeze, and the sheer joy. The idiots sat at the table with a correctness that approached implausibility. They handled their silverware perfectly and passed the plates as if they were normal people, educated in the best family etiquette. The two women looked at them with satisfaction. A half hour later Marcianita gave the mental command and the four of them were shut in the dauphins' room as if they were about to fabricate a monstrous creature.

They uttered not a single word; they only received the cerebral orders. Neither did Inesita understand for certain what was happening. But with that infinite instinct of the wretched who long to find a path to salvation, thorny though it may be, she entered the room and saw the pair of idiots on the beds. Marcianita had not been capable of saying anything to Inesita, and only upon seeing her sons were undressing and that perhaps she should not prolong the suffering of her invited guest, did she whisper three or four words in her ear.

Neither of the two women, during the events in progress or during those that followed, remembers with certainty what those words were. What is certain is that Inesita was petrified to see surge from the bodies of the two idiots a pair of rude, deformed tuberosities, as erect as what she perhaps had yearned for one day in her maidenly paralysis. Marcianita stood behind the wheelchair. The idiots looked at the women as if about to perform a sexual act that involved undressing them by force. The hermetically sealed room. The beds rattling with the rhythmical movements of the pair of masturbants. The breathing of two panting mouths. The dark room filling little by little with an indescribable light. The idiots, spreading their legs, opening their mouths, emitting guttural ultrasonic sounds, their hands passing rapidly over their organs, their eyes on Inesita. Suddenly, the explosion. The immaculate cries of white liquid on their hands. The beam of light in the eyes of the two witnesses. The idiots' unicorns pointing at Inesita's wheelchair. Both boys' hands open, displaying their whitish produce. The sound filling the room. The light blinding Marcianita's eyes. Inesita had long ago entered a limitless trance. Throughout her invalid limbs she felt a tingling similar to what one feels in a leg that has fallen asleep in an uncomfortable position and is set back into motion. In her soul, in the depths of her purity, she had a sensation which had not been repeated since the night when the bazaar lived its last riotous moment.

The light disappeared when the idiots stopped emitting their ultrasonic gutturals. Marcianita understood perfectly and, before leaning over the paralytic guest to bid her to rise, she thought schematically of what she should do to convince her sons that it was not the masturbating that cured, but rather the special sounds. Then, still blinded by the unprecedented splendor that had enveloped her, Marcianita Barona stretched her hand out to the only woman who, in her childhood, had offered her the gift of friendship. As she did so, returning from her trance, Inesita surely believed it was the hand of the aide-de-camp at the coronation in Cartagena leading her victoriously down the runway. She timidly declined to rise, but the certainty in Marcianita's eyes and the continued snorts of Bartolomé, splayed out on the bed, nude and flaccid, induced her to comply. It was two twenty-three in the afternoon. Sixteen years before, she had been consigned to a wheelchair. Ten minutes later, scared, fearful that her incapacitation would return because the effect might wear off, Inesita ran two, three, four meters, and stopped to look at Marcianita. The expression of joy that Tuluá had observed in its queen on the dawn of her return from Cali with the departmental beauty crown, the smile of satisfaction that not even the wheelchair had stolen from the paralytic queen shone forcefully in the heavens of Tuluá.

At three in the afternoon she did not wait for the car to come from her house. Having walked the three blocks that separate La Rivera and Tuluá, holding the hand of her miraculous hostess, Inesita waited for a car to pass by and pick her up. The first to pass, as if to fulfill an appointment with destiny, was Nina Pérez, who was coming down from Picacho in a friend's car. Upon seeing Inesita on foot, holding out her hand to stop the car as if she were any hitchhiking tourist, Nina screamed with the same violent force of her morning songs, bewildering the driver; and before the car had come to a complete halt, she was out of it with all her obesity, screaming ceaselessly, "Miracle,

miracle, miracle!", reminiscing aloud, "She has the measurements of Miss Universe, miracle, miracle, miracle!"

And atop her friend's car, with the queen of Tuluá inside, as beautiful as at the height of her reign, Nina Pérez could not figure out how to awaken Tuluá so it could see that Inesita González, its paralytic queen, had been cured. After crossing Black Bridge and starting up the avenue by the river, Nina had Inesita get out and ordered her friend, also infected with happiness, to drive ahead and blow the horn to open a path of honor for the queen who, miraculously cured, walked once again.

Marcianita was not at their side. Instants after Inesita entered the car she again closed herself in with her idiots. But Nina did not stop shouting. "Miracle, a miracle by Marcianita Barona's idiots, they cured her, they did it! Miracle, miracle, miracle! She has the measurements of Miss Universe!" And one by one the people of Tuluá emerged from all their hiding places; and following Inesita a multitude, and others on the corners, and cars honking. When they reached the Boyacá Park and when Aminta, who had come running, her eyes popping out of her head, heard the racket that Nina was making and saw Inesita completely cured, walking without anyone's help, she did not know whether to run back to call Miss Maruja and Toño or to drop to her knees to give thanks to Our Lady of Perpetual Help. The crowd ended up by trampling her, and she by losing consciousness of the happiness that had seized her. At that precise moment someone who had disregarded Father Phanor's orders climbed the tower and rang the chimes. The firemen sounded their sirens and for minutes Tuluá experienced the carnival of ecstasy that it had prepared that November eleventh when Inesita was to be crowned the national beauty queen. They strewed flowers in her path. Nina's cries were lost in the uproar. Tear-filled eyes and goose bumps marked those who had lived through her paralysis and Tuluá's traumatic suffering. Those who had heard from their elders the story of paralytic queen Inesita, and had seen her many times roll by in her wheelchair down the streets of Sajonia, were boundlessly astonished and shouted as avidly as those who wept. And the children, those who were not able to hear the tale of the paraplegic queen, acted as if it were familiar to them, cheering until they were hoarse, while she, with the elegant manners that she surely would have borne to receive the national crown, walked shakily home in the midst of such a throng.

The most emotional moment came not an hour later when the crowd arrived at Marcianita's house at La Rivera. It came when, at the door of Inesita's house, her mother and her brother, lost in a cadaverous pallor, saw their daughter and sister—their queen—arrive surrounded by a crowd that set off firecrackers and cherry bombs, threw flowers, and screamed frenetically. Their paralytic, who had left at ten in the morning in a wheelchair, now walked back home under her own power. The crowd seemed to grow silent for a fraction of a second, for the instant when Inesita reached the threshold of her house and was lost in the single embrace of her mother and brother. Then Tuluá exploded, and those who had not cried before burst into tears at that moment, and those who did not really remember which queen it was or did not know the story of the beauty who had the measurements of Miss Universe, pretended to be well informed. And when the door of the house was closed and happiness again overwhelmed the frightened Aminta, Nina Pérez, with the same voice as always, as if she had not already spent an hour shouting, turned the crowd toward the house at La Rivera.

The news was already distorted. The idiots had cured Inesita González. No one knew the details because Inesita, dumbstruck with happiness, had trouble telling Nina just that they were the ones. The rest showed in the satisfied face of the queen as she passed through the streets that she could not traverse during her interrupted reign. But the people were not motivated by gratitude, much less by Nina. They were going to meet Marcianita's idiots, to prove themselves their masters by making them appear on the balcony. They were the miraculous idiots of Tuluá. They were the idiots of the bazaar. The spirit of exploitation. The glory that had befallen the city.

They forgot, nevertheless, that Marcianita was Marcianita Barona, the daughter of Doña Manuela and Father Tascón, the wife of Nemesio Rodríguez, separated from her husband, the mother of the idiots. They did not remember her history, nor her origin, and despite their surrounding the house for more than an hour, trampling her lawn, and shouting that they wanted to see the idiots, Marcianita opened neither door nor window. And neither Bartolomé nor Ramón Lucio came out on the balcony to receive the homage of a village that was more than grateful, that was crazed with the knowledge of being the master of such marvels.

That same night the radio stations broadcast the news as of prime national importance. "News from Tuluá indicates that a miraculous cure has been worked by a pair of mentally retarded boys." The radio stations had neither the memory of tape recorders nor the archives of the newspapers which, the next day, on the first page, in large letters to remind the readers of Inesita González's unequaled beauty, ran the story with a picture of her being crowned the Valle beauty queen. At eleven that morning in a small plane at the Farfán airport, a commission of newspaper writers and photographers arrived to interview the reconstituted queen. They did not take the pictures of her in a bathing suit that they had taken sixteen years before, but they were astounded at how, in spite of the years, a woman could preserve her beauty. One of them, who was bound to have many followers as time passed, dropped the hint in his report the next day that in Tuluá it was rumored that the one who was posing could be Inesita's sister. There was no way to convince those who did not know Tuluá that the fable was false because Inesita had no siblings other than her one brother. But the power of the subsequent miracles, the certainty with which Tuluá accepted her idiots and proudly displayed her paralytic queen healthy and ambulatory as if nothing had happened, finally occasioned the demise of that theory, which reemerged more than once in the final days.

The other newspapers and radio stations called endless attention to the miraculous cure. Since it had become so widely known throughout the nation, many believed it, and in some remote place in their memory they recalled the handicapped queen who had filled whole pages in the newspapers. They did not respond immediately because the idiots were not photographed or interviewed, and all the stories about them were by word of mouth. But some of the many who remembered nurtured the hope of going some day to Tuluá to be cured of their ills by the pair of miraculous idiots.

Marcianita, meanwhile, stayed confined to her house, measuring the consequences of her sons' supernatural act. At the culminating moment she had already estimated that the miraculous power lay in the ultrasonic signal they emitted and had begun waging a campaign to convince her sons that the power lay there and not in their mastur-bation. She could not take recourse to mental power because in sexual matters a puritanical scruple had governed her since her birth; but after much thought she decided to take a chance and make use of her control over them once more. If on the afternoon of the cure she had had sufficient strength to close doors and windows and not to give in to the vain temptation to display her idiots on the balcony, she would also have the means to convince them that masturbation was not the best way to produce their curative effects. Of these matters she knew very little; she had once read about onanism in the *Home Medical Guide* and had heard her mother speak ill of those who masturbated, but she never had occasion to discuss such a topic with anyone or to educate herself beyond the limits of that book. But she was convinced it was evil, pernicious, and she was not going to drain her sons' vitality by having them masturbate at the same time as they worked their miracles.

The morning when the reporters and photographers arrived and vainly knocked on the doors of her house and climbed the trees to try to take pictures of the interior and in some way catch a glimpse of the idiots, she went into a trance. Seeing an armadillo limp by, she concluded that there was only one immediate way to cut short her sons' miraculous masturbation. She crushed the animal's paw, wailed dolefully, and called her idiots. She gazed at them, giving the mental commands that only they understood, and with her wizardry made them produce the guttural sounds with no need of masturbating. Seeing the armadillo walk normally with its little paw magically cured, the two idiots exchanged malicious glances, taking note of their occult truth. Marcianita relaxed but did not open the doors or windows and did not even go out to inspect the trampled lawn that the demonstration on the day of the miracle had left. She kept her sons' miraculous power to herself.

She fed them almost as she had in the first days of their instruction as robots; she let them do whatever they pleased, play with the armadillos, look at the Swissman's gifts, cut jasmines for new flower beds, and she waited. She was unswervingly certain that at some moment Inesita's marvelous miracle would attract not reporters but someone who really needed curing. They tried to deceive her; they almost succeeded, but the traits of her heritage—half-lay, half-religious—braked her in time.

Three days after the photographers and reporters from the little airplane had tired of knocking on doors and taking pictures of only the exterior of the house to publish them alongside the photo of Inesita in the newspapers, a vendor of *justarazón* leaves arrived at the door. Since the only way to soothe the sore that had formed where Nemesio had belted her was with an infusion of *justarazón*, no sooner had she heard his call than she wanted to buy some. She was already cured and had no need of them, but the plants had been disappearing as the land was cleared, and the leaves, dried or green, had the same curative effect, just in case. Someone from Tuluá who had seen her collecting the leaves of that plant in the first days of her lump-cum-hump had tipped off the reporter. He dressed like a peasant and smeared himself with dirt as best he could. In his bag he put the camera and the leaves of the rain tree that are called *justarazón*, and raising his newsroom voice he called from the corner by the Ruices'. Marcianita responded. She did no more than loosen the window chain, opening it a crack to peer through at him. She observed him carefully through the tiny slit, told him to wait a moment, and opened the window completely. Something told her that there was deceit in those *justarazón* leaves, and in fear she chose not to open the door. The reporter guessed what might happen: having decided not to miss the chance to snap a picture of the idiots' mama, he took out his camera as she unhooked the chain, and before the sluggishly humped Marcianita's could take into account what was happening and close the window again, he succeeded in getting a shot.

The next day a picture of Marcianita's stoloniferous figure trying to close the window appeared in the Bogotá papers. The murmurings of Inesita's miracle again took flight, and the radio stations and newspapers sent out more reporters to try to break the siege on the house of jasmines. On the sixth day the arrival of Brother Andrés for the benefit festival arrested their attention. For the first time Marcianita could open the doors and windows of her house. The alpinist-Marist brother's spiders, lizards, and snakes deflected the interest in the miraculous idiots for at least a day. Marcianita was sure that sooner or later she would no longer be able to stave off the avalanche, but during those days she persistently prepared her sons for the new function with which life had entrusted them. She wove new suits for them, furnished the tiny balcony with special seats for their interviews and visits from afar, and, seated in the chair where she had also anticipated their birth (and her mother, the arrival of the gray mare), she awaited the moment to commence the main attraction of the bazaar into which her life had been converted.

XII

Long before Chuchú arrived at the door of the big house that
Don Jesús Sarmiento donated to the Franciscans so that they could
found their monastery in Tuluá, her fame as God's favorite and the
benefactress of mankind had already blanketed the countryside. Dressed
in black as if observing an eternal mourning that many attributed to the
Christ of Good Friday, who made her cry like nobody else, Chuchú,
whose last name has never been known, is the point of contact that
Tuluá has maintained with God and His angels. Many of the dying have
called out in their death rattles to that strange woman who, protected
behind thick green glasses, seems to show them, at the end of their
lives, the sure path to heaven. The organizer of the festivals of San
Francisco, the principal pilgrim on the Holy Thursday nocturnal hike to
Buga's Basilica of Our Lord of Miracles, the bearer of Veronica's veil
in the procession on Holy Saturday, the first voice in the chorus of
mourners of the Blessed Sacrament congregation, she has taken
communion, on her knees before the altar of the Immaculate in the
temple of the Franciscans, every day of her life. Wherever she passes in
her daily stroll, she leaves a trail of ineffable perfume. She has not so
much as looked at a man and has never attempted to serve as witness at
a wedding ever since the afternoon on which, swimming through what
seemed like endless tears, she followed the bier of Edgar Bastidas, her
intended, whom she was to marry the next Saturday.

That night she anointed herself with ashes and, kneeling before
the monumental Christ at the head of her bed, swore eternal love for the
man whom typhus, in less than a week, had carried to the tomb. On her
lips would never again appear a smile, and, instead of words of love,
her teeth were witness only to the spewing of prayers and more prayers.
No one has prayed so much as Chuchú. No one has spent so much time
kneeling as this woman who is surrounded by ejaculations, prayers to
the Almighty Lord, and secret invocations to San Francisco de Sales
that start at six every morning. But never has she so much as interceded
so that a marriage would not fail or so that one that was foundering
might be restored to perfection. She accepts requests for all sorts of
intercessions but will not pray for a marriage, a sweetheart, or any
amorous prospect. Nor does she attend weddings, and when someone
decides to get married at the six-thirty mass, she, wrapped in her black
gown, prudently exits from the temple. She comes back at seven for
communion, but for nothing in the world will she witness the
consummation of the sacrament at which she was stood up. For years

she has lived in Blanquita Lozano's house, but no one knows if she is Blanquita's sister or just one of the four women who stopped by and ended up staying. She leaves at six-fifteen and does not return until three in the afternoon when, on her knees at a prie-dieu that she keeps in front of a niche full of saints, she begins her labor as God's favorite, opening a bound green notebook, and invoking line by line the favors that have been solicited throughout the day.

Although nobody knows exactly when she began her labors, she did not undertake her intercessions until Edgar Bastidas was buried, on the afternoon when she drowned in tears. If it had been before, Paulina Sarmiento would have set her to praying to counter the effect of that daughter of sin. Besides, her chances for success in such activity before the heavenly dominions were slim. Another thing she does not do is to invoke souls in purgatory. For Chuchú, although she lives with the word Satan on her lips, believes neither in that nor in Hell. Because she stays in God's grace, she fears neither the demon nor his malignant spirits, but she flees the anger of San Gabriel the Archangel, who has scourged her more than once when she has had evil thoughts after six in the evening, while finishing her intermittent prayer.

She eats only at Blanquita's. For breakfast she has nothing but communion; there is no delicacy more exquisite than communion, she says, fingering her rosaries while having bread and coffee at home. Because her schedule is so tight, she has no lunch anywhere. At twelve-fifteen, finishing up the Magnificat—her arms outstretched like a cross in front of the altar of the Most Holy Trinity in the church of San Bartolomé—with the scorching sun and not the slightest intention of removing any of her black gowns, Chuchú walks from one end of town to the other. Monday, Wednesday, and Friday she goes to the diminutive farm of one of Blanquita Lozano's brothers-in-law. Tuesday, Thursday, and Saturday she leaves San Bartolomé for Toño González's, which is at the farthest extreme from Blanquita Lozano's husband's brother-in-law's farm. Between San Bartolomé and her midday destination, Chuchú spends an hour to an hour-and-a-half. She does it sometimes as exercise and other times as a sacrifice for the expiation of her carnal sins. Regardless of whether it rains, thunders, or lightnings, Chuchú does not alter her scheduled routine. Whether covered with a black rubber raincoat and aided by an umbrella that many find gives her the appearance of a medieval witch, or stuffed into swamp boots, she is relentless in her tour through the byways of Tuluá.

At three in the afternoon, when she returns to Blanquita's house and takes out her prie-dieu, she accepts only a glass of water. At six-thirty she has supper. A half hour later, covered to the head in black ruffles, she climbs under the blankets and prays continuously, without even a second's interruption, in order not to allow to enter the evil thoughts that almost always torment her in the evening. Sometimes she has yielded to them, and her mind, clouded by prayers, feels almost like an oasis reveling in immodesty. But when she realizes she has sinned, the fantasy is dispelled and, fearful of the presence of the Archangel with his relentless whip, she lashes herself with a hair shirt that Father Saavedra of the Franciscans gave her one afternoon to do penance. She has been a lover of sacrifices for redemption. She firmly believes in the value of martyrdom, and once a year, between the second and third Wednesdays of Lent, she covers herself with ashes, fasts on bread and water, and presides over the collective penance of at least a hundred persons who do the same as she. Almost all are beneficiaries of her divine intercession. If she has not done someone the favor of relieving a toothache, she has obtained for him or her the bank loan that has spelled eternal salvation. Everyone else is a friend of the beneficiary or a future recipient of her heavenly interventions. During the seven days of the week of atonement, she, ash-covered, invokes the angels with prayers found in no book but which she repeats with such dignity and ability that many have believed she recited them by heart. Finally, free of all burdens, together with her companions in martyrdom and fasting, she intones a Te Deum as thanks.

Because she has never gotten involved with incurable illnesses or insoluble problems, no one can say she works miracles. She simply invokes her saints, the virgins, and the angels, and hopes that the natural order of things will come to her aid. At no time has she entered into the monastery of the Franciscans, for whom she does much more than a hundred monks, nor has she considered becoming a nun herself. But some of those who have felt favored by the celestial communication she has facilitated for them have often wanted to give her a monk's robes to wear in place of her inevitable severe black. Gifted with a mythological ability to convert the impossible into reality and four stones into bread, Chuchú can practically be said to have constructed the Franciscan monastery. She did not organize a bazaar like Marcianita Barona's, much less a festival, because she does not patronize events where men and women commingle. But by asking at every door, speaking not so much with the cherubim and seraphim of the celestial army as with mayors and governors, with their wives and children, she has made possible, at the site of Don Jesús Sarmiento's house, a school and a monastery with all the modern conveniences. As a reward, the Community of San Francisco de Asís conferred upon her the Medal of the Third Order and, in time, the title of Friar Chuchú, the only woman in Colombia and indeed the world to be so honored.

The news spread like wildfire the afternoon when the Franciscans let it be known. Chuchú had just arrived at Blanquita's house and was on her knees at her prie-dieu looking through her notebook at that day's requests for intercession. Father Saavedra, with his voice of an ancient organ and his face like a champagne cork, arrived almost choking, brandishing the letter from Rome that bore the good tidings. Chuchú, unshakable, listened to him as she knelt at her prie-dieu. She lowered her eyes and perhaps entered a trance. The next morning, dressed in a black tunic she must have made during the night, Chuchú arrived at the Franciscans' temple. The bells rang as if the one entering at that moment were the first priest Tuluá had ever had or the bishop it has spent its whole life awaiting. Incense invaded the images and altars of the church. The full pews saw her enter with her head uncovered and the black veil of her tunic dragging on the floor. Since that day Tuluá has counted on Friar Chuchú not so much for the glory and honor of the community of San Francisco as for its tranquility. As one of the ladies of the many religious congregations said, that incomparable woman was Tuluá's lightning rod for divine ire.

The new title did not make her change any of her pastimes, much less her methods. She has continued going from one end of town to the other at noon to collect in her notebook the favors she should solicit, and to dress in the same black outfit she has worn almost since birth. She has not had a single friend and has had absolutely no relationship with those who have not requested her intercession. She is one of the few women in Tuluá who has not gone to Isaac Nessim's shop, but that has not kept her from being a customer of his. Along with all her virtues as one favored by God, she combines her power of persuasion and her capacity for comedy. With the first she has gotten one person or another to handle her commercial dealings so that she does not have to see people she does not know, people who do not respect her, or people who might perhaps be inspired to entertain an evil thought. Her modesty reaches such extremes that she would be absolutely incapable of going to a shop to purchase underwear. Blanquita, or one of the other women who live in her house, runs such errands for her. She has convinced them all that it is materially impossible for her to find the time to make such a purchase, when the truth is that she does not live except to convey not a single evil thought to those about her. And when someone stares at her she rushes to her prie-dieu, prays more fervently than ever, and that night lashes herself with the Archangel Gabriel's hair shirt.

Once she went so far that Blanquita was about to intervene by calling Father Saavedra. Walking along the highway to Toño González's cabana, Chuchú passed by the stream where the women from the Morales district usually do their laundry. Dressed all in black, she caused an incredible stir among the pubescent boys who bathed there naked. The oldest, seeing her coming, swung his whole member in the air. Chuchú almost died. In order to cross the bridge she had to pass right by the naked adolescent. She looked at the ground pretending to be blind, but a distant nocturnal temptation made her fix her glance (purified by thick green glasses) on the boy's member. The rest of the boys noticed, and when she passed by in shock on her way back from the cabana, three boys just like the one who had first drawn her glance waited for her, naked, at the bridge. Aware of her presence only a few yards away, and perhaps aware that she was an inconceivably chaste woman, they started to fondle themselves. With shouts in keeping with their age and state of excitation, and informed by who knows whom, they combined her name with their droning acts. Upon hearing it in a tone much stronger and more lascivious than usual, she barely managed to cross the bridge and run for her life so that, choking and spouting tears as on the day of her Pasto fiancé's burial, she could kneel and shake at her prie-dieu. She did not eat that night, and during the whole period of darkness Blanquita heard her whipping herself with the hair shirt. The next morning they found her collapsed, her back one single ulcer. They rubbed it with lemon and salt, cleaned it with alcohol and merthiolate, and called Father Saavedra.

Chuchú took to bed for a week. Dr. Uribe sent pills to help her sleep, and Blanquita gave them to her in her coffee. The night they stopped giving them to her, Chuchú recreated in her mind the troika of boys masturbating before her. She ordered a dozen masses celebrated in repentance and walked down the street as if, rather than suffering from a raw back, she wore a chain between her knees. All that happened quite some time ago. Nevertheless Chuchú has not stopped reliving it in all her moments of weakness, and when upset she again flagellates herself before the archangel can appear in her room to do it.

People who have recently seen the doors to her intercessions closed attest to her other quality, her capacity for comedy and histrionics. Feeling imaginary pains, Chuchú has simulated an attack of hysteria that almost makes one believe she has bone cancer. Seated in front of her icons, insistently thrusting her fingers and toes into hot salt water, gesticulating in such a way that those who see her pity her imaginary pain, Chuchú has interrupted her labor as an intermediary, her walks from one end of town to the other, and her jottings in the green notebook.

As God's only favorite and the medium blessed with his powers, she awaits—with certain excitement—the moment when the thunderous miracle working will come to an end and she can silently recover the role which for so many years she has played with consummate skill.

XIII

Tuluá, which thanks to Inesita González's cure appeared overnight on the front pages of the daily papers and on prime-time radio and television, must have never thought that in less than a week the eyes of the nation would again focus there with much greater interest than that provoked by the idiots. Brother Andrés's arrival at the benefit function, which for at least a day deflected the curious gazes away from La Rivera to the Marist brother's spiders and lizards, marked the beginning of an avalanche whose only limit would be the one produced a few hours ago by destiny.

Since Brother Andrés was a national figure, a columnist for all the major newspapers, and the successful scaler of all Colombia's snow-covered peaks, the news that the spider *Metropolus* had bitten him and that the special antidote was not obtained the first or second day, that the whole world rushed to his aid, that the emperor of Japan sent experts in ophidian bites, that he was in a cataleptic state in order to slow the spread of the venom—all this and much more that the journalists invented relegated Marcianita and her idiots to near oblivion. But certain that there would be no turning back from what was well underway, she waited with the same awesome calm with which her mother yearned for or feared the arrival of the mare, every evening at seven in the house on the Boyacá Park. Perhaps because of that serenity (when, at noon on the eighth day of waiting for a cure for the agonizing Brother Andrés, they knocked on the door of her house and clouds of reporters and photographers descended upon her from an ambulance and a battery of cars), she neither altered nor accelerated her step but emerged on the balcony with a bough of jasmines, gave orders for them to lower the stretcher with the semi-conscious Marist brother, and—without opening the door—by simply appearing, she was able to accomplish the cure.

The moment they laid the stretcher with the dying man on the lawn—which in those days was still green—Marcianita tossed the bough from the balcony and had them place it on the agonizing spider trainer's chest. Then she deserted the balcony for some ten minutes. The silence and impatience grew in the reporters who hovered like birds of prey, waiting for the miraculous news. The whole country was hanging on Brother Andrés' health. Since there was no other news, since the war in Vietnam remained as stagnant as it had for the previous six years, since the governments continued doing the same things with the same people, the only newsworthy figure was that alpinist brother, newsman, photographer, spider trainer, and recipient of the Order of the Rising Sun from the emperor of Japan. Marcianita knew it well. Step by step, she had observed the details of the tragedy and the progress of the poison through the organism of the man bitten by the *Metropolus*. She had foreseen with such simplicity that, prior to the cure, Nature was imposing itself on the events. The bough of jasmines had been fanned over the agonizing brother because she had decided, in one of those days' luminous moments, that although natural powers are the only ones susceptible of exploitation, her sons' supernatural powers would see her through to better times than those she had spent with Father Tascón's endless gold coins. "Let the jasmines lie on his paralyzed limbs," Marcianita suddenly declared from the depths of the room behind the balcony. Those who were next to the stretcher rushed to do as they were bid. They had not yet finished when the silence became a murmur and the flashbulbs of cameramen and photographers indelibly captured the moment of the idiots' appearance. "They are brighter than those stupid things," cried Marcianita from the same depths as before. The journalists desisted and then the pair of idiots, dressed in red and black brocades, opened their mouths and raised their hands as if holding something. No one heard a thing, but dogs barked and the pair gesticulated as if they were producing an indispensable sound. The brilliant light blinded everyone; cameras took photos, and those who did not close their eyes had to lower their heads to avoid the supernatural brilliance emanating from the balcony.

When they could see again, the idiots had already closed the doors of the miraculous overlook and Brother Andrés had begun to deflate; he opened his eyes, said his first words in several days, and squeezed the bough of jasmines between his hands. The reporters, even the most incredulous ones who had come by car, rushed to be the first at telephones and teletypes to spread the news. The photographers galloped off to develop their film. No one could find anything; the idiots' extraordinary resplendence overexposed every photograph. The only ones that came out were those taken a moment before the brilliance, when the photographers had lit their lights and Marcianita had shouted to douse them. The slight figures of the miracle workers were hard to discern in the midst of the brilliance of their brocades. But with those impressions, and the ones with which in amazement the reporters filled sheets and sheets of paper, the news of the miraculous cure of the alpinist-spider trainer reached the four corners of the world.

In Tuluá it was received more with astonishment than glee. Inesita's cure practically incited a carnival. Brother Andrés's cure did no such thing. Instead, fear trickled in through all the crevices of the houses and seized even the city's most insignificant inhabitants. Few managed to have sufficient foresight to anticipate that a few days later this pair of cures would shake the world and turn topsy-turvy everything that had up until that day functioned with monotonous regularity. Things were so sped up, so prodigiously accelerated, that no one could pretend not to be taken by surprise by the radical change in customs.

The first place to become congested was the Office of Tele-communications. There were not enough telephones; the lines were insufficient. Some desperate reporters went to Buga the day of Brother Andrés's cure to send urgent communiqués, and even when they encountered the problem of the city employees' not permitting them to put Tuluá in the dateline because they were calling from Buga, so many words were sent that, in order not to appear to be capitulating, the employees ended up feigning ignorance. Those from the magazine *Seven Days* outdid themselves inventing lies. They obtained in who-knows-which old house some snapshots of a certain Marcianita, the daughter of a Vallecaucan farming couple, and deflected, perhaps forever, the truth about the origin and probable explanation of the idiots' miraculous power. Nemesio Rodríguez, who perhaps still lives in some inaccessible part of the universe, was portrayed as deceased in the construction of the Pacific Railroad, a victim of malaria. The idiots turned out to be not so idiotic and Marcianita did not appear with the hump that doubled her over to her feet but rather with a likely radi-ological accumulation on her back that was perhaps what produced the beam of infinite light and set the dogs up and down the block to barking.

The second site of congestion was the Ruices' store, just before the house at La Rivera. Since it was the only house for three blocks around and the only place where soft drinks were sold to quench the thirst of long hours' awaiting the appearance of the idiots, the throng reached such levels that the vendors, desperately seeing themselves soon incapable of keeping up with the demand, after years of casually selling three or four drinks a day to those who passed by on the way to Picacho, requested the aid and protection of the police. They ordered as well from the distributors case after case of English Cola and cigarettes not by the box but by the carton, as if their store were not the miniscule avocation they inherited from their grandmother but rather an immense casino where people drank and smoked as if there were no tomorrow.

Some reporters and others who were just curious or skeptical set up tents in the fields around Marcianita's house. There they sought shelter from the sun and took turns awaiting the idiots' next appearance on the balcony. Cripples and beggars arrived, but since no one came with Brother Andrés's ballyhoo or Inesita's affection, neither did the balcony open nor did the hoped-for cure take place. For the doors to be opened for Brother Andrés it was not sufficient for one of the ambulance attendants merely to knock. Marcianita had yielded to the pleas of Dr. Fajardo from the hospital, the first to be convinced of the idiots' miraculous powers. He was the only person who could approach Marcianita and actually the only one other than the Swissman Hayer who could persuade her to lend her services. He had not examined the boys since the day of his initial treatment, but in the depths of his intelligence he understood that they possessed something that neither he nor anyone else could control. It was he who arranged for the ambulance and the cure at that precise hour and no other. He took the precaution of taking x-rays and consulting with three other specialists in a thorough examination of Brother Andrés before sending him to La Rivera, and with those notes and others he made regarding Inesita González, he began his famous book on the cures that only now, after selling out three printings, has been contested by some readers.

The second day after the Marist brother's cure, the pilgrimage had reached such proportions in the area around the Ruices' store that the three blocks that separate La Rivera from Tuluá looked like the entrance to an ant hill. The green lawn that had surrounded Marcianita's house, her adobe wall, and her bower: completely trampled. The tranquility that Marcianita had guarded jealously was about to disappear entirely. After the reporters said that the jasmines were the probable external curative element—and since Brother Andrés had them clutched in his hand at the instant of the miraculous light—the pilgrims' insane desire for the flowers had Marcianita concerned for her adobe wall and her bower. Among her plans was to establish a schedule for the sale of plants and flowers, but if people were going to come with such desperate curiosity, she would have to change her approach. At four that afternoon, with the tents practically hidden by the crowd that made walking impossible, even though it moved like a millennial mob itself, Marcianita could stand no more and went out onto the balcony. It was for no longer than a second. Chuchú, who was also among the thousands of curious onlookers in attendance at the idiots' house, described Marcianita's fleeting appearance as a sacrilegious parody of the Pope's appearances on the balcony of the Vatican. Marcianita rose up to give a desperate cry. "I need Dr. Fajardo! It's urgent!" and she again closed the balcony doors. No one in her house was sick as many,

instantly disillusioned, believed. It was that he was the only person with
the authority to request from the mayor a large detachment of police to
disperse the people who, in order to pick the miraculous jasmines, were
trying to knock down her adobe wall and her bower.

And a half hour later Dr. Fajardo arrived, making his way with
difficulty through the crowd. The news had reached the hospital by
word of mouth. An hour later the police made the rubber-neckers
retreat to a distance of five yards from the house, and Marcianita, more
secure, planned a schedule of appearances and cures for her idiots after
they produced a third miraculous cure. Before that third cure, she
would not put her sons on exhibit. She had to choose very carefully and
do it with as much publicity as the first two times. The paralytic queen
and the brother bitten by the spider *Metropolus* were two good cases,
but one more was needed to convert their miraculous actions into
limitless acts, capable of carrying their ultrasonic waves to places where
the real would merge with the imaginary.

Many reporters had already returned to their headquarters. A
few remained to await new developments. The comments in *The Press*
continued, but they were no longer the full-page reports of the two
previous days. The majority of the curious pilgrims of the past two
afternoons were from Tuluá or nearby towns. Marcianita understood all
that, but since, having never had any friends, her communication with
the outside world was nonexistent, she did not go out to converse with
the people of Tuluá or to learn of more tragic cases. She waited,
trusting that the next day, early in the morning, along with the crowd
that would show up at dawn, she would find the possibility of a
miraculous demonstration of the type she desired.

And at nine in the morning, while the people were blanketing the
lawn anew, as if—thanks to her perpetual communication with
destiny—she directed not only her miraculous idiots, Tille Uribe made
her appearance carrying in her hands Carlos, the nearly lifeless parrot.

Throughout the whole night, as the culmination of a process of
many days, Tille Uribe was at her parrot's side, shining an infra-red
lamp on him, anointing him with anti-inflammatory poultices, and
uttering the prayers she found in her brother Enrique's book of
Masonry. Carlos, who had been her faithful companion for years and
years, her unthwartable lover, seemed definitively incurable, with no
future other than death. She could not accept the idea of her Amazonian
parrot's disappearance. He had accompanied her in health for years, and
the miraculous drug to restore him from his infirmity had to exist. As
days passed, the hope that Brother Andrés's serum engendered in

Tille Uribe diminished. The night before his appearance in the idiots'
neighborhood, the spoiled parrot's palpitations became practically im-
perceptible. For a day and a half after she learned of Brother Andrés's
cure, Tille harbored the idea of taking her parrot to Marcianita's house.
But the unfavorable impression that the hump-backed woman had
made on Tille the day she saw her searching on a bicycle for a doctor,
and the remote feeling of respect for Marcianita that her parents had
fostered, made her prolong her meditations and delay her arrival at
the miraculous house. At first she planned to wait for the brother's
convalescence and continued with the serum therapy that no longer had
any effect, but when she appeared at dawn that day at La Rivera and
Carlos continuously emitted a hoarse, moribund cry, his feet numbed
with cold, she decided to take the chance. The only way to get any
attention was to take her father along. No matter how much heaven and
earth were opposed to Marcianita Barona, Dr. Uribe had tended to her
in her deliveries and the idiots' diagnoses. Many years had passed since
that time. Dr. Uribe no longer practiced medicine and could stand up
only with the assistance of a walking stick. There was nothing left of
his distant glory except his scalpel and the rotund voice of his best
years. So Tille had to sit on the edge of her ancient father's bed starting
at six in the morning, to convince him that now was the moment to do
what he had always wanted to do for his unmarried daughter, destined
to die of cancer. At eight-thirty in the morning, when she managed to
persuade him and to leave for the Boyacá Park carefully escorting
the famous Dr. Uribe, who had not been seen for more than fifteen
years and whom many believed to be dead, Tuluá, frightened as it was
by the lively acceleration of the miracles, was not affected. But more
than one person seeing the ancient doctor believed that, amidst so much
miraculous chaos, time was running backward.

The car could not draw any closer than the Ruices' store. The
dense crowd blocked the way like ants fleeing from chlordane.
Fortunately, Tille had anticipated this, and at the store she trotted out
the wheelchair that the ancient medicine dispenser of Tuluá used for
many hours each day. It took forty-five minutes to traverse the three
hundred meters from the Ruices' to the police line. Many people helped
them along. The presence of Dr. Uribe and his respectable elderliness
created something capable of confronting the highest divinity and
worthy of the miraculous potential enclosed in Marcianita's house.
Knowing this, Tille made use of her wiles to follow the wheelchair
which, through the efforts of the driver and the helpers, stopped right
in front of the balcony of miracles.

"Marciana, Marciana, Marciana." What remained of Dr. Uribe's ancient, awesome voice resounded. Tille had no intention of knocking at the door. If she did, Marcianita or the police would bar her entry. But neither Marcianita nor anyone else in the house could deny the groans, almost from beyond the tomb, of the ancient doctor who had helped her bear the idiots. Tille Uribe, confident, her diaper-swaddled parrot in her arms, awaited the moment.

Marcianita recognized him before he spoke. Her capacity to sense at a distance the people who had passed through her life put her on alert. When she heard the almost unique cry of "Marciana," which only he and certain spirits employed, she opened the balcony doors, made the multitude tremble, and intensified the depressing moan of all who had gathered that morning. Without saying more than "Dr. Uribe, Dr. Uribe," and crossing her arms, she sent him an embrace from a distance, forgetting that she had stopped speaking to him many years before, and initiated the third miraculous cure at the house of jasmines, making official for Tuluá and all Colombia the presence of her supernatural idiots.

For a few moments the police were incapable of keeping the crowd five yards from the house. On the balcony, her fine zebu's hump making her look always down and never up, before producing the delirious spectacle that the presence of the idiots before the parrot eventually became, Marcianita had the brilliant idea of creating a walkway similar to those used to bathe cattle, thus avoiding problems with the police. Only after she mapped out her immediate plans did Marcianita open wide the doors to the diminutive balcony and retire to the depths in order to await the appearance of her slow, clumsy miracle-workers.

It would have pleased her greatly to heal and rejuvenate Dr. Uribe, but on Tille's face and in the immobile arms of that solitary woman, perhaps as filled with suffering as she in her own emotional life, she found what she had been searching for ever since. With her mental powers, she conjured up a third fantasy cure, one bordering on the unreal. Dr. Uribe's daughter's parrot was just the thing. The appearance of her two dauphins took a little longer than usual. The delay allowed time for reporters and photographers to draw near and for the incredulous enemies of their mythological abilities to see everything so clearly that they would never again be able to deny their power. It took exactly sixteen minutes. One of the correspondents described it that night in a special radio report from the miraculous city of Tuluá where a pair of mental retards could cure people as well as animals by simply tossing jasmines at the stricken. When the seventeenth minute began, silence shook the crowd's fragile structure. A unanimous cry which must have reached even the dwelling of the elders filled the space around Marcianita Barona's house. In the background, framed by the diminutive balcony, the pair of idiots. The people did not know whether to applaud or shout, to cheer or weep, to drop to their knees or climb on their neighbor's shoulders to catch a glimpse of the miracle workers. There was unique and total hysteria. The only exceptions were Dr. Uribe and his daughter Tille. They were exactly in front of the balcony, mute with fear, terror, or the estrangement that the pair of supernatural creatures inspired. Tille did no more than stretch out her arms and show the idiots her squalid, moribund parrot, panting, with his lackluster feathers drooping over his bound claws. Those in the back, those at the entrance to the house, those who had managed to reach the curve at the Ruices' and see the balcony from a distance with binoculars, with human eyes that would shortly go blind, saw nothing more than an infinite splendor centered on the balcony. It was for only a few seconds. Then the cries, the thundering and riotous "Miracle, miracle, miracle!" Tille Uribe, paralyzed with joy, watching her ancient father rub his eyes to regain his vision, saw Carlos on her shoulder, full of the life that only instants before had been abandoning him, with his feathers as brilliant as in the days of his youth, a chatterbox as he had always been. The balcony was shut, and the crowd walking down the road to Tuluá was declaring that a miracle had once again occurred. The reporters were interviewing Tille Uribe; the ancient Dr. Uribe was asking for air and begging for a pathway to his car. Everything all at once, blanketing the pious and the unfaithful, the believers and incredulous, shouting incessantly, repeating like an echo: miracle, miracle, miracle!

Marcianita meanwhile was conversing with the head of the police detail that surrounded her house. Early the next morning they would increase the buffer zone to thirty yards, and workmen would mark out a long walkway that would run the length of the house, passing before the balcony. The police would be unnecessary next to the house but would be needed to prevent tramplings at the entrance to the walkway. In this way the brilliant idea emanating from the moment of Tille Uribe's parrot's cure was put into practice.

The repairs took three days. During that time many curious people were gathering to see from afar the miraculous house and the work being done. When everything was completed at dawn of the third day, the police took their new posts. In front of the balcony was a gigantic platter on top of a large table. There, those who filed by would deposit the alms that would make it possible for Marcianita Barona to escape that modest, monotonous regimen she had kept for almost half a century, rationing out Father Tascón's inexhaustible gold coins.

On a piece of paper, in India ink, very neatly done, almost as if by a printer, was the schedule of the miraculous idiots' appearances. Monday through Friday from nine to eleven-thirty A.M. From four-thirty to six in the afternoon. Saturdays and Sundays from eight to ten in the morning and from four to six in the afternoon.

The jasmines were not put up for sale as she had planned. Instead, foreseeing a future exploitable as never before, each day she dedicated her free hours—those that she did not spend waiting, seated in the room with the balcony, for the intermittent splendor that the idiots produced only once each shift—to the meticulous cultivation of thousands of jasmine seedlings.

The first days, when the pilgrims were none other than Tuluá's neighbors and the crowd was not yet what it has been these last few days, the cures took on a generalizable character and favored chronic illnesses over complete paralysis. Alvaro Bejarano's wife, from Buga, was the first to leave her crutches leaning against the wall of the house. She arrived the day after Tille Uribe's parrot's cure, but she found that the idiots would not attend to her until the walkway was completed. A car had hit her five months before, and although the doctors had said she would be completely cured, without casts or wounds, she could not stay on her feet except with a pair of crutches. Her husband helped her out of one of those many little Renaults bought nowadays by poor people who want to feel rich. In front of the Ruices' store, his in-laws, who were perhaps the first to foresee the chimney-less industry that was growing, organized a parking lot on the land where the shopkeepers had once kept four cows and a couple of starving horses. That is how Alvaro Bejarano's wife came to be one of the first in line on the day the schedule of appearances on the balcony was posted and the new walkway was inaugurated. They arrived at eight-thirty in the morning, certain that since it was a weekday, they would not find too many people, but they had to wait until she nearly fainted, holding herself up on her crutches with difficulty until the afternoon appearance. The reflection of the aura that the idiots emitted at exactly eleven did not reach her. Although the people passed before the idiots in a file that moved slowly but surely, the crowd was such that they did not even get close to the curve at the Ruices' and could not see the splendor from the balcony. In the afternoon they passed by it, just at six, when the idiots sent the infinite splendor surging forth from the palms of their hands. More spectacular than in the morning (and not according to the group that was close to the house but rather to those who were in the meadow across the way), the cry of miracle rose from the mouth of one who was said to be mute from birth. Alvaro Bejarano's wife's cure was most sensational. Because Bejarano, wishing to erase the acts of infidelity he had committed while his wife was paralyzed, spread the news embellished with the metaphors of the poet he always wanted to be and never was, the next day the place was filled with pilgrims from Buga, bringing with them a thousand and one infirmities.

At first she felt a tingling in her feeble legs. Then an emptiness in the pit of her stomach. She did not quite have time to say "Alvaro" when her crutches dropped and she walked with the same ease she had had until the day the car hit her. "Miracle, miracle, miracle!" repeated the incalculable chorus of those who were still enraptured by the idiots' splendor that evening. It seems that more than one person was cured at that moment. At noon a lady arrived at the Ruices' store with her hand wrapped in rags and gauze, and when she left around seven that night the Ruices were sure they saw her with the white strips in her unbound hands. She wore a happy expression and simply asked them what Marcianita would like. They did not know what to tell her and merely commented, in the midst of that starved mob demanding immediate service, that Marcianita was an expert at embroidery and cultivating jasmines.

Three days later, the cures having been repeated several times, near and far from the epicenter of the idiots' light, with the radio and the press insisting on the extraordinary case of Marcianita's sons to the point of turning it into a news item every bit as national as Brother Andrés (who was completely restored by that time), that same woman with the rags and gauze who had conversed with the Ruices that night and who, by various methods, they had determined was cured, came back to the parking lot. She got there at five in the morning, at the time when the Ruices, still exhausted from the night before, were getting up to make *arepas* and sell pots of black coffee as if they were serving factory workers leaving for home. She arrived in a pick-up truck full of boxes. Three helpers carried them amidst the many pilgrims who had been arriving since midnight to wait their turns to pass before the idiots. She got as far as the table that held the platter, but instead of tossing bills and coins as so many did as they passed by, she left the three big boxes. That was the start of the contribution of objects, which so many people chose to bring out of gratitude to the idiots.

After that day Marcianita picked up the platter of contributions every night, sorted the gifts as to quality and type, and divided up the packages. She counted the money and stored it in big, black suitcases. At eight the next morning, leaving from the rear of La Rivera, crossing the brook, going up by the power plant instead of down the road by the Ruices', one of the servants would carry the booty to Tuluá and turn it over to Don Alonso Victoria of the lottery agency. Marcianita had made an arrangement with Dr. Fajardo that an ambulance would pick the servant up three times a week with the boxes of clothing that she would distribute among the poor in Gota de Leche or at the antituberculin clinic. In that same ambulance they brought the groceries and carried the black suitcases of money. Dr. Fajardo received nothing for his services, but he maintained the hospital and charity ward in great style. No one knows how much Marcianita has helped in those good deeds all these months, but given Dr. Fajardo's reaction a few minutes ago when he heard the news, many people in Tuluá are tallying up, recognizing that they are the ones who were right, and not the reporters or Lieutenant Caravalí.

Those first days no one noticed the great piles of coins and bills that Marcianita must have collected. Hoards of people arrived day after day, night after night, to see the idiots' miraculous cures. Many left cured of their ills, so it mattered little to them how much the idiots made. The idiots reveled not in apparitions, nor spoke of religion or anything of the sort; they simply made use of their powers. At least that is how the thousands who passed daily by their estate at La Rivera understood it. But neither Chuchú, nor the Archbishop, nor the church, nor so many others who thought they saw in the idiots their major competition understood it.

The first to feel the drop in clientele were the Redemptionist fathers in Buga. The miraculous Christ in the basilica, admired and venerated by all residents of the region, had been acquiring a modest importance before the splendor of the Tuluá idiots' miracles. The lines that led up to the tabernacle where the so-often-destroyed-and-as-often-reconstructed-one opened His arms rapidly diminished. The tables for votive candles, which used to run the length and width of the basilica's lateral aisles, were reduced to the main altar, and upon moving them the fathers had to post a notice saying that the health and hygiene of the pilgrims made it necessary to do away with them. The sale of relics, of Brother Champagnat's oil, of water from Guadalajara, of slivers of the soap that the Indian woman was using three centuries before when she found the miraculous image while washing clothes in the river, of all the soapwood rosaries that were made of Saint Peter's tears, everything —the whole miraculous megillah—came to a standstill. For the first time since the day they began to construct the basilica and monastery, the caretaker-father had to spend money from the safe and reduce the shipments of stamps for the missions and funds for the headquarters in Burgos. "The month of anguish," it was called by some lay brothers who were the first to have half of their daily food ration cut out. "The month of skinny minnies," the father superior called it, sending news of the defeat to the central facility. "Satan," screamed Chuchú when she learned of the vacuum in which the Catholic village of Buga had left Our Lord of Miracles. But it was only for one month. Thirty-nine days later, so many buses arrived in Tuluá that the people fit neither in the Ruices' parking lot nor in the few hotels near there, and Buga, always big on hospitality, was converted into the residential center for the pilgrims, and the basilica of Our Lord of Miracles lavishly recovered its former miracle-working status. There was not a pilgrim who would arrive in Tuluá and not go to Buga to see the basilica of Our Lord of Miracles. The thrust of the new miracle working was so great that the Redemptionist fathers were almost penalized by their superior when they refused to read the Archbishop's pastoral letter. But by pretending to be blind or deaf and by sending enormous contributions for the cult and for diocesan expenses, they avoided the peril.

Marcianita also avoided many dangers. However much she continued to toss jasmines at the sick people a few minutes before the divine idiots rose from their seats and stretched out their hands to radiate health, the jasmines she had tried to propagate did not develop with the speed or perfection she desired. She once again had free time while she waited for the jasmines to grow, and she could clean out the empty shelves she had filled with new plants. She ignored the care of the armadillos and dedicated herself to weaving new tunics and brocades for her sons. She made so many and such a variety of styles and colors that since each one had a matching hat of the same material, which the idiots wore while they were on the balcony watching the endless masses of pilgrims file by, many people believed (and the story grew) that there were not two idiots but many more. But they were the same Bartolomé and Ramón Lucio Rodríguez Barona who had been born either shitting in their mother's belly or after her case of German measles. Marcianita made them some very comfortable seats so they could sit and greet the people who passed along the walkway under the balcony, and they, obeying the one who had been directing them like robots for years, would not change their ways for anyone else.

Never before had so many people been seen at their feet. Rather than frightening them, the many days, months, and years of absolute confinement to which Marcianita had subjected them converted them into happy, distant spectators. The faces were constantly changing; very few people returned. No one came close. The balcony was ten feet above ground and Marcianita opened the door to no one and gave no private consultations. The only avenue of communication was through Dr. Fajardo, and the idiots, sufficiently removed from the crowd, found a type of amusement that neither the armadillos nor the jasmines had given them in their fourteen years.

XIV

When her son was four years old, Rocío Jojoa took him to his grandfather's gunpowder factory. Despite the love potions and coffee dregs she had used to read the child's future, he reached an age that according to his Putumayan ancestors was the precise time to steer him toward a profession. He would go to school for as long as they could afford the paper and books. The rest of the time he ought to spend learning the same profession that his grandfather had learned when he arrived from the Sibundoy Valley and was first dazzled by the brilliance of sulfur and the bang of black powder. She had had no more children, but she was not in a position to accord him even the limited educational facilities Tuluá could offer. Not only was he Nemesio Rodríguez's bastard son; because she had been unwilling to divulge the father's identity, he was registered with the notary as the child of an unknown sire.

His grandfather took him in with the same cruel indifference he himself was received with that gray morning when his father had led him by the hand to Timaná Hill and showed him Lake Guamez below. His grandfather had tossed sulfur on a rock, set it off with a firebrand, and with three drops of muriatic acid and potassium permanganate he had revealed a dazzling world to his first grandson born outside of Sibundoy territory.

He showed him compassion if not affection. He taught him to read so he would not have to go to school and suffer the stigma of bastardy. He himself had attended Father Fiori's school with the Capuchin monks of Saint James. Following his teacher, he had moved to Tuluá when the gunpowder factory was founded. As he learned the trade and language, he found among his teacher's books the stories of Sacco and Vanzetti, of the death of Señor Cánovas, and the sacred texts of Bakunin, all in the same language which Father Fiori, in order to protect him from the other Capuchin fathers, had taught him. He had no need, in order for his grandson to learn to speak the Spanish of the government officials, to give him the same calamitous and monotonous classes the priest had offered the grandfather on so many mornings; from the very start he directed him in that strange language that enabled the boy to read the texts of his powdermaker-mentor. No one else in Tuluá spoke the language. As days passed, the child became much more of a recluse than his great-great-grandfather, and a much better powdermaker than his grandfather. Because he had to use Spanish to handle customers and spoke it with his mother every night, he did not forget the language. He turned out to be the spitting image of a Putumayan Indian without ever having learned a word of the Sibundoy dialect of his elders. At the age of ten he loaded rockets for feast days and *novenas* with perhaps greater ease than his teacher. By the time he was eleven he had read about or discovered a new process for the construction of Roman candles. He practiced as much as the powder reserves would allow. He spent entire days at his task, forgetting his reading in search of innovative discoveries. Always at his side, his grandfather, every day seeing less, every day more of a fanatical anarchist.

On his twelfth birthday his grandfather let him dress up on Sundays like the other boys on the block. They closed the powder works and left as gleeful as a grandfather and grandson going off on a fishing trip. Instead of a fishing pole, they carried a packet of concentrated powder, two slow fuses, and a box of matches. These were skillfully wrapped in banana leaves beneath some *pitahayas*. With this package they got on the bus for Buga. Still with it, but without the *pitahayas*, they got off near the basilica of Our Lord of Miracles. The boy asked nothing during the trip. He knew better than his grandfather the explosive power stored in the package, but he did not make the slightest attempt to disobey his orders. They casually went up to the sanctuary of the miraculous Christ. To the pilgrims, the devout old ladies, and the vigilant sacristans they were a couple of Indians with a bundle wrapped in banana leaves. Although years later, immediately following his grandfather's tragic episode, the boy perfected his craft as a powdermaker with veritable impeccability, it was impossible for him to surpass the role he played that afternoon in the basilica of Our Lord . of Miracles.

On his knees, pretending to be the most Catholic and faithful of the pilgrims, the old man remained motionless before the main altar, staring up at the tabernacle ceiling. The boy, tiny like a good Sibundoy, bored, playing the role of the carsick traveler, went to sit down on the prie-dieu at one of the confessionals. He put down his packet, inserted the fuse between the banana leaves, lit his incandescent match as if he were taking out a bonbon, protected himself from view by choosing the darkest confessional, whimpered continuously like a small child calling for his grandfather, appeared at his grandfather's side seeming to interrupt the supplication, and abandoned the atrium of the basilica, almost dragged along by the spitting mad Putumayan Indian. They walked calmly to the bus station, bought their tickets for Tuluá, and were pulling in to San Pedro exactly a half hour after lighting the incandescent match, when a deafening explosion shook the sacred cloister, sending the confessional flying.

At noon the next day the grandfather, impassively following his normal routine, bought a newspaper. He read the details of the explosion, the explanations of the reporters and the Buga police, and the names of the detainees, and then he passed the paper to his grandson, who was engrossed in the fabrication of fireworks for the *novena* of the Immaculate Virgin in the parish of Trujillo.

For neither of the two, not the grandfather (steeped in combat of that sort, in which he had engaged every eleven months for many years) nor the boy (his daring apprentice), did the news cause any greater impression than hearing that their fireworks for the *novena* of God the Son or for the feast of Mary Magdalene turned out to be unsurpassable and that the parish priests would rehire them. During all that time a boundless affection for his grandfather was taking shape in the boy. He cared for the old man as no Sibundoy Indian would have done. Taking care of food, clothing, sleep, and rest for the old man, the boy shared deeply in the life and feelings of Father Fiori's disciple. What he imitated most was his grandfather's dexterity in making powder figurines, respecting his grandfather's hands as much as he revered the man himself. He would not permit him to wash them with the same lye soap that worked so well to remove even impenetrable sulfur stains. For him he created a soap of *chambimbe* seeds which he kept in a large earthen jar within the master powdermaker's reach. He practically walked in his grandfather's footsteps and with time equaled and even exceeded his ability. But he made light of that skill and insisted on recognizing the old man as his master and guide. By playing along with the odd anarchy that his grandfather still persisted in teaching him, he avoided the typical confrontation between professor and pupil.

The old man could not get his grandson to surpass him in this field as well. The difficulty of training, the excessive theoretical burden, the lack of incentives to refine the ideology all kept him at a distinct advantage over his disciple. Ten months after the attempt on the basilica of Our Lord of Miracles in Buga, the pair of anarchists directed their steps toward the cathedral in Palmira. This time they did not carry the explosives wrapped in banana leaves. Unearthing concepts from a collection called *A Treasury for Youth*, which his grandfather had received as payment for a castle of lights he had fashioned for a poor parish priest, the grandson loaded his timer with a charge of smoky black powder. The explosive fit perfectly within a leather-bound Bible, one of those that Nacar Colunga sold house-to-house with a picture of Mexico's Archbishop Garibaldi on the frontispiece. The occasion could not have been more propitious: the ordination of the first Black priest in the archdiocese. They wrapped the Bible simply, in plain paper, to make it look as if they did not want to soil it. They lined up before the cathedral door, and when the bishop decided the offerings of the faithful could be placed on the table, the adolescent mestizo, almost doubled by the weight of such a book, went alone to the table. The crowd of believers carefully watched the worthy gesture of the boy, dressed in his Sunday best but awkwardly bundled up as if wearing two layers of clothing.

While Rocío Jojoa's son carefully deposited the Bible, his grandfather, having already bought the tickets, was waiting for him at the bus station. The timer would allow for only twenty long minutes. The noisy tick-tock would be masked by the choir and the reed organ. The boy would cover the distance quickly. Instead of returning to his place in the pews he marched straight back to the cathedral door and, at a moment when no one could see him, headed for the bus station. Before catching the bus that was passing through, he went to the bathroom and discarded his Sunday clothes, with both the sorrow of an adolescent who has only one outfit and the conviction of a consummate anarchist. He got on the bus, and when it was reaching Amaime, the Bible in the cathedral blew to smithereens, raising a cloud of smoke so huge that the firemen, convinced by the cries and the smoke that there was a blaze, arrived before the police. The shock wave sent some of the medallions left near the Bible flying like shrapnel. The next day's newspaper reported that a very well-dressed mestizo boy had been seen a few minutes before the explosion. Because the clothes were found in the bathroom at the bus station, and given the circumstances, it was supposed that the anarchist was one of the members of a Trotskyite group at the University of the Valle in Cali. No one ever suspected the Putumayan powdermaker, much less his grandson, who seldom appeared in public and even less frequently waited on customers.

A day and a half after this exploit, nevertheless, something the Putumayan called an error (but his daughter read in the coffee grinds as punishment from the gods) put the grandson in charge of the powder factory. While packing a charge of nitrous powder into the head of a statue of the Child Mary of Caloto for the fireworks display on the eve of her feast day, the old man either squeezed the cartridge too tightly or else did not measure the acid accurately. His hands, the skilled artisan's hands that his grandson venerated, flew to pieces. The explosion was not very great, but very little was left of his prodigious hands. Three whole fingers flew halfway across the patio where, fortunately, the statue was being prepared. The old man was left with only stumps which, considering all the options and well aware that he would draw the attention of the authorities if he went to the hospital, he took care of himself by burning off what was left of them against his daughter's hot cookstove. The flesh on the old man's two arms sizzled. The grandson could not tolerate the spectacle or the pain. Crazed, he went to buy penicillin for his grandfather at the pharmacy. The Putumayan healed with time, but Rocío Jojoa's son could no longer evade his fate. In charge of the powder works, filling orders, and practically supporting his family, he seemed older than his thirteen years.

He never lost the hope of seeing the old Putumayan Indian restored. He was left after the cookstove cauterization with three fingers on the left hand and a stump with tiny beginnings of fingers on the right, and the boy often dreamed that his grandfather sprouted new limbs like a tree. Absolutely unbelieving in the miraculous powers of the saints and relics the priests brought in sympathy for the one whose powder had brightened their feasts and novenas, he grew hopeful again only at the prospect of turning to Marcianita's idiots.

At first, for almost six months, he was one of that spectacle's opponents. He did not go to La Rivera and only learned of the details because his grandfather would meticulously read to him from the newspapers while he worked double time, filling in for the amputee. The old man was even less likely to show up out there. He was very aware that his mutilation was incurable, but no other illness bothered him. He took pleasure in the news because he saw that the competition with the church's miraculous saints was making an impact. Maybe because of that awareness, or simply because of his handicap, he did not direct his anarchistic battery against them.

The grandson, on the other hand, never once thought of the negative effect the pair of idiots was having on the church and the cult of miraculous saints. From refusing to recognize their powers at first and confusing them with charlatans, he came to respect them as the months passed and finally to idolize them as the ones who could restore his grandfather's lost faculties. Refraining from further anarchistic activities after the one in the Palmira cathedral, he was drawn a little closer to a respect for religion. The Putumayan Jojoa's manual debility did the rest. For several months the grandson thought it over carefully, and it finally became an obsession. His mother, reading the coffee grounds, sensed it. Since she felt that her husband's other sons should not meet *her* son, she took it upon herself to prevent his going to

Marcianita's the two or three times she saw him intent upon taking his grandfather. She never mentioned to her son who his father was, and since her father had always already left for work when Nemesio Rodríguez arrived, *he* never knew. But the grandson's desire to see the master restored began to grow, to grow along with the tales of the idiots' marvels. So yesterday, when Tuluá decided to go in great waves to Marcianita Baron's house, Nemesio Jojoa, after spending the whole night measuring his thoughts as if they were doses of highly explosive gunpowder, overcame his mother's prohibitions and convictions and finally decided to appear this morning before the idiots.

XV

When Chuchú, decked out in black with a purple ribbon at her hem, arrived at the office of the Bishop of Palmira and his *tulueño* secretary Father Gómez, she was received with the same peevishness that must have been shown to Mary Magdalene. The first seven buses of the uninterrupted stream that would arrive on pilgrimages from that day forward lined up in the streets of Tuluá, causing a traffic jam and an unprecedented blossoming of Tuluá's commercial and touristic capacities to such an extent that tomorrow, when all this may perhaps have ceased, many will see the end not of a time of prosperity, but of the mere possibility of subsistence.

Since the arrival of those buses, and even before, the road to La Rivera had been lined from one end to the other with little stands like the Ruices', which sold Coca-Cola and coffee and later grew into restaurants and souvenir shops. The pictures that Oswaldo López, who came from Cali, took with a telephoto lens were reproduced, and the pair of idiots, seated on their chairs or with their hands open an instant before giving off the light, were sold framed, wholesale, retail, on multicolored bottles, on gilded copper bracelets, and in miniscule telescopes. There was not a single pilgrim who would not make the long three-block journey from the highway to the miraculous house and who would not buy at least one of these photographs; with time, the image of the pair of miraculous idiots was displacing that of the Sacred Heart, exalted in every home in Colombia. The prices varied according to the gullibility of the shopper or the incurability of his illness. They never ran out of pictures because the ladies of the magazine *Experiences in Cali* stole the negative from the photographer López, and what they did not make selling the tacky publication they made with the negative. Every Monday, chattering incessantly among themselves as they always were, even while embroiled in their most intimate tasks, they frequented the pilgrims' way. From stand to stand, from restaurant to restaurant, from sale to sale, reeking from smoke from the frying pans and from the foul odors of the numerous latrines, they peddled the photographs of the pair of idiots, demanding immediate payment. It was a fabulous business, much greater than that of the sale of jasmines, but nothing compared to the business that grew out of the use of toilets.

First the Ruices' in-laws set up behind the parking lot a wooden outhouse that one month later was converted into the site for unloading invalids who could not be carried. With the disproportionate growth in the number of pilgrims, one latrine was not enough; in time it constituted a feat to be able to walk past certain places; the smell was so intense that people were guided by it to take care of their necessities and to deposit more waste in the same place. A majestic idea occurred to Don Belisario Concha, who had sold toilets his whole life. He bought a small lot in the area of Don Hernando Rivera's house, about a hundred meters above the beginning of the road, and set up a septic system so complete, with running water direct from the aqueduct, that the neighbor had no choice but to move out of his house and convert every last closet into another collection of toilets. Every "sitting" was worth a *peso*, a urination, fifty *centavos*, a hand wash, twenty. In time, Don Hernando built a special bathhouse on the back patio and charged five *pesos* for a shower. Since no matter how early the pilgrims arrived (only last night, as if they foresaw today's splendid spectacle, they arrived continuously from the end of the six o'clock showing), they always had to wait through at least one show, there was no one who did not make use of Don Hernando Rivera's sanitary services or the porcine privies of the stands, restaurants, and stores that line the road from Tuluá to La Rivera. Attendance has been so great in front of the idiots' house that whether it rains, thunders, or swelters, there is a crowd awaiting the appearance of the pair of miracle workers who each day cure more and more people, causing amazement in those who benefit, ire in those overlooked, and protestations among those who never manage to come. But persons like Chuchú are turned into enemies.

In spite of everything, these enemies have been in the minority. Those who have not been able to come to Tuluá in these years of glory and curation have relied on their friends or neighbors for photographs of the miraculous idiots, a little jasmine plant, the extract of perfume that is sold in almost as great a quantity as the pictures, or bits of dirt, lawn, or air from the surroundings. People have arrived out of nowhere. Some brought little boxes in which to carry off pieces of the gravel that had to be spread on what was La Rivera meadow. So many people trampled it and so many downpours fell that the time came when it was converted into an incomparable, stinking mudhole, awaiting a solitary ray of sun that sometimes would scarcely take off the chill. Others would carry bottles with stoppers they would remove to collect the air from the region of the house, air corrupted by the presence of thousands of pilgrims attracted by the story in *The Press* to the effect that air brought in bottles from the miraculous site of the idiots had cured all the inmates in the Manizales tuberculosis sanitarium. A few have been content to come at night, pass with difficulty through the area, and depart without witnessing the miraculous act. They are not capable of tolerating the daily congestion or the waiting until the next day, having to rest against one of the few unoccupied trees, on one of the cement benches that the Rotary Club placed at the entrance by the curve at the Ruices', or in one of the buses that line up in the special parking areas on the shoulder of the road to Tuluá. But every one of those who bring boxes or bottles carries off pictures, perfume, or jasmine plants. Those who merely show up and see the place to satisfy an eternal curiosity, all—absolutely all—are bearers of a profound respect for the site, for the idiots, and for the different stories that circulate about them.

The interpretations that arose regarding their miraculous powers almost always came from the mouths of the first cured or from the reporters and photographers who saw the cures of Brother Andrés and Tille Uribe's parrot. No one could interview Inesita González because she either refused an audience or answered in nothing but monosyllables. Fourteen months had to pass, people had to forget that the most prodigious cure, the first one, had been that of crownless Queen Inesita, before one of the many foreigners who came as reporters could turn her again into a legend, and his version of the story into a true hecatomb. During those fourteen months, reporters came from the world over. Japanese with special lights to peer through the splendor that the idiots produced in their cures. Austrians with super-powerful lenses to capture on film the magical eleven o'clock act. Bulgarians and Romanians collecting data with which to make a movie. North Americans spending mountains of money to film and interview those cured. Frenchmen measuring the intensity of the voices that repeatedly cried miracle. Italians climbing into giddy helicopters or digging tunnels to enter the idiots' house, every day more impenetrable. No one, however, could interview Inesita González, because she, radiant with beauty, always had a timely refusal on her lips. It took a Swiss reporter—accompanied by the dean of the Lausanne Medical School, whom Hayer had already tried to convince at the beginning of the miraculous cycle—to be able to interview her, and her answers were transformed into limitless pandemonium for the ignorant adolescents of Colombia, America, and a major part of the world—as far as the news could reach.

From Switzerland they wrote to Inesita's brother Toño, a graduate of their medical college. They did not stay in his house because they wanted to avoid converting his home into a hotel for relatives eager to meet the miraculous idiots; but they were invited there for lunch, and Inesita granted them a long interview, telling them everything only she and Marcianita knew. They wrote it all down, and when—twenty days later—the news came out in banner headlines in the national *Press*, and was repeated in newspapers almost all over the world, a wave of adolescent masturbations began to perplex psychiatrists, psychologists, parents, and headmasters. There was not a boy who reached the age of feeling his masculinity erect who did not try to duplicate the idiots' powers. Since she explained that when the idiots performed their curative masturbations their cries had risen in tone until they were lost and only their gestures remained, the boys who read the news transformed by translation from the original French were caught in their onanistic exercises by the explosive cry they would let loose at the culminating moment. There was no father, mother, or older brother who did not put his ear to the bathroom door every time his son or adolescent brother would shut himself in to take care of his necessities, to see if the millennial cry imitative of the idiots would come from there too. A case became known of some students who, at the time of their examinations, would masturbate right in class, sure of summoning sufficient mental strength to pass the exam. It was a bigger fad than Superman or Tarzan. Everyone wanted to try, and since many said that after masturbating they truly felt an increased mental capacity and an unprecedented ability to surmount unfavorable circumstances, the wave of masturbations grew and grew until it reached unsuspected proportions.

Priests in their sermons, bishops in their pastoral letters, doctors on television, parents at mealtimes, headmasters at school assemblies, professors in class—everyone who could speak joined in the campaign to quell the uprisings. The dangers of masturbation were brought to light. They were exaggerated to such an extent that it was said that masturbation was much more dangerous than marijuana, which is harmless at any rate. Only now, months after Inesita broke the news with astonishing candor, has the fad diminished a little, but only in the sense that the masturbants no longer scream with such ferocity.

Things were as they had been with the pair of miraculous idiots since the beginning. Breathtaking. Brutally breathtaking. The shops and restaurants sprouted up almost overnight. The ordinances against driving cars on the road to La Rivera, the parking lots on the shoulder of the highway to Tuluá, the gravel on the patio, all came about too quickly. It is not known if the one who gave the orders was the mayor, the chief of police, or Dr. Fajardo, but just a couple of months ago Marcianita, tired of seeing so many people up to their knees in that damp sand that was spread in front of her house every two weeks, canceled the appearances of the idiots for a week while an asphalt surface was laid at her command, paid for with the platterfuls of money collected. Tuluá then knew that the directrix of the project resided in the remote emptiness of the idiots' house. It was perhaps the valve that opened the floodgates that will barely close today. The sale of jasmines on the seventh day almost set it off, but at that time there were so many people cured by the adolescent pair's miracles that they either did not believe the denunciations or turned a deaf ear, because it was worth spending a little on jasmines to have such undeniable miracle working.

Marcianita got her own way, and not by using such unscrupulous ladies as those who sold the photos; she had every one of the stands from her house to the highway, starting with the Ruices', which was the first and only permanent one, sell all at once the one thousand three hundred fifty-nine jasmine plants she had carefully planted and cultivated ever since she had the brilliant idea of selling a memento of her sons' miraculous powers. From those plants the shopkeepers took cuttings. When these ran out, they came up with more jasmine plants, and whether they were brought from Manizales, Medellín or Barranquilla, from the banana zone or the remote Guajira, they were sold at the stands with the claim that they were cuttings from the plants that Marcianita had raised and from which came the little white branches that the idiots waved at the pilgrims just before every appearance of the light. Many made extracts from the leaves and flowers. Others made perfumes, and there was even someone who made medicinal balms. Some reporters denounced the growing business, others penned warnings of deceit, but no one paid much heed. The cures attributed to the idiots' light, to the photographs, to the bottles of air, and to dirt from La Rivera were so numerous and of such magnitude that those who issued the warnings were finally denounced as incredulous hypocrites. The crutches, the artificial limbs, the canes, the oddest but most representative elements, came to cover even the last open patch on the wall of Marcianita's house, and it became necessary to build a shed to store all the implements of all the paralytics or invalids who were cured simply by passing under the ray of the idiots' light, by the foot of the balcony, or in the distance by the curve at the Ruices'.

Many were really cured, but others were fanatics who through the power of suggestion were led to announce their cures when they were hardly a remote illusion. The cries of miracle blanketed the crowd, the crutches were left in the designated shed, and the invalid left on the shoulders of the crowd, only to have to buy another pair of crutches as soon as he was put down.

The most hopeless case was that of one Jaime Córdoba, a lawyer with a degree from the Javeriana, who, because of his bowing so often to the ladies, developed a tumor on his spine, to the point that his closely cropped head was replicated just a little above his buttocks. The intelligence of two heads did nothing to arrest the paralysis. He arrived one morning, supported by a pair of crutches and convinced by the ladies selling photographs (to whom he bowed until he kissed their feet) that the idiots would cure him. Someone had shown him the picture of Marcianita closing the window, and since her duplicate head was just like his, except that Marcianita's was near her head and his was by the buttocks, he blindly believed he would be cured. He was accompanied by his only remaining friend, by some of the unscrupulous ladies, and by the photographer López, contracted by him specifically to provide authentic proof of his cure.

They arrived at three-thirty in the afternoon. Since he was crippled, they drove him in as far as the Ruices' parking lot. The line of pilgrims anxious to pass by the idiots at the nine o'clock viewing reached as far as the curve by the Ruices'. They were a little farther back, with a view of the miraculous house. López, the photographer, took quite a few snapshots of the line of pilgrims. Still a friend of the thieves, he had come in spite of the theft. He left the others to go to the shed where, draped across cots, the many incurables waited for the idiots' healing ray of light. He caught grimaces, abnormalities, tragedies in his Yashica. Logically enough, the one he photographed most was Córdoba. Since he had two heads, one would always turn out all right. The two ladies who accompanied him and his friend chatted with him, encouraged him, helped him hold up his crutches, painted for him a glorious future, and convinced him he would be completely cured.

Oswaldo López, inspired by the idea of vengeance, did the same when he was not busy taking pictures. They waited for six hours until the moment when the balcony doors opened and the tiny figures of the pair of idiots appeared, wrapped in their brocades, their heads covered by the essential caps, and their eyes cast timidly at the crowd before them. They sat on their chairs making faces or playing with each other in an ongoing joke about those below and filled the two hours watching the file of thousands of pilgrims—sick people, healthy people, curiosity seekers, and victims of incurable birth defects, contagious ailments, or unsatisfied needs. Córdoba's group—López and the ladies—passed before them ten minutes before eleven. When the idiots got up to open their hands and create the light, eleven minutes later, the group was already leaving the walkway they had followed. At that moment the crowd stopped shuffling, stood motionless wherever they might be, awaiting the culminating effect. López made such an effort to persuade Córdoba that the ladies, more convinced than the ailing one, ended up believing him. Instead of taking photographs of the idiots, he turned his lens on the faces of the two ladies. The curative light rays appeared, and he snapped the shutter of his camera, both before and after. At the same time he continued talking and, aided by his neighbors who were impressed by the faith of the group that hoped to see cured the one with crutches, he succeeded in convincing Córdoba that he *was* cured before the miraculous rays had ceased. He took away the crutches; the neighbors threw Córdoba up on the shoulders of the throng in front of the house shouting miracle, miracle, miracle. And Córdoba, convinced of his cure, abandoned his crutches and left on the shoulders of the multitude.

López only clicked the shutter on his camera and a month later, when Córdoba was still paralyzed, unable to walk even with crutches owing to injuries suffered by being carried aloft, he organized a show with the pictures of the "cured" man and of the ladies who had stolen from him the negative of the picture of the idiots.

The case was ignored, even by Lieutenant Caravalí. Those who were not cured—and there were many—did not appear in *The Press* or in the infinite accounts of those healed by the pair of idiots, much less in the final tally included in every edition of Dr. Fajardo's book. Córdoba's case was made known through the tales the photographer López invented to publicize his show, but it was taken mostly as a joke, and no one blamed the idiots. There were quite a few cases like this: many crutches, wax hands, and canes that were left in the shed were needed again by their owners, who, deceived by a delirious crowd, had discarded them forever. There were those who went into debt not only for the cost of the journey to Tuluá, but also for a new pair of crutches, because the desire to be cured and the magnificent cries of miracle, miracle, miracle had led them to toss their crutches into the shed.

But if those cases served only to increase the victims' debts or to delude for a while those presumed cured, the most dramatic and complicated cases for the authorities of Tuluá, and for the pilgrims who sometimes were not prepared for the spectacle and passed out by the dozens, were those cases of seriously ill people who came in desperation to find health, only to encounter death. Sclerotic septuagenarians who suffered their final stroke in the crowd. Advanced cancer victims, weakened from standing in one place for three hours, who dropped dead in their tracks. Perpetual asthmatics who wheezed in the great void, breathing contaminated air. In general, none of those deceased brought assistants or identification. They were so bent on gambling all or nothing that they went to the idiots prepared to die. First the municipality of Tuluá and later Dr. Fajardo's hospital (whose endless funds are only now suspected to have been donated by Marcianita) took charge of their burials. The crowd did not pick them up, and many cadavers remained for hours and hours, until the pilgrims had stopped filing by, before the Red Cross could come to carry them off.

The spectacle grew alarmingly, but much more alarming were those with contagious or unsightly diseases. Lepers with their limbs gnawed away by the disease, evil-smelling ulcers, rags soaked in bloody pus; consumptives drowning in coughs and aphrodisiac death rattles, vomiting blood with every effort; splotchy-faced syphilitics, panting with their inflamed hearts; women with terminal breast cancer, wearing transparent clothing, easily removed at the moment of the miraculous light; deformed pilgrims, with three hands, without arms, with only one leg, simultaneously frightened and enlightened; arthritics with their fingers gnarled like the number three, their joints deformed. They all came without anyone's making room for them, suffering a crisis of conscience, or having the Red Cross orderlies remove them.

The respect the location and the miraculous idiots infused in them blanketed all without exception. Men and women, boys and girls, healthy and ill, the faithful and the non-believing, those with more chance of being infected than of being cured have filed by, keeping an appointment with their destinies, with the absurd chance of recovery.

No one has been cured since the supernatural light of the pair of idiots was extinguished, but people continue to believe that the photos, the jasmines, or any other objects in which the miraculous ray of light lodges possess the same curative powers. In the living rooms of innumerable Colombian houses, objects touched by the beam of light warrant a special place and compete with rosaries from Fátima, water from Lourdes, or relics from the Holy Land.

But Marcianita's miraculous bazaar has had enemies as well as friends. They are not those prevented from being cured or those who at some time passed by the supernatural balcony but failed to derive the expected benefit. They are frenetic partisans estranged from human power, those of rationalist vigor, and—what few have been able to understand—some fanatical owners of dogs, which have been barred from entry since the first days.

The dawn when Isaac Nessim confused the dogs' uproar with the warning of a Tokyo-like earthquake, Marcianita noticed that something strange emanating from her vital innards was disturbing them. When the Swissman Hayer departed healed she rapidly confirmed her impression, and the day after the cure of Tille Uribe's parrot she hung a notice next to the schedule: NO DOGS ALLOWED. It seemed strange to many people, but the prohibition did not stop those who took the bazaar as a Satanic sequence. There have not been many, five or six at the most, but they have all come away with dead dogs. The rest of the dogs of Tuluá do not venture within three blocks, despite the abundance of scraps there. If there had been more, surely the scandal and the explanations would have come from the enemies of the miracle working, but since none of the five or six dog owners has talked with reporters or protested the deaths, the matter has remained closed to all but a handful of observers. No one has investigated the case, and those like Lieutenant Caravalí, who used it, have suffered the consequences.

But without a doubt the two greatest enemies of the miraculous bazaar have been the Bishop of Palmira and the newspaper columnist Pangloss, both coincidentally dog owners. The two have been nourished by the Satanic tales of Chuchú, shrouded in her black gown.

From the first instant when she saw Marcianita Barona appear in the distance on her balcony and she took it into her head that this was a sacrilegious parody of the Sunday appearances of the Holy Father on the balcony of Saint Peter's in Rome, Chuchú decided to collect all the data and evidence to the effect that Satan haunted that site, the idiots, and their mama. As if it were a trial against the heretics of the colony, she believed herself the embodiment of the Inquisition and followed a corresponding scenario to the letter. She did not have to dress like Don Juan of Mañozga, much less run naked through the streets, as the Cartagena inquisitor had done. She maintained her custom of collecting requests for heavenly intercessions, but at the same time she would ruminate about the way to present to the bishop an airtight case, one so well founded as to produce within minutes an explosive excommunication. It did not cross her mind to communicate with the beyond to intercept Marcianita. Well she knew that the moment her signature appeared at the head of a letter, the avalanche would be immediate. She consulted with her confessor, still maintaining enough of a conscience so as not to injure Marcianita and her idiots without first justifying herself. It did not matter that she could clearly see how in the end they were going to drive Chuchú out of business; in any case, whether or not there was a legitimate rationale, her scruples would not permit such an outcome. But not only did the attempt at an inquisition seem right to the Franciscan father, who was fearful of losing clientele at his temple; the next day he filled out the protest petition form based on the community's usual concordat. Chuchú copied it with drawing paper and an eyebrow pencil, and before sending the first letter to the bishop, she—as the only female monk in Colombia—turned to the local director of the community, the venerable Father Uribe, magnificent rector of the University of San Buenaventura. He answered her at once, telling her she had his full support to continue the investigation intended to prove that the demon was behind it all, and that as of that day he had directed his Holy Office to contact his superior in Rome, advising him of the gravity of the situation in his beloved Tuluá.

When the many pilgrimages were under way and the road to La Rivera was turned into a gigantic bazaar where they sold smoked meats, portraits of the idiots, essence of jasmine, cuttings of that same plant, bottled air from the idiots' environs, relics touched by the supernatural pair's luminous rays, and even chances to enter into the heavenly realm, Chuchú addressed her first letter to the bishop and sent the first photographs to the columnist Pangloss. Delaying his response considerably, Monsignor did not answer Chuchú right away, but Pangloss, thirsty for material for his rationalist column, cut loose a cry to high heaven and dubbed the La Rivera pilgrims lunatics. Condemning those who scurried there as fools, he showed how it was all nothing more than a product of popular mawkishness and a consequence of Catholic fetishism. At first neither the newspaper nor the readers paid any attention, but after he had insisted on the theme week after week, and Brother Andrés had written an article attesting to his cure by the pair of idiots, and the whole superstitious world had bought copies right and left, he launched a frontal attack, calling the "divine idiots" swindlers, Marcianita a schizophrenic, and the pilgrims a bunch of suckers. Chuchú almost died of joy. She was one of the few people who saved that afternoon issue of *The Spectator*. At five in the afternoon, before the idiots spread their miraculous rays over the pilgrims, all the copies of the paper that reached Tuluá were piled at the entrance to the Ruices' store. And before six they were placed within sight of the idiots, who instantly seared them with their magical rays. The reporters permanently assigned to the supernatural epicenter spread the news by teletype. Pangloss stopped writing for a month, did not deal with the theme of the idiots when he began to write again, and although recently he has again expressed similar views, he does so in a way that at least maintains a scientific façade. When Chuchú learned that the papers were burning, she carefully cut out the article and, retelling the story in her own words, submitted it to the rigors of the anti-heresy memorandum she was compiling. When Monsignor's answer arrived, she had the dossier ready. She took it in an immense folder to the bishop's office, waited as long as was necessary to see Father Gómez, and upon being received in the brilliant hall she sank to her knees, kissed the archbishop's ring, and like a disco-dancing marionette, bopping from one end of the room to the other, she tossed out everything she thought might convince the dignitary. It did not work out quite as planned, but the bishop's immediate reaction was much more clamorous than Chuchú had expected.

Dressed with full episcopal pomp, under a canopy carried by six gentlemen of the Holy Sepulchre of the Palmira Cathedral, attended by Father Phanor, and looking solemnly at the curious people who returned his glance a hundredfold, Monsignor appeared in the vicinity of the idiots' house. He could not get as near as he had hoped because no sooner had he arrived at the curve by the Ruices' and seen the idiots framed by their balcony than, as if they felt a sudden urge to rush to the bathroom, they got up from their seats, opened their hands as they would at the appointed hour, worked the miracles there was time for, and closed the balcony doors. Forthwith, a nameless downpour ensued which muddied everything right up to the episcopal canopy. The bishop was saved from falling into the mudhole because, protected by the canopy, he was able to reach the Ruices' store where they, being old-fashioned Catholics, received him with countless honors until the rain stopped.

Many criticized the action of the Bishop of Palmira, calling it ridiculous, unnecessary, and impulsive, but the cries were soon stifled. One pastoral letter, which not even the Viceregal Archbishop had been capable of issuing, left the office of the Bishop of Palmira. Marcianita and her idiots were excommunicated from the Catholic religion they had never belonged to, and the site of the pilgrimages was declared a place of damnation and a seat of Satan. It was the first of three letters the Episcopal See dedicated to the idiots, all equal in their vacuousness.

The Church has not cured us, replied Brother Andrés in a newspaper column. His superiors admonished him, forbade him from writing again, but thousands and thousands of Colombians agreed with him; rather than serving as a prohibition, the warning caused more and more people to come to La Rivera and appear before the miraculous idiots.

The call to order by the Archbishop of Bogotá and the Primate of Colombia in his sermon on the seven words of Good Friday did not work. Or if it did, it served only to incite revolutionary ferment among the priests and to broadcast the image of Father Hurtado Gálviz ranting at the top of his lungs on the radio and television, in the newspapers, and from any available soapbox that the idiots were saints, chaste and pure like no one else, and that La Rivera could well be another Lourdes because miracles were not the exclusive province of civilized Europe. He was a gratuitous defender of miracle working. Marcianita never received him in her seclusion; her communication with her father's brotherhood had always been nil, and she was not going to change for just any opportunist who happened along. But without a doubt, the newsboys' exploitation of Father Hurtado's attitude and the endless harangues he delivered before the radio microphones raised the idiots' level of affluence and success to even greater heights.

From all of Colombia came voices of support, from the clergy itself, through Father Hurtado. Since he was from the diocese of Cali and not from Palmira, he was not under the Bishop-Inquisitor's jurisdiction, but Chuchú did succeed in punishing him. On more than one occasion, helped by an awl she hid in the sleeve of her dress-habit, she approached the pick-up he drove to Tuluá and slashed its tires to shreds. Other times she planted tacks in their path, and the day she was able to get close to him, she surreptitiously stained his white soutane with a perfume bottle full of black ink.

Clamorously applauded, Father Hurtado was a raging success. The idiots assumed the position of gods and shed the guise of medicasters which the media had previously assigned them. Were it not for the waves of masturbations that overran America, Father Hurtado would have supported them to the end. Inesita's sole affirmation that the idiots had worked their cure by masturbating before her made Father Hurtado's theory fall flat. Since he based it on the pair of idiots' purity and chastity, such an insinuation made him appear resoundingly ridiculous. He closed his trap and did not return to Tuluá. And even though he did not write a single word against them, his unexpected silence was taken for what it really was: a manifestation of repentance for his error.

Marcianita rested in seclusion. Through all the months of miracles, of daily appearances on the balcony, the most dramatic moments occurred during the time of Father Hurtado. She knew that sooner or later she would have to receive him because he was without a doubt the greatest defender of her ideals and her powers, but she continued firm in her conviction that her only contact with the outside world should be Dr. Fajardo. Her private life had been scarcely modified. Everything else was adjusted to fit in with the schedule of public appearances. They stopped caring for the armadillos, forgot about Diego Hayer, hermetically sealed the doors and windows, no longer breathed in the green meadows of the surroundings, and limited themselves to strolls on the jasmine patio. While her idiots presided over the multitudes of pilgrims from the balcony, she embroidered their suits, which they never wore twice in the same month. Her hump bent her skeleton to unforeseen extremes until Dr. Fajardo sent her enormous quantities of vitamins, together with the receipts of her consignments, to bolster her fragile constitution and the idiots' hardiness.

They continued to eat as if ingesting still another meal were the only thing that mattered to them. On not one of those days were they ever sick or weary. They spent twenty-two months, day after day, healing thousands of people and watching endless processions of incurables, curiosity seekers, fussy agonizers, reporters, and photographers. All they did was watch. Marcianita spoke with no one, other than with Dr. Fajardo three or four times. Through letters and written communiqués she maintained contact with the outside; compelled to continue her sons' miraculous work with no sense of the ultimate endpoint, she seemed to be obsessed. Actually, sensing the end was near, she was driven by hypersensitivity. She did not know to what extent her idiots were inexhaustible fountains of wealth, and she often claimed to feel tempted to travel for three or four weeks, with all expenses paid by Brazilian public corporations, Indian maharajas, chiefs of state, or Swiss hospitals. The power of her sons' luminous rays was immeasurable and incomparable. There was no precedent for such a power, and no text indicated how long the miracles could go on working. Often she was assaulted by the idea that her sons were marionettes. Or that they were Martians and she had never really had sons. She finally accepted the idea, quite correct from her standpoint, that the Martian was Nemesio Rodríguez, who had impregnated her and then departed for his world forever. It seemed strange to her that, as much as her sons' miracles were known worldwide, there were no signs of life from the magical idiots' papa. Either the sea had swallowed him up or death had come to him very early. Perhaps that is why she found consolation in the hope that her sons' powers would last forever, and for months on end she forgot about the possibility of their depletion.

Tuluá, in the meantime, was transformed from a quiet town into a tourist attraction. It was saved from the avalanche because La Rivera was on the outskirts and few people, in pursuit of the trail of miracles, passed through the village streets either beforehand or afterwards. Since there was an unspoken agreement not to build hotels or to turn homes into boarding houses, the new faces that were seen within the city limits were generally relatives of the inhabitants from times past who came to see the idiots. The sixty or seventy buses that arrived daily from all parts of Colombia and America stayed no longer than necessary. Those that arrived during the night filled the main highway or the area around the road to La Rivera, and there they would wait, with their passengers aboard, for the victorious dawn and the curative rays of light. Some who came from afar would stay in Buga. That town, built on guile, with its miraculous Christ who was losing clientele, the sale of sweets along the highway, and its crystalline fountains and fruit juices, was the one that managed to carry off the lion's share of the whole miraculous process; and when the twenty-two months were over and the number of cured people from Colombia and the world was beyond calculation, Buga seemed not to shrink but rather to grow and grow, like an inexhaustible cascade.

During those months, the bishops issued three pastoral letters; *The Press* fought the miracle working; Chuchú continued to send reminders to all the columnists, to the World Health Organization in Geneva, to the Pan American Union in Washington, to the Ministry of Health in Bogotá, and to the Departmental Secretary of Hygiene; but in spite of all this and the many enemies of the prodigious pair of idiots, the crowd rallied every day in greater numbers. Cures were so abundant that Marcianita Barona, revitalized by Father Hurtado's praises, with the wave of masturbations forgotten and the main square paved as far as the curve by the Ruices', consolidated her powers and began to pave the way for the end of her existence and the eternal glory of her idiots.

XVI

Since seven last night the dogs have been barking as much as they did that early morning when Isaac Nessim confused their protests with an earthquake warning. The disturbance ran rampant until a few minutes ago, but few people actually heard it. Since half of Tuluá took to the streets and the other half undertook a maddening pilgrimage to the idiots, no one has paid much attention to the uproar, much less to the gray mare that appeared out of nowhere in the Boyacá Park when the bells chimed eight.

In spite of the specific prohibition against animals on paved streets, there are those who believe the mare flew from the Abad's ancestral mansion, where, progress notwithstanding, animals are still kept. The only one who noted anything unusual was Pacho Montalvo, one of Don Jesús Sarmiento's cowboys, who, bent over by years and gray hairs, and seated on one of the park benches watching the beast's strange appearance, recognized the mare he had chased for a whole night with ropes and muriatic acid. He has not dared tell anyone for fear they would re-commit him to the Cali insane asylum, where they had put him for staring at the sun; but, ever on the alert, early last night he called the district police so a few agents would come to restrain the beast which, according to him, was ruining the plants and lawn of the Boyacá Park.

It was a spectacle similar to the one he participated in with Don Jesús's other cowboys. Only two policemen came from the squadron of carabineers they brought after Caravalí's departure, but they struggled so hard and so in vain to lasso the animal that Pacho Montalvo decided it was the same beast. The dogs kept on barking madly and the mare ran incessantly about the park, always evading the policemen's threatening maneuvers. When she stopped she looked broodingly for Manuela Barona's old house, sniffed despondently at the door and walls, and returned to her repeated trotting about.

Witnesses to the spectacle asserted that the mare did not move from the side of Marcianita's house, but the two policemen and Pacho Montalvo saw her race alarmingly round and round the Boyacá Park. At ten the carabineers decided to desist, as did the mare. Slowly, with the gait of a coach horse, the beast headed down the streets she had not yet traversed. Pacho Montalvo, exhausted, did not follow her, preferring to go to sleep. He had no reason to go up to the idiots, and there was no way for him to connect one thing to the other. He had simply seen the gray mare again, and she had again avoided being caught by the police. Smelling from afar all the people closing in on her, retracing every block covered, trying to find a certain house by its scent, she continued her reconnaissance of the town. In two places she managed to smell something that set her to trembling, but either the scent turned out to be false or very weak, or it did not suit her purpose. The first opportunity was in front of old Dr. Uribe's house. Passing by the first time, she quivered from head to foot, but then she lost contact. Returning to where she had been, she recognized a scent and stopped short. The dogs barked desperately, drowning in a single uproar. She was about to trot over to Tille Uribe's door when the parrot screeched at the top of its lungs, "The ship came in, the ship, the ship, the ship," and kept repeating itself incessantly. Either the mare got frightened or the parrot's racket put her off the scent. She went by again but no longer sensed anything. She continued her search, street by street.

Those who shuttled between La Rivera and the city had no time to notice the mare that sniffed about so stealthily. Nor did she have time to stop for them; confused by the sensation at the parrot's house, she hunted for the same smell at other doors. With so much running in circles, she passed by Nina Pérez's house, where the gathered people overflowed the doors and windows, joking and celebrating, happy and riotous. It was very hard for her to get close, and if her forelock had not stood on end, she would not have strode along this block. Feinting, pretending to be Chucho Zafra's silly mare, she approached the door through which the most people were spilling out. She did so gingerly, but scarcely had she drawn near, shaking from head to foot for having found what she was hunting for, when she had to retreat. Nina Pérez, rising slowly but steadily, with a strong beat and an attentive audience, began to sing, "The boat is leaving, leaving with the fisherman." It was just as it had been with the parrot: the feelings were lost and the mare had no choice but to trot up the street, behind the pilgrims on their way to La Rivera. She smelled everyone from a distance, trying to home in on the key scent, but with the parrot repeating his phrase or Nina singing or the dogs barking, she found the task impossible.

Finally she arrived at the entrance to the road to La Rivera, where the human ants that pressed forward absolutely blocked her way. She stopped near the bus parking lot and watched from there for the least congested moment in order to enter the ant hill easily. All night long, amidst the distant barking of Tuluá's dogs, there was not a free instant for the mare to approach. In the wee hours, tired of being shut out, she followed her intuition and leaped one of the wire fences around the stands along the road. She trotted as far as she could, jumped another fence, still another, and arrived at Hernando Rivera and Belisario Concha's urinals. There she encountered brick walls and had to detour to the south, clear three more fences, and turn again in the same direction in which the human ant hill flowed. About fifty meters from the Ruices' house, she smelled something that disturbed her. From one of the back gardens of the stands she had passed, almost from the stand itself, came the unmistakable scent. She stopped, perked up her ears, made certain of the odor, and cautiously headed toward the garden. The smell was that of a jasmine plant in full bloom. She managed to see it from afar and, crazed, she tried to jump the bamboo fence that had been put up to protect the plants. She did not notice that someone was there, and when she tried to jump in to eat the flowers, an old insomniac with a staff cried out, "It's going, it's going, it's going..." and the mare experienced the same frustration she had been feeling all night.

She walked. She stopped before the great concentration of humanity at the foot of Marcianita's house in the early hours. There was no way she could close in, and while she was trying, looking for an entrance, dawn overtook her. She humbly bent her legs and, sprawled like any old mule, she swallowed her impotence alongside thousands of pilgrims awaiting the opening of the balcony doors. The dogs continued to bark, but the people made such a din or were so used to the noise that they paid no attention. The mare could do no more; the light of day destroyed her sense of smell and the best she could do was wait for nightfall to renew her search.

She found a place from which to watch Marcianita's house and the movements of the crowd, protected by a barbed-wire fence thick enough to hold back the multitude of pilgrims that awaited the appearance of the miraculous pair. She isolated the smell of the jasmine plant, and with the morning breeze she smelled anew the aroma coming from Marcianita's house. Unfortunately, the light of day impeded the functioning of her olfactory mechanism, and resignedly she awaited dusk.

At least that is how things appeared to the pilgrims who, tired of standing in one place, set eyes on the gray mare that sadly searched for a comfortable place at the base of the fence and watched them as if searching for an explanation. To many, she seemed to be a common, everyday mare, but there was more than one person, specially endowed to glimpse the beyond, who found indelible traits of some unknown animal. The special luster of her coat, the elegant shape of her ears, and the essential well-being behind the assumed sadness, placed her at the center of the glances of those who awaited the apparition on the balcony.

Tuluá, strangely tilted toward La Rivera, found no merit in the gray mare that returned their glance. Tille Uribe's parrot, driven almost to distraction, paced up and down in his cage, incessantly repeating, "The ship came in, the ship came in." Nina Pérez had not been able to shut off her refrain of "The boat is leaving, it's leaving, it's leaving with the fisherman." And the dogs would not put an end to their barking.

A few minutes ago, when the great explosion filled the pilgrims with hysteria and Marcianita with eternal glory, the gray mare galloped back over the fences she had leaped to get there. Even though many believed she was frightened by the shock wave and the screaming, Pacho Montalvo, seeing her gallop past his park bench, bound for the Abad's mansion, had his doubts. Only now has the dogs' barking seemed to subside.

XVII

No one attended so faithfully and broodingly as Isaac Nessim. Entire nights staring at the ceiling, hearing Lieutenant Caravalí's unmistakable breathing, whole days tending the counter at Salón Eva almost like a sleepwalker, waiting for the hour when Caravalí would go off duty, the Dutch Jew wondered whether or not the miraculous idiots could cure illnesses of the soul. Timidly he approached from a distance two or three times. He did not join the endless procession of pilgrims, but he did watch from afar the ant trail into which the road to La Rivera had been converted. He grew as enthusiastic as his skepticism about life would permit, returned to his store, and at night, looking into Caravalí's eyes or separated by the darkness, he asked the officer's opinion. He did not find it at all favorable. The lieutenant not only said he did not believe in those vulgar prodigies; he was in fact bored to death with the complications they had caused for the district police of Tuluá, a peaceful town since the violence had ended. Not a day passed when they did not have to inspect the pilgrims' path to carry off the faint, attend to the dying, pick up unidentified bodies, or testify to the dents suffered by cars and buses in their race to have their passengers take their turn before the miraculous light. It was not that he did not actually believe in the curative effects of the abnormal pair. It was that by nature he hated anything that caused him problems. He had never even gone up there in person; he handled the difficulties from the map table at the district headquarters.

Actually, the real reason for his discouraging Nessim from visiting the site of the miracles was something very akin to a fear of losing him. The owner of Salón Eva had suffered no illness other than the bishop's gonorrhea. He was unknown in the Tuluá hospital. Since his friends were few, he did not have occasion to visit anyone. The doctors hardly bought anything from him. He never had a cold, never lost a tooth, never even had a bunion. But some rare intuition converted his gonorrhea into an illness of the soul and even after the venereal disease was cured, his spirit found no ease. His illness often ruined his appetite, leaving him no recourse but to gaze into the mirror of fate. He grew bitter in his loneliness and could not make the final decision. If the idiots cured him, Lieutenant Caravalí would lose his chance to control the merchant. His passion grew as a function of the tragedy Nessim harbored in the depths of his soul. Caravalí had discovered the key to his terror, and when it was time for lovemaking he would play with it with Dantesque finesse. By the intensity of the color of a mole on

Nessim's neck, he was tipped off as to whether the merchant was longing for his past or remembering it with anger. When it was the former, his hands, rough from handling so many policemen, pistols, and rifles, would alight on Nessim's body to remind him of his father's tickling on the night he would never again relive. The times when Nessim remembered his past with anger, Lieutenant Caravalí called on all his authoritarian powers, bellowed like a despot, sank his teeth into the Jew's skinny buttocks, and in the hour of love treated him like the most wretched and sickening of whores.

But Isaac Nessim, making a supreme effort to shed his skepticism, pondering every night, every morning, every minute, meditated until deciding to see the idiots and find a cure for his soul's illness. He consulted no more with Lieutenant Caravalí, included him no longer in the emptiness of his dream. He simply and plainly decided to go before the idiots and seek redemption from his spiritual malaise.

Early one morning, after having learned of the miraculous cure of one of his customers who had been committed for years to a psychiatric asylum, he whispered his decision in Caravalí's ear. The lieutenant did not bat an eye, gazed at the ceiling as if the light were coming from there, took the Jew's hand, and simply said to him, "Your consultation should be private." He said no more, knowing full well the value of lapidary words in the mind of Salón Eva's proprietor; he dressed and went out as if nothing had happened. Inside he was dying. Nessim had played the card of independence he had so feared, and he could only anticipate the results with anxiety.

It did not take long. For several weeks Isaac delayed his decision and the fulfillment of his desire to line up like so many thousands of pilgrims. He thought it over again methodically. With the acuity of a merchant with almost half a century's experience, he calculated all the possibilities. In the end, only a couple of options were left: Dr. Fajardo or the maid. He investigated carefully in order to convince himself he was not mistaken. Those two were Marcianita's means of communication with the outside. Few persons knew it, but he was certain. When he was positive, he again told Caravalí, and the latter, more familiar with housemaids than the women's underwear salesman was, advised him to talk with Dr. Fajardo. It would be possible to convince the maid, and the lieutenant's danger would be reborn. The doctor was well known for his integrity and respect, and even if he were given a thousand Salón Evas, he would not betray his relationship with Marcianita.

Once more Caravalí won, and it was Dr. Fajardo who delayed the moment of the Dutch Jew's appearance. The doctor first smiled; all Tuluá knew of Nessim's ailing soul. Upon hearing mention of a private consultation, the doctor saw his sense of propriety almost sink before his immense desire to serve a man who had done no one any harm but had been tormented his whole life by the tragedy of loving other men. The smile misled Nessim, and although the doctor told him a few minutes later that he had no contact with Marcianita and was not in a position to help him, the ambivalence of his facial expression offered the merchant remote hope. He spent several days in front of the hospital office longing for the instant when the doctor would come out and, moved to pity, tell him that he would help arrange a private appointment with the miracle workers. But since a month passed and Doctor Fajardo did not appear, but rather solidified his position, Isaac Nessim returned to his office with tears in his eyes. Pointing a long, skinny finger like an Egyptian mummy's, he pleaded with the doctor to serve as his intermediary. Caravalí was right; not even tears moved the hospital director. The denial was categorical, implacably categorical. Nessim looked at him intensely and, with his index finger still erect, signaling the end of his hopes and obliging him to seek the cure in public, left the office. He spent the whole rest of the day thinking about the best approach to use with Marcianita's maid, how to promise her the moon and get her to arrange a private appointment. To be received secretly was an obsession. As much as Tuluá was aware of his queenliness, he tried to convince himself that no one knew of it. He wanted nothing less than to endure the ridicule of those who would see him going before the supernatural pair because the least they would believe was that his gonorrhea had reappeared. So he pursued the second possibility obsessively. He did not run the risk of going to the girl. He would have nothing to do with females other than to sell them merchandise. Caravalí, on the other hand, had interacted with them as a policeman, a person, and a lover. In trusting the lieutenant, seeing him as affectionate, visionary, and powerful in a town incapable of doing anything other than obey him, the owner of Salón Eva made another mistake.

He entrusted the policeman with the task of convincing the maid, of conveying to her that she would find a world of glory and comfort if she could arrange an appointment for Nessim. He gave Caravalí absolute power to spend up to a hundred thousand *pesos* if necessary. He could have spent half the amount or exercised his powers as district commander and kept the money for himself, for he knew how much more the Jew had, but that was not his goal; in spite of accepting the task, he would not take a single cent. A week later, having fully reported to Nessim the maid's refusal, Caravalí arranged for two police officers to stake out the hospital ambulance and the transfer, both coming and going, of Marcianita's helper. The lieutenant did not tell his friend, but the latter—after all, the greatest salesman in Tuluá—learned of it through his informants, and perhaps at that precise moment Isaac Nessim lost confidence in Caravalí.

They continued to sleep together, making love in the melodramatic tones that were their wont, chatting about their sorrows and their problems, but the old Jew now aspired to nothing more than sexual encounters with the lieutenant. He did not inform him of his decision when it was made. He made the decision driven by what was left of a vital force within him. At four o'clock one morning when Caravalí was on duty, he left his house filled with great anticipation. He believed in his heart of hearts that on that particular day the illness of his soul would be completely cured. No one believed more in miracles than the wretched owner of Salón Eva. Nessim took his place at the end of a long line of pilgrims who were already waiting for the miraculous moment at nine A.M. Like one more pilgrim, unknown to almost everyone except for the shopkeepers and restaurant owners along the way, who no longer cared who walked by in the early morning in search of health or out of impertinent curiosity, he waited for the moment of the idiots' appearance on the balcony. He gushed faith from his elongated fingertips, from his diagrammatic face. He walked slowly until he passed under the balcony. He gazed on the idiots as if on eternal glory, as he would have looked on his parents if they had returned from the beyond which had once swallowed them up. He said nothing to them although he was tempted to do so. He did not look at them with the passionate expression he wore with Dr. Fajardo the times when he went to seek his help. He believed that by simply passing beneath the balcony he would enter into a curative trance. It was still forty minutes before the moment when the rays of health would emanate from the hands of the extraordinary Gideons, but at that instant he already felt the joy of the cure.

There followed forty minutes of frustration for Caravalí, who only then noticed that Nessim had not opened the store, and forty minutes of happiness for the merchant. The lieutenant ran to La Rivera without leaving any word for Nessim. There were so many pilgrims, and at that hour they were squeezed so tightly together, trying to receive at least a particle of the luminous curative ray, that they blocked his way, and from the far side of the curve by the Ruices' he saw the emission of the ray that would obliterate his unhappiness. But it did not bathe Isaac Nessim—as he had so hoped and the other had feared even more. And then the Jew's supreme faith evaporated completely, for he realized without being told that he had not been cured. Caravalí believed the opposite and neither expected nor called on him that night; the next morning, when the store was again closed and Nessim again went before the idiots, the lieutenant not only decided never again to set foot in his friend's house, at least for as long as he was so concerned about his spiritual health, but he also conceived a macabre plan to convince Nessim he was wasting his time.

He did not have to implement it. Isaac Nessim, with a faith whose origin he knew not, repeated the morning hike in quest of his cure. He again felt the same joy as soon as he spied them on the balcony. The irritating sensation was repeated when the rays blanketed him, but he did not manage to feel glory oozing from his pores. He abandoned the site of the miracles with his index finger pointed accusingly at his conscience. Convinced as he had been that he would be healed, he now came easily to admit that he would never be free of his emotional burden.

At three in the afternoon, seated at his desk in the office of Salón Eva, having just waited on one of his clients who bought two brassieres and one girdle, Isaac Nessim Dayam, the fifty-nine-year-old Dutch Jew, shot himself in the temple. The night before, Lieutenant Caravalí had again steered clear of his bed. So the news made the policeman feel guilty, and in his solitude he reacted against the idiots.

Tuluá buried Nessim with honors he had never dreamed of. It seemed everyone agreed that solitude in life should not carry over into death, and in grateful homage the burial was as well attended as if the deceased were Father Phanor or Nina Pérez. As the bier headed for the civil cemetery, where he had to be buried for lack of a synagogue, Lieutenant Caravalí, certain of not being included in the dead man's will, exercised his power, and in a folder in which he stuffed old collected photographs and new ones ordered taken from that day on, he accumulated what later became the great dossier against Marcianita Barona de Rodríguez and her idiots.

He thought about it so much and in such minute detail that he almost equaled Nessim's brooding before going to see the miracle workers. He studied everything in depth. He chose the reporters who could spread the news and calculated the precise moment to make the denunciation. Perhaps the impact would have been stronger if his methods of collecting information had stuck closer to the general norms of propriety, but he used crude, strongman tactics, and what could have been a sincere contribution was frequently a contentious smear, more the fruit of terror than of collaboration. He forced beggars who had never expected any kind of cure from the idiots to sign documents attesting to the fact that they had not been cured by them and that they had lost their crutches because of the pressure of the crowd. In many cases, they did not even use crutches and had gone to La Rivera only to try to raise their incomes as beggars and not for the health they stated had been denied them. He demanded press passes of some photographers before they could enter the site, and since they could not produce them, they were given their freedom only in exchange for some cheap pictures of the pilgrims' path, which were included in the folder. He detained Chuchú, who in her whole life has never harmed a flea and who, from wandering the streets of Tuluá so frequently, could well have been a most obsequious informant and archivist. He found no other way, there being so many, to make her appear at police headquarters. From so much begging her pardon and her collaboration, the intrepid action of her detainment did not prove to be as destructive as it might have been. Between the two of them, they agreed quite practically on the central aspects of the accusation. They filled these in with details that they, prisoners of hate, considered invaluable and succeeded in writing the document in such terms of pious expostulation and admonition that the central point almost came to be the rallying cry for the idiots' gratuitous enemies. They did not think much about contrived facts, much less about scientific data. They simply compiled with peasant logic and common sense an inventory of their observations. They had such an effect and made such an impact that the myth of the curative idiots appeared to be debunked once and for all in Colombia.

The report was sent to the national commander of police but was also turned over to a group of reporters capable of sullying the image of Saint Francis of Assisi. The next day *The Press* did no more than comment with extensive headlines on the manner in which the myth of the idiots was destroyed. Caravalí and Chuchú, nourished by their own vengeance, wrote up a communiqué with seven points. They made the thing so gloomy and damaging that for a few moments, as the news circulated about the country, the denunciation enjoyed absolute credence.

It is categorically contradictory and inadmissible for the Colombian church, state, and people, said the communiqué, that a pair of idiots who are the presumed workers of miracles on the incurable, should be incapable of removing the horrible hump from their mother, who has lived tormented by that martyrdom for many years. Even the most uncivilized beings have demonstrated filial love, whose manifestations have been immediate. But it is even more serious, continued the communiqué, that the people of this nation have been swindled by the infantile game of the identical twins. All of Tuluá has known since long before Inesita González was queen that she had an identical twin and that the one who appears parading through the streets and disturbing the peace is the one who was never paralyzed. But since it is difficult to change a mistaken opinion, we include with this report notarized affidavits of sick people who went to be restored to health and who continued in the same lamentable state after having spent their life's savings to reach Tuluá. Colombia ought to take note, stressed Lieutenant Caravalí's report to his superiors, that the pilgrims' path from Tuluá is a loathsome road where all types of infectious diseases abound and proliferate because there is no limit on the number of visitors, there being insufficient toilets and latrines for such a multitude. Besides, and national public opinion is already well aware of this, the people who daily die along the way cannot be collected until several hours later, often putrefied and having contaminated other passersby. The dead dogs, and no one knows why the idiots so hate those animals, are often not collected and the people trample them to mincemeat, creating a new hub of infection in the majority of cases. For all these reasons, concluded the report, the authorities should become acquainted with the dangers presented by the idiots and take the necessary measures to avoid harm to the Colombian people.

The impact of the release was brutal. An immense chill ran through the owners of the restaurants and stores along the road from the highway to La Rivera. But the next day, when a rationalist botanist wrote an article that tried to reinforce Caravalí's thesis, saying that the jasmines sold around La Rivera were all extremely dangerous because they belonged to a wild species which, since the beginnings of botany, has been used as a poison, the owners of those establishments, Brother Andrés from Manizales, and Hernando Giraldo, a columnist from *The Spectator* who had become the idiots' official defender, organized such a campaign that Lieutenant Caravalí's scandalous inquisition was minimized. Within seventy-two hours they collected money from everyone in Colombia who had been cured in order to pay for a full-page ad for a whole week in three newspapers with national circulation, denying the lieutenant's claims and showing the photographs of Brother Andrés agonizing and then cured and of Queen Inesita paralytic and then walking, and reproducing a certification from the curia of Tuluá and from the González family indicating that she was their only daughter. But while those heroes made their moves from other cities in defense of Marcianita and her sons, in Tuluá the owners of the food stands, the parking attendants, those who carried the ill, the vendors of soft drinks, cold water, and jasmine plants, those in charge of Belisario Concha's sanitary service, those of Hernando Rivera's, the Ruices, the dumptruck drivers, the paving contractor's workers, the town notary who since the start of the miracles had not stopped signing resale deeds, the extra telephone employees, and even the waiters met one morning. Abandoning their combat positions, in an unprecedented display of unity supported by all of that day's pilgrims, they descended upon the police headquarters. If not for Caravalí's supreme ability, they would have destroyed the building. He fled in an army jeep that came from Buga to help control the situation and never again showed his face in these parts.

A little while ago, before the police reported the truth to Marcianita, she thought about Lieutenant Caravalí. During the days of the national scandal that he had provoked, she lived all the incidents in detail. She cut out every one of the paid ads that the cured people published for her sons, and if she did not find the reason for the lieutenant's vengeance, deep within herself she caught an intuitive glimpse of his motives. She did not lose hope. Only on the day of the demonstration against the police and the resulting disturbances did the number of people gathered around her house diminish. On the other days, and as a demonstration of the idiots' curative prowess, the crowd reached the same levels it had maintained for months and months. She had acted with great discretion in not making public the monies collected on the platters which some days amounted to tens of thousands of pesos. Doctor Fajardo modernized his hospital, installed equipment he in no way could have otherwise afforded, and along the way he bought stocks and bonds in the name of the "La Rivera Society," the title under which Marcianita registered her sons' wealth upon selling the farm her husband had left her.

But one day, bored with hearing the murmur under the balcony, which tired her sooner than her sons, she decided to buy some adjoining land. It was the only time she left the house since the beginning of the cures. With her hump prominent, she opened the door of the house and through the thick of the crowd that sometimes recognized her as the mother of the idiots and other times as just another sick person searching in vain for a cure, she went out to the notary to sign a deed for the lands bordering hers at La Rivera. They were no more than seven acres, but the public was so sensitive to such matters that if the Tour de Colombia had not arrived at that time and all the cyclists, curious to meet Marcianita and hopeful of feeling super-endowed and winning the championship, had not made a stop before the idiots, the clientele at La Rivera would have dwindled.

The miracles did not stop happening; they may have even increased in number and quality. From the Swissman Hayer's cure to those of leukemia victims there was a great distance, but the public strangely forgot everything but the evidence of personal enrichment. The purchase of the land, the only public act performed by the hump-backed Marcianita Barona, who almost touched the ground under the enormous weight of her deformation, was an unforgivable blow. They had resisted Caravalí's call to vengeance, but they could not overlook this. Nevertheless, the Tour de Colombia saved her, if not by means of her idiots, then yet miraculously. So many reporters came, and the national and international press so spotlighted a Cochise or an Alvar Pachón filing before the balcony of the pair of prodigious curers that the next day the crowd grew as if inflated by powerful winds. The dramatic scenes of cures of paralytics who walked again, of mutes who spoke anew, of deaf persons who again heard were repeated daily, and perhaps only on those days, with all critics silenced, could Marcianita say that her sons were a national institution.

That was hardly two months ago. Tuluá has continued to enjoy certain guaranteed benefits. Buga has been enriched by the hotels that have been built, and by the thousands of persons who formerly had no job and no way to earn a living and now found themselves set for life. Tomorrow, unfortunately, although many people will continue to file past the balcony that the municipality will order rebuilt to resemble the one in memory, it will not be the same, and everyone is filled with regret. Perhaps Marcianita may be the one most affected, but only Nina Pérez, still resplendent today with a halo of light similar to the idiots', is truly traumatized by what happened a short while ago.

Just yesterday, compelled by some unknown fate, because she was never a true believer, she decided to go before the idiots. She did not sing in the morning, as she had been doing uninterruptedly since the day she went deaf and feared becoming mute. She shouted like no one else when the idiots appeared on the balcony of the house at La Rivera, stunned her neighbors, managed to break a few eardrums, but continued marching toward the cure. She had decided to come while she was wallowing in her bed waiting for dawn. She heard a distant voice in her dream and awoke with a halo of light that she still bears today. In none of the previous months did she want to present herself before the idiots. Many came to believe that she had sought her deafness and derived satisfaction from suffering a life of isolation. No one understood Nina's behavior, and much less so when they remembered that she had been the discoverer of Inesita González's miraculous cure. At the burial of Isaac Nessim—whose spiritual illness was the only one that could not be cured—she shouted at the top of her lungs, "How miraculous must the idiots be if they even found a cure for Nessim's ills." Few understood her; only the parish priest considered it an explanation for the suicide. Silent and withdrawn as he had been ever since the pastoral letters of his bishop failed to staunch the avalanche of heresy triggered by Marcianita's sons, he expressed his opinion with difficulty that day to those around him in the door of the rectory as they watched the funeral pass by. But even so, Nina Pérez had no faith in finding a cure in the house at La Rivera.

When they healed Brother Andrés she considered going. An aversion to national notoriety prevented her from seeking a cure on that occasion. On the day of the cure of Tille Uribe's parrot, she closed doors and windows to resist temptation. It was as if she did not want to be better, as if her happiness were in being stone deaf. Chuchú succeeded in believing that Nina's nonattendance on the pilgrims' path could be interpreted either as a show of friendship or a sign of disbelief, and one afternoon she tried to convert her to the true faith. The witch's cry is still ringing in the ears of the only woman priest who has existed in Colombia. At that point her only response was a continued refusal to go before the idiots. Nina almost came to be the conscience of Tuluá, which, for reasons both unmistakable and inadmissible, ignored the grandeur of the event before it. She came to the idiots' defense when Lieutenant Caravalí promoted the alliance with Chuchú, and she crushed the press. She did not contribute to Hernando Giraldo's ads, but she collaborated faithfully with Tille Uribe in collecting the funds. She cheered the Tour de Colombia in her great soprano tones and often brightened the looks of the pilgrims who came to Tuluá, making her rhinoceros fatness jiggle with every step, but only yesterday did she appear before the prodigious possessors of curative light. As soon as she heard the voice in her dreams suggesting catastrophe, she sang to reassure herself of being alive, even though it was three in the morning. She woke up her indignant neighbors who did not know whether she was dying or going crazy. It was not time to sing nor did she have a reason to wake them. She went out along the road to La Rivera singing canticles as though at the dawn rosary. Many people followed her; many more joined her group when they reached the pilgrims' path. Everyone who at that hour was sleeping on the buses, waiting for the morning show, got off and, singing along, followed her voice like rats trailing the Pied Piper of Hamlin.

The pitch rose at exactly nine o'clock, when the pair of idiots appeared, decked in brocade, on the balcony of Marcianita's house. Nina marched slowly until she was situated directly in front of the site of miracles. Marcianita sensed her at a distance as she had sensed the presence of Tille Uribe the day she came with the doctor and her sick parrot. She came out on the balcony with her idiots, breaking her custom to the contrary. "NINA," she shouted from the curvature of her hump. And Nina Pérez, suckled from that moment by the supernatural powers of the idiots from whose hands the light emerged, heard for the first time in many years, and, seized by a panic caught from those who witnessed the cure, she shouted as perhaps she had never before managed to shout in her morning cantos, "MIRACLE, MIRACLE, MIRACLE!"

Tuluá convulsed and, shaking off her centuries-old lethargy, awoke to realize that the idiots were much more important than it had admitted until that moment. En masse, those who had come but once out of curiosity as well as those who had never come near at all appeared morning and afternoon, yesterday and today, in front of Marcianita Barona's house. It was like a final wave, like an unquenchable thirst that attends the draining of the last drops of water in the canteen. Nina's cry had been felt in the conscience of all Tuluá's inhabitants. There were no more reporters to announce in banner headlines news of the cure. Much less television anchormen to convey the prodigious act to the rest of the world. It was Tuluá as a whole that turned upside down, repentant, to convince itself that Marcianita's idiots were its own, that in its bosom it had nurtured the supernatural power that had been granted to no other town. Filing by silently or noisily until just a short while ago, it gave its testimony of acknowledgement of that truth.

This morning, when new waves of pilgrims arrived at the universal focus of miracles and the crowd squeezed together as never before in front of the balcony, the idiots appeared dressed in white for the first time in their curative history. Marcianita Barona, who while they were healing Nina Pérez felt the end was nigh, had cut jasmines all night and when she was tired had gone to sit in the rocking chair where she had so often anticipated so many things. Brother Andrés, without knowing of Nina's cure, was wakened in the early hours by a wind that entered his room in the Marist Brothers' academy in Manizales. He dressed as best he could, woke the school bus driver, and without asking the permission of his superiors, he had himself brought to Tuluá. Inesita González learned about Nina at nightfall, upon returning to her family's farm. At eight in the morning, at the same time when Brother Andrés arrived at the entrance to the pilgrims' path, she got out of her car. They did not have to greet each other to feel the same need and to break into unexplainable tears. Tille Uribe's parrot flew about his cage and repeated over and over, incessantly, "The ship came in, the ship came in, the ship, the ship..."

Marcianita's jasmines, cut in nocturnal despair, started falling on the pilgrims bright and early. An unmistakable aroma filled the space from the curve by the Ruices' to the home of the supernatural pair until just a little while ago. At exactly nine-twenty Nemesio Jojoa made his entrance at the covered walkway. In his hands he carried hope. At nine thirty-one he was in front of the balcony. Marcianita felt it in the depths of her hump; the idiots rose from their comfortable seats as if to render homage to the eminent visitor and raised their hands as if to perform a miracle or to beg for mercy. The crowd bellowed like crazy and an explosion that filled with smoke the diminutive balcony from which the cures were worked put the finishing touches on the enormous effort that Marcianita had been making since dawn.

Fragments of Bartolomé's cap hit her face as she sat in the rocking chair. Pieces of Ramón Lucio's flesh peppered the faces of those surrounding the anarchist. The blood that the shrapnel drew from many arms and heads of those nearest the balcony prevented the crowd from lynching Nemesio Jojoa, the son of Rocío Jojoa and an unknown father, a powder-maker by profession, only fifteen years old according to the official police report that the radio stations repeat continuously, remorsefully spreading to the world the news of the death of the idiots.